DEBTS & DIAMONDS

THE DEANA-DHE DUET
BOOK 1

BEA PAIGE

GRITTY, ANGSTY, DANGEROUS ROMANCE

DEBTS
and
DIAMONDS

BEA PAIGE

FOREWORD

Dear Reader,

This book Debts & Diamonds is book one of the Deana-dhe duet. It is a standalone duet that you can read independently of my other series and still enjoy.

However, these characters do have a cameo in the Academy of Stardom series, and Their Obsession duet. Of the two, Their Obsession duet (The Dancer and The Masks, The Masks and The Dancer) features them more, and the events in the epilogue of this book tie in with the events in the epilogue of The Masks and The Dancer. You *don't* have to read Their Obsession duet, but I think it will give you more insight into Cyn particularly and her relationship with The Masks (the Deana-dhe's enemies, who are mentioned in this book) as it will add to the richness of their story as a whole.

But, you don't have to. It's entirely up to you!

If you don't already know, all my stories are set in the same world with cameos appearing across the series / duets I've written. If you're interested in reading my books below here is the recommended reading order.

PLEASE NOTE: all series / trilogies / duets are self-contained and can be read on their own and there is no need to read all my books listed below to enjoy any series. This is merely for the die-hard fans who want to immerse themselves in the world I created.

Happy reading!

•**The Brothers Freed trilogy** (Reverse harem romance) - featuring Hudson Freed (Grim's best friend), Bryce and Max.

•**Academy of Misfits trilogy** (Reverse harem romance) - featuring Ford, Asia and her other 'bad boys'; Eastern, Camden and Sonny, as well as cameos from Grim and Hudson Freed.

•**Beyond the Horizon** (M/F age gap romance) - featuring Malakai and has cameos from Ford, Asia and her other 'bad boys'; Eastern, Camden, Sonny.

•**Finding Their Muse** (Reverse harem romance) - featuring Asia from Academy of Misfits.

•**Academy of Stardom series** (Reverse harem romance) - featuring Pen and her Breakers, with cameos of Grim and Beast, Hudson Freed, the Deana-dhe, and Asia (off-page).

•**Their Obsession Duet** (Reverse harem romance) - featuring Christy and her men The Masks. This duet also has cameos from Grim, Beast, Ford and Camden. This duet also introduces The Deana-dhe.

•** **Grim & Beast's Duet** (M/F romance) - prequel to all of the above stories, and includes cameos of characters from many of the books listed above with the exception of Finding Their Muse series.

•**The Deana-dhe Duet** (Reverse harem romance) This features Cyn aka 'Thirteen' who appears in Their Obsession Duet and her love interests, The Deana-Dhe, who cameo in Academy of Stardom and Their Obsession Duet.

CONTENT NOTICE

There are some scenes in this book that you may find triggering, including bullying, and childhood trauma (murder of a parent, off page).

BOOK PLAYLIST

You can find **Debts & Diamonds** on my Bea Paige spotify playlist.

My favourite track has to be Teardrop by Massive Attack. The second I heard this song I knew it would be the theme tune to the Deana-dhe duet.

This book is dedicated to Mum & Dad.
You've both had a rough year health wise and I'm so grateful
everyday that you're both still here. I love you both eternally and no
matter the time, night or day, I'm there for you both always. Never a
burden, always an honour.
Your girl x

"Love, love is a verb. Love is a doing word. Fearless on my breath..."

~ *Teardrop, Massive Attack.*

PROLOGUE

Arden - present day

I should feel disgust at the knife I'm holding in my hand, but all I feel is relief. Relief that I've finally taken back what belongs to me, to *us*. My deceased father's skin might be wrapped around the handle, the butterfly tattoo he wore inked across his throat now stretched thin and faded with time. It should sicken me. It doesn't. This knife and my father's murder has become a symbol of who and what we are.

His death birthed us: the Deana-dhe.

Arden Dálaigh.

Carrick O'Shea.

Lorcan Sheehan.

Brothers in arms. Purveyors of truths and lies. Dealers of Debts. Legends.

We're the men criminals fear above all else.

Our power comes not from brute force, though we have that in spades. It comes from truths hidden and lies uncovered. Everyone has secrets they wish to hide from the world, and we're very adept at unearthing those truths and bartering with them. You need information, we have it. You want to blackmail your enemy, we can help you. For a price.

No money crosses hands. We don't deal in property either, or precious gems and metals.

We deal in debts.

A truth for a debt of our choosing that we will cash in when the time is right.

It could be a year from now, five, ten, longer, but don't get complacent, we never forget a deal made. We will always call in that debt, and if you refuse to deliver on your part of the deal? Well, put it this way, death isn't the worst thing we can do to you.

Cynthia O'Farrell knows that better than anyone.

1

Cyn - fifteen years old

"Your room is situated in the east wing of the dormitory. Breakfast is at seven am sharp. The school day begins at eight-thirty am. Your father has already arranged for your personal belongings to be delivered. They're in your room. Tomorrow you will meet your study partners and your therapist," the school's headmistress, Ms Weatherby, reels off as she strides in front of me along the stone corridor in her low heels, plaid skirt and high-neck, ruffled shirt.

I never wanted to come to Silver Oaks Institute, a school for the psychologically damaged, but my father had other ideas, and despite begging him not to send me, he did so anyway. What Niall O'Farrell wants he gets. Always.

"Do you understand?"

Of course I don't answer. I *can't* answer.

She stops walking, looking over her shoulder and down her nose at me. "Do you understand?" she repeats, her posh accent grating to my ears.

I nod. *Yes.*

Pulling in a sharp breath through her flared nostrils she nods. "Curfew is nine pm. Anyone caught out of their room after this time will be punished."

If I could speak, I would question what kind of punishment she's talking about. But as I can't, I simply follow her, my trainer clad footsteps quiet where hers are loud.

She stops at the end of the corridor and pushes open a heavy wooden door. It squeaks on its iron hinges, the sound making my teeth go on edge. My face must pale, because she gives me a fake smile before stepping into the dimly lit hallway beyond.

"Old buildings like this are full of noises. You shouldn't worry, it's the quiet that you need to fear."

My eyebrows draw together in a frown, and I expect her to laugh, telling me that she's joking. She doesn't.

A shiver tracks down my spine at the way she smirks in the darkness, and whilst I'm not easily scared, I am cautious enough to know that I need to avoid this woman at all costs. Which is a problem, given I'm alone with her right now.

"We're almost to your room," she says, another smile swarming up her face like wasps across discarded ice-cream. It should be comforting to know I'm finally going to be able to rest after spending most of the day travelling, but it isn't. Not when she holds the key to this wing of the dormitory.

I give her a tight smile. The second I'm alone I'm texting my father. There's no way I'm staying here. No way. This isn't where damaged teenagers go to get fixed, this is where they go to die, and I'm not willing to end my life at the hands of some psycho headmistress with a chilling smile and a penchant for cheap perfume and plaid material.

"Well, come along then," she insists.

But despite my fears, just like the obedient girl I was brought up to be, I follow her.

Like everywhere else I've passed through today, this portion of the dormitory is quiet. In fact, since I've arrived at the institute, I haven't seen another student. Not one. Perhaps they're all in class or therapy sessions with tweed wearing, cigar smoking psychotherapists.

Or perhaps they're all dead, a soft voice inside my head whispers.

Clamping my lips shut on the scream that wants to break free from my chest, I fold my arms tighter around myself. Keeping my eyes fixed firmly on the back of Ms Weatherby, I force my feet to move and remind myself that I am the daughter of Niall O'Farrell, a man no one, especially not some uptight, freaky schoolmistress, wants to get on the wrong side of.

He's fearsome, and has a reputation that stretches across the whole of Southern Ireland and the United Kingdom. My father is not someone you choose to mess with, and he's certainly not someone who'll stand any harm against his only child. Even if that child is a disappointment, as well as a freak.

"This is your room," Ms Weatherby says, stopping outside of a door halfway down the hallway. A little further along is another door, and I can't help but wonder who my neighbour is.

"Arden Dálaigh."

I frown, my gaze meeting Ms Weatherby's.

"That's his room. I'm assuming that's what you wanted to know?"

I keep my expression neutral and wait for further information. Usually, when someone is greeted with silence they fill it with the sound of their own voice. Ms Weatherby is no different.

"His father was murdered, and he went off the rails, so to speak. I would steer well clear of him if I were you. He's trouble, that one. No amount of therapy will fix that young man, not an ounce of empathy in his body. Lost it the day his father died."

Something about the dismissive way she talks about this boy I've never met and the trauma he's so obviously been through, angers me. Most days I'm glad I can't speak, but there are occasions where I wish I had a voice so that I can really tell people what's on my mind.

Bitch.

"There's no need for that look," she says, waving her hand in my face as she scowls at me. "I'm only telling you what you'll find out soon enough. You'll thank me for the heads up. Steer clear."

If Arden is someone I need to stay away from, it begs the

question why she roomed me *next* to him. I think Ms Weatherby is the one without any empathy, or any human decency for that matter, or maybe she just has a really messed-up sense of humour.

"Well, I'll leave you to it. Here's your key. Don't lose it," she instructs with a sniff as she drops the key into my open palm.

Then she's gone.

I heave out a long breath then unlock my bedroom door and push it open, coming face to face with a boy lounging on my bed, smoking a cigarette. At a guess I'd say he was no more than a year older than me, if that.

What the hell?!

I stand in the doorway, my mouth popped open in shock.

"You know she's right. You should stay away from me. I *am* trouble," he says, turning on his side, his mud-covered boots dirtying up my white sheets as he taps the ash from his cigarette, the soft lilt of his accent deceptively kind sounding.

My gaze drops to the hot ash floating towards the threadbare rug covering the wooden floor. It sizzles a little at the contact, and I have the sudden urge to rush forward and stamp my foot on it.

"Your room is much nicer than mine," he continues, swinging his legs over the side of the bed, his wet boots putting out any possible fire. "You've got a lot of shit too."

His assessing gaze tracks across the room to the worn leather trunk filled with my possessions. It's an heirloom, and my dad insisted on me using it to transport my belongings. Our family crest is emblazoned in gold leaf on the lid, an ostentatious display of nobility and wealth that makes me die a little inside.

"It's locked," he points out.

I fold my arms across my chest, resisting the urge to raise a sarcastic brow.

Of course it's locked.

Inside my trunk are all the things that are most important to me aside from my clothes, none of which I want this arsehat to see. On instinct, I lift my hand to my chest, my fingers trailing over the key that's resting there on a long piece of leather string. He notices, and I immediately pull my hand away.

"That's the O'Farrell crest. I'm guessing *you're* an O'Farrell?" he asks, looking up at me from beneath his curtain of black hair.

I nod. My hackles rising at the intense way he studies me with his liquid amber eyes.

"Daughter?"

I nod.

"So it's true then… you don't speak?"

Chewing on the inside of my cheek to stop me from glaring at him, I nod again. *Yes, it's true.*

The tip of his cigarette sizzles as he draws in a deep breath, then blows it out, smoke curling upwards like a snake, following his words into the air. "That's fucked up."

No more than you are.

My ugly thoughts must reveal themselves on my face because he barks out a laugh.

"We're all fucked-up here. Comes with the territory."

We stare at each other, me wondering how he was able to

interpret my thoughts so easily, and him enjoying making me feel uncomfortable with every passing second that he remains seated on my bed. How did he get in here anyway? And more to the point, what does he want from me? Or is this simply intimidation tactics? Either way, he's beginning to piss me off. Not that I'll show him how affected I am.

Swinging my backpack around to the front of my chest, I unzip it and pull out my notepad and pen, discarding my bag in the process.

This is my room, I write, showing the page to him.

"And?" is his obnoxious reply.

And you should leave, I add, keeping my anger at bay by schooling my features into a bland expression. I've learnt that allowing my emotions to sit on my face like an open book is worse for me than hiding them. People give up trying to get me to speak when all they're faced with is a neutral expression and indifference. I like the protection it affords me.

Crushing the butt of his cigarette directly onto the side table beside my bed, he stands, striding over to me. "Make me," he says.

Loosening the tight grip my fingers have on the pad, I swallow down my frustration and force myself to not react. *I want you to leave.*

He laughs, then quick as a flash, snatches the notepad from me and chucks it over his shoulder. It lands with a thud on the floor behind him, and my chest tightens with pain. I know it's only a cheap, lined notepad but it's my only form of communication, and throwing it away is akin to silencing me. I'd wanted to learn sign language, but my father didn't want me to draw any more attention to myself and forbade it. When he realised I was never going to talk again, he allowed me to communicate with a notepad and pen, but surreptitiously. God forbid I was too obvious about it.

"What's the matter? Did I hurt your feelings?" he goads, snorting with laughter.

I want to tell him that I'm sick of being silenced, of not being heard.

Its been the same for as long as I can remember, even before my mum was brutally murdered before my very eyes and I lost the ability to speak.

Good little Cynthia, be seen but not heard.

Don't misbehave.

Be *quiet*.

When Arden takes a step forward, his steel toe-capped boots touching my trainers, I stand my ground despite not giving him any sign of the fury whipping up like a storm inside my chest.

It doesn't matter that he's almost a head taller than me and I have to look up at him whilst he smirks down at me. It doesn't matter that my slight frame is overshadowed by his broad shoulders or that he brings his hand up to grip my face, I remain calm in the face of his unprovoked anger.

"Interesting," he mutters, his grip tightening on my jaw even as he lifts his other hand and gently slides his fingers over my lips, confusing my already overstimulated brain. "So stoic, I wonder what it would take to hear you scream?"

His voice is a warm caress even though his words are as sharp as a knife, and just as threatening.

"You'd better bench that thought, Arden," another, slightly deeper, male voice says from behind us.

Arden's grip loosens a little, but he still doesn't let me go. "Things were just getting interesting, you're spoiling all my fun," he complains to whomever is standing behind us. "I haven't found out her secrets yet."

"I bet," is the stunted response.

"What's going on, Lorcan?" Arden asks with an annoyed sigh as he looks over my head.

"Dr Lynch is on his way. You've ducked out of too many therapy sessions and he's pissed. Better get your story together or face a week in solitary. You know how much that place sucks."

Solitary? That doesn't sound good.

"Fuck!" Arden swears, letting me go abruptly. He takes a step back and glares at me. "This isn't over."

I blink up at him, all my courage from before draining from my body. If he doesn't leave soon he'll witness just how much he's gotten to me, and I can't have that.

"Arden," the boy at the door urges. "Come on. You've got to go."

"Now you know who I am, *Little Mouse*," he says, staring back down at me and ignoring his friend as his fingers stroke down the column of my neck. "But if you tell your father about our little *chat*, I will have no problem sneaking into your bedroom in the dead of night and wringing your neck."

His fingers wrap around my throat, squeezing tight enough to tell me that this isn't an empty threat, that he means every word. "Do we have an understanding?"

I nod my head, trembling.

He smiles. "Good. Now move!" he demands, releasing me from his hold.

With a heaving chest, I step out of his way, my back pressed against the wall as he strides past me and out into the hallway beyond. Bile rises up my throat, threatening to break free from my pursed lips, but I swallow it back down, refusing to show how bothered he's made me and how much emotion is brimming inside of me from our brief interaction.

"Whatever you've done to piss him off, I wouldn't do it again," the boy in the hallway says, a sympathetic note to his voice.

He swipes a hand through his white hair as he tracks his gaze over me, his ice-grey eyes, and the paleness of his lashes, skin and hair stunning me momentarily. He's beautiful.

I give him an automatic nod, then curse internally. *I* haven't done anything wrong so why am I nodding like I'm admitting culpability? Before today I hadn't even met the guy. I don't know him, and I don't want to know him either. Whatever his problem is, it's got nothing to do with me.

"If you want to survive your time here, you should do whatever you can to please Arden," he continues, the tone of his voice changing from one that's sympathetic to coercive. "And that extends to his best mates as well..."

My spine snaps rigid, warning bells ringing once more, but I force myself to relax, meeting this boy's gaze with a neutral one of my own. Who the hell are these people?

"I'm Lorcan," he says with a tip of his head as though I spoke that question out loud. "I'm the nicest of the group. You'll meet Carrick soon enough. He's stuck in solitary right now, and he's gonna be tense as fuck when he gets out. I'd watch your back, he likes to prey on nice girls."

Without thinking my actions through, I stride towards the door and slam it in his face, locking it.

My back hits the door, my legs giving way as Lorcan's laughter taunts me from the hallway, and as I sit on the floor of my new home for the next few years, I can't help but wonder what I did in a former life to deserve the hell of this one.

2

L orcan - Present day

"Cyn, it's time to start fulfilling your debt," I demand, my fist pounding against her door.

The moment we showed her to her suite twenty-four hours ago, she barricaded herself in and hasn't stepped out since. Gritting my teeth on my waning patience, I swallow my annoyance and lighten the tone of my voice.

"You've not eaten or drank anything since you arrived here. You must be hungry," I point out. Truth is, she didn't *arrive* here, not of her own accord anyway. We called in her debt and it didn't matter that she wasn't ready, she didn't have a choice but to come with us.

Just over a year ago she came to us requesting the name of the man responsible for the death of her mother, a death she witnessed at just four years old that led her to losing her ability to speak.

We gave her that information in exchange for the murder of her childhood friends and our bitter enemies, The Masks. Except the night we stole her back from The Masks, Arden changed her debt, allowing his cousin, Christy, the honour of killing The Masks for kidnapping her, and forcing Cyn to make a drug called diamonds for us instead.

It's a risk, of course, keeping her here. She is, after all, the daughter of Niall O'Farrell, one of the most feared bosses in Ireland. Not that it matters who her father is, he may be feared by many, but not by us. And whilst her late mother's family, the O'Briens, are friends of the Deana-dhe, we don't owe them a damn thing. Cyn made a deal with us several years ago, and we're calling in that debt now. Neither of the warring O'Farrells and O'Briens can change that fact.

They know the score, as does she.

"So you're going for the sympathy tactic. I see that's working well," Carrick says with a heavy dose of sarcasm as he watches me from the other side of the hallway with his coal black eyes.

"I'd rather choose the path of least resistance, brother," I shrug.

"Sympathy never worked before on Cyn. She saw through your *kindness* when we were kids and she'll see through it now."

"Go on then, smartarse. What do you suggest?"

He grins, a sly smile jerking his lips upwards. "I thought you'd never ask."

Shoving me aside, he curls his fingers around the door-frame, then lifts his foot and slams it into the door. On the third kick, it flies open.

"There," he says, stepping into the room. "Brute force wins out over sweet talking every damn time."

If he wasn't my best friend I'd hate him a little bit right now. "You're gonna need to fix that," I point out, stepping into the room behind him.

"Fuck the door. If she insists on barricading herself in we'll just remove it altogether," Carrick retorts, striding down the entrance hallway and into her bedroom suite. "FUCK!"

"What?" I ask.

"She isn't here."

"What do you mean, she isn't here? Where the fuck is she?" I ask, stepping around him.

Her bed is made, the duvet pulled tight over the mattress as though she hasn't even sat on it, let alone slept in it.

"Cyn?!" I call out, striding over to the door in the corner of the room where her ensuite bathroom is located. I know before I even push it open that she isn't in there either. "Fuck!"

I check under the bed and in the wardrobe before tugging on the sash window, but like all the upstairs windows it's nailed shut. Never questioned why that is until now. Maybe this was more of a prison than a monastery. Not that she'd get very far even if she had been able to escape through the window. Our island is small, remote and surrounded by an ocean with powerful currents that will drown even the strongest of swimmers. It's why we made it our home. No one can get onto the island without us noticing and whilst we're positive no one is brave enough to take on the Deana-dhe, it pays to be cautious, especially when we have someone so valuable living here with us.

"And you still don't think she's a witch," Carrick remarks dryly as he twists on his feet and searches the room, as though expecting Cyn to appear out of a wall or something.

"She's a healer, Carrick, not a witch," I reply.

He shakes his head, sneering. "Whatever you need to tell yourself, brother."

"She can't have gotten very far. Come on," I say, ignoring his dark mood as I pass him by and head back downstairs.

Carrick chuckles darkly as he steps into stride beside me. "If she wanted to play a game of cat and mouse, she should've said."

"This isn't a game, Carrick. She's here for a reason, and you and I both know we can't afford to lose her."

"Lose *who*?"

"Arden..." Carrick begins, then slams his mouth shut when he notices the scowl on our best friend's face as he steps out of the living room.

"Well?" he insists, a muscle ticking in his jaw.

"Cyn's not in her room," I say, cutting to the chase.

Arden isn't a man who minces words, and neither am I. We're as close as we are because we understand each other better than our own flesh and blood ever could. There is no bond stronger than the one we share. I expect his anger, understand it.

Arden's eyes flare dangerously, the golden hue turning fiery. "Where the fuck is she?"

"I'll check the grounds and the beach," Carrick says, grabbing his coat from the hanger by the front door. He's gone before we're even able to respond.

"Why bother, she can't get off the island," Arden says, though I note the hint of uncertainty in his voice.

"I agree, but she's also stubborn and has a reckless streak. If anyone would try to escape, it'd be her," I say, acknowledging what we're both thinking.

"I underestimated her," Arden says, snaking his fingers roughly through his hair.

"Wouldn't be the first time," I say.

He doesn't argue because he knows I'm right.

"I'll check downstairs."

"I'll do upstairs."

He spins on his heel, and I call after him. "She's here somewhere."

The brief nod he gives me is the only indication he's heard what I've said.

By the time I reach the kitchen, the last room to check because it's the furthest part of the house to where I started, I'm cursing how fucking huge our home is and how many hiding places there are. Like Carrick suggested, this could've been a fun experience if there wasn't so much at stake, and I can't help but recall how we enjoyed a little game of cat and mouse when we were teenagers. Well, *we* enjoyed it, I can't speak for Cyn.

Pushing those memories of our time at Silver Oaks Institute

aside, I open the kitchen door only to find her standing right before me.

"So this is where you've been hiding," I say at the sight of her. She's wearing an apron wrapped around her waist and a sheen of sweat across her forehead as she stirs some liquid in a large iron pot on the kitchen table. "What are you doing?"

She glances up at me, her expression calm as she jerks her chin towards the seat at the end of the table.

Sit, she silently demands.

"You do realise Carrick is out in this shitty weather searching for your broken body at the bottom of Briars Point," I say, glancing at the darkening sky through the kitchen window as I pull out the stool and sit down, refusing to look too closely at how my body slumps in relief. It's probably fatigue. I haven't slept well in years, pretty sure insomnia is a condition designed to bring down even the hardiest of men.

She gives me a blank look that says nothing and everything at the same time. *This fucking woman.* How many times have I received that very same look from her over the years? Too many to count, I can assure you. She intrigues and frustrates me in equal measure.

"So what's the deal?" I ask, picking up a twig from a pile in front of me, wondering what possible use it has.

Cyn can make something out of the randomest of shit. She's gifted, some kind of genius in the art of herbology and has an encyclopaedic brain when it comes to knowing everything there is to know about every species of plant, flower, shrub and funghi. Not to mention minerals and precious stones.

Arden believes she's an alchemist, a person who is able to turn base metals into precious metals, and who is connected to the spiritual and metaphysical world in a way other people aren't. He believes she can manipulate the chemical makeup of any object and turn it into something else.

Carrick believes she's a cailleach, a *witch*. He took an immediate dislike to her the moment they met back at the institute we all attended as kids. That hatred has twisted into something even more dangerous.

And me? I believe she's a healer, someone who has an innate ability to understand what ails a person and goes out of her way to help them even if they don't deserve it. Even if they're men like us. She's selfless and kind, proving that time and again over the years.

She's everything we're not.

Either way, she's an obsession none of us are able to shake for differing reasons.

She's *trouble*.

"You barricade yourself in your room for a whole day and night and then suddenly this morning you wake up and decide to start..."

In my periphery, Cyn picks up her pen and jots something down in a leather-bound notebook before she grabs the lined pad next to it and scribbles a message, then holds it up for me to read.

I didn't barricade myself in. The door was unlocked this whole time.

"It was?" I can't help but laugh, shaking my head at her tenacity. "Carrick just kicked the door down."

She shrugs, placing her notepad on the table and returning her attention to the huge pot of liquid. If she could speak, I'm pretty sure she'd be calling us all eejits right now. She'd be right too.

Peering at the dried herbs and flowers scattered across the table, I ask, "What are you making anyway?"

Dipping her head over the pot, she inhales deeply. Her eyes flutter shut and her cheeks pink up as she breathes in the scent, which frankly smells less than pleasant. But my olfactory sense takes a back seat when the sun breaks through the clouds and douses her in a golden halo, somehow making her seem impossibly beautiful.

Swallowing hard, I drag my gaze away.

Like I said, she's *trouble*.

It's tea. It will help me to remain calm, focused. I'll need it if I'm going to fulfil my debt, she writes across her notepad, her expression neutral despite the grief she must be feeling.

"That's fair," I reply, choosing to take the road less travelled and remain neutral, if not exactly friendly. Arden and Carrick will more than make up for it once they find out she's been here all along. I know my best friends, despite her doing nothing other than what comes naturally, they'll want to punish her.

Why?

Because she made us feel *fear*.

And the Deana-dhe aren't afraid of anything or anyone.

Except maybe her.

Arden fears the thought of anyone, including her father, using her gift for their own gain. As far as he's concerned, Cyn is our property. *She's* valuable, and whilst we've always prided ourselves in putting worth in things other people don't, like information, we understand that her value is something that cannot easily be bought, or found elsewhere.

Carrick fears her abilities, what she can do. It's unsurprising given she managed to kill him back at the institute when we were teenagers. The fact she warned him not to taste the tincture or that she brought him back to life with her quick thinking is neither here nor there. He blames her for the nightmares that have haunted him every night since.

And me? I'm afraid of how much I like her. I can't bring myself to hate her like Carrick, or keep her at arms length like Arden. Carrick thinks I'm putting on an act. I'm not. I like Cyn. I always have. But liking someone isn't part of the Deana-dhe's modus operandi.

We intimidate, scare, bully, overpower. We rarely hold out the hand of friendship.

Chewing on the inside of her cheek, Cyn holds the pad in her hand, her pen hovering over the paper like she's trying to decide whether she wants to converse with me more. Eventually, she seems to make up her mind and scribbles something down.

Do you want to try some?

"Of your tea?" I pull a face. "It doesn't smell good."

It's delicious.

"I'm not convinced."

She shrugs.

"Did you make this for The Masks before we took you from them?" I ask, wanting to know what her relationship with them looked like, needing to understand how someone like Cyn, so pure, so good, could end up being friends with those sadistic bastards.

Cyn looks at me, her expression a blank mask just like it always is when we mentioned her childhood friends. It's the first time I've brought them up since we took her from them a few days ago. We might've called in her debt giving her no choice but to come with us, but let's not be mistaken, we did it to seek revenge on The Masks as much as we did for our own personal gain. The look on their faces when we arrived at their castle and called in her debt was worth all the trouble finding their secret lair.

"Well, did you?" I insist.

She refuses to respond, her loyalty to the three men angering me.

"You and I both know that the world is a better place now that they're no longer alive in it," I remark, noticing how she flinches at my words.

Regret instantly makes me want to apologise, not for speaking the truth but for hurting her, but I swallow it down because I will never understand her friendship with those despicable fucking men. Their deaths, as well as the death of their father, Malik Brov, a couple of years prior, was a blessing. Good fucking riddance to them all. My only regret is that it wasn't one of us who had the pleasure of taking their lives.

"They deserved everything they got, Cyn," I add, hating how her love for them still exists despite knowing how evil they were.

But just like she's so adept at doing, she ignores me, compartmentalising her emotions. If she feels grief, she doesn't show it. Instead she places her pad and pen back onto the table, picks up a ladle and scoops up some of the liquid, pouring it over a sieve and into a jug. She does this several times until the jug is full, then she pours herself a glass. Even the colour is off putting.

"Didn't anyone ever tell you not to drink something that's a hazardous neon yellow?" I ask, watching her curiously as she takes a sip of the tea.

Her expression changes from one of masked indifference to satisfaction as she licks her lips and offers me the cup with a jerk of her chin.

"No. Definitely not," I say, looking from the cup to her face and back again.

Go on. She urges with her eyes.

"I was never a fan of yellow, it makes my skin look sallow," I deadpan.

The tiniest hint of a smile plays about her lips and I'd be a liar if it didn't do something to me.

"Fine!" I say, reaching for the cup. I take it from her, then hold my breath and raise it to my lips, hesitating when Cyn's eyes flick away from me and widen in horror. From her reaction I know who's just stepped into the room.

"What the fuck do you think you're doing?!" Carrick shouts as he smacks the cup out of my hand and it flies across the kitchen smashing against the cabinet on the other side of the room. "Have you lost your mind?"

One minute Carrick is glaring at me, his black eyes wild

with rage, and the next he has Cyn pinned against the kitchen cabinet, his actions snuffing out that brief moment of happiness I witnessed moments before.

And *that* angers *me*.

Later when I think about this moment I know I'll question my actions, and the sudden well of protectiveness that shoved my deep-seated loyalty to Carrick and our brotherhood aside as though it meant nothing. But for now I act.

"Get your hands off her!" I shout, grabbing his shoulder and yanking him backwards.

He stumbles, releasing Cyn. His cheeks are ruddy with cold, but his enmity is an inferno as he turns on me, his best friend, his brother.

"You really think that this act you've got going on is going to get you in her knickers, huh?"

"No."

"Because it won't," he snaps, jabbing his finger into my chest. "She didn't *want* to fuck us before and she doesn't want to fuck us now. The *only* reason she gave us her virginity was because we were high and she could curse us whilst we were under her spell. Have you forgotten the agreement we made after that night?"

"No, I haven't," I respond, doing everything in my power to keep myself under control, because like it or not he's hit a nerve.

I *do* want to fuck her. On the rare occasions that I've managed to grab a few hours of sleep, I've dreamt of nothing else but her. That night we took her virginity and sealed our pact is forever etched into my fucking memory. For years I've craved the taste of her skin, thought of nothing else but the way she silently came, her body shuddering with pleasure as we fucked her. It was literal heaven on Earth, and no one I've been with since has come close to making me feel the same way.

No one.

"You're acting irrationally. It's not poison. I watched Cyn drink it herself," I argue.

"And? She's smart, she could've taken something before you got here to counteract whatever that fucking poison is!" he shouts.

Admittedly, I hadn't thought of that. Carrick's right, she is smart, but is she really that cunning or that devious? In truth, my instincts tell me no, that her goodness couldn't allow her to behave that way. She was friends with The Masks, for fuck sake. Those men were evil personified. She had to be a saint to be friends with those motherfuckers.

Or evil herself...

"You're letting your dick lead you by the nose, you fucking eejit!"

Before I'm able to respond, Cyn lifts the wooden ladle and slams it against the kitchen table, efficiently drawing our attention back to her.

"What, *cailleach*?" Carrick sneers, though I see the surprise in his expression.

It isn't often that she demands attention. For the most part she exists in a state of quiet calm, and I don't just mean not speaking, but her whole way of being is quiet. She rarely does anything to draw attention to herself. She dresses plainly, she doesn't make any big gestures to make up for her lack of sound. She just exists, like a wraith.

Haunting us with her presence.

But not this time.

This time everything about her is big, loud, attention-seeing, and we're both enraptured. Most likely for differing reasons, but enraptured nonetheless.

With her jaw clamped shut, Cyn picks up her notepad and pen, and scribbles furiously across the paper. Her anger is a series of bold and violent lines across the page, forming words that stun us both.

You're right. I could kill you. I've thought about it for years.

"SEE!" Carrick roars, lunging for her.

Cyn dodges him, running around the table with her notepad and pen grasped in her hands.

"Back the fuck up!"

Carrick falters, giving me time to restrain him whilst Arden steps into the kitchen. It doesn't take him long to figure out what's happened.

"So this is where you've been hiding," he says, his voice eerily calm.

I watch how Cyn reacts to his presence, the way she straightens her spine further as though readying herself for a fight, yet her chest and cheeks heat, indicating a deeper emotion. There's always been something more between them, some kind of attraction. Maybe it's because they've both been gifted with extraordinary talent, or perhaps it's the unexplainable magic that runs in their veins. Because if Cyn is a witch, then Arden's a seer, just like all the Dálaighs in his family are.

"You've helped yourself to the herb selection I bought for you," he says.

She nods. *Yes.*

"Do you want to tell us what's on your mind?" he asks, calm as fuck on the outside, but I know him well enough to see how much she affects him. The tiny muscle twitching beneath his right eye is his biggest tell. He's barely holding onto his restraint.

Her eyes drop to the pad she's holding and her face screws up in concentration as she writes. A moment later she holds it up for Arden to read.

I will honour my debt. I will make diamonds. I will do what you want. But I cannot do that if I'm having to watch my back all the time, she says, pointedly looking at Carrick.

"He'll back off," Arden clips.

"The fuck I will!"

Arden narrows his eyes at Carrick. "You *will* back the fuck off."

"You actually trust her?" Carrick asks in disbelief.

"I trust that she wants her freedom, and the only way she's going to get that is if she fulfils her debt. She can't get off this island without us, and she won't until she's done."

Cyn nods, briefly catching my eye before writing another message.

You let me work. You give me space to do that, and you resist the urge to hurt me. Those are my terms. If you break them, I will do what you so desperately want to do, she warns, glaring at Carrick.

"Yeah, and what's that?" he taunts back.

I'll end my life, so you don't have to.

Carrick's black eyes narrow on Cyn. "You don't have it in you."

Don't I? she writes, and then with dignity born from a woman who has endured suffering and survived, she returns her attention back to her work and ignores us all once more.

3

Cyn - fifteen years old

"So *you're* our study partner?" the black-eyed boy sneers, a smile curling up his face like some demented clown as he drops down into the seat opposite me.

"This is Carrick O'Shea," Dr Lynch says, giving the boy a warm smile as he pushes his glasses up his nose and addresses us both from the head of the table, situated in his office on the far side of the campus. "And this is Cynthia O'Farrell."

"I know who she is," he responds, folding his arms across his chest as he stretches his long legs out under the table and studies me just like a hawk might its next meal.

He's wearing a thick, black, cable-knit sweater and dark

blue jeans, and looks every inch the deviant Lorcan warned me he would be. I try not to flinch as his gaze trails over my body, taking in my grey hoodie and loose jeans. There's nothing remotely sexy or attractive about my outfit, but the thoughts running through his mind are easy to interpret.

"I hope you'll be respectful and welcome Cynthia into the school with grace and kindness."

"Of course, Doc, we wouldn't have it any other way."

His voice is as lyrical as Arden's and Lorcan's but it has an edge that speaks of dark deeds and deviousness. I don't like it. I don't like him.

"Good," Dr Lynch says, jotting something down on his notepad.

Carrick's smirk, and the obscene way he pumps his fist when Dr Lynch isn't looking, tells me that he hasn't got an ounce of grace or kindness in his body, just like his friends. He wants me to react to his lewd behaviour. I don't. I've become adept at ignoring people, Carrick is no different.

Dr Lynch looks at his wristwatch. "Where are Arden and Lorcan? I can't start this session without them."

"On their way over. Ms Polithy is having issues with her... *pipes*," Carrick replies, the innuendo completely lost on Dr Lynch. "She needed a helping hand."

"Oh yes, this building is very old. Always a pipe bursting and in need of repair," he responds happily. "I'm glad that they're choosing to listen to my advice and actively seeking to put their newly acquired skills to the test. I knew that the practicality of a plumbing course would help to focus their minds. They both need to engage their hands and their brains in order to get the best out of their therapy."

"Oh, yes, they are certainly putting their new skills to the test," Carrick replies, hiding the salacious glint in his eyes behind a swathe of brown hair.

Whilst I wait for Dr Lynch to catch on, I can't help but wonder if he really is that stupid or if he's choosing to ignore Carrick's very obvious, very disturbing, innuendos because confronting them would mean acknowledging that the pair are probably having sex with a teacher right now.

"And what about you? Are you enjoying your singing lessons? You have a very expressive voice, and it's a useful tool to channel unwanted emotions and spin them into something positive."

Singing lessons? It takes a great deal of self-control to hide the smirk desperate to unfurl from my lips. Somehow Carrick notices my glee, despite doing my best to try and hide it, and I make a mental note to stand in front of the mirror later, replaying this moment so that I can practise schooling my features.

"Why the fuck did you bring that up?" Carrick grinds out, glaring at me, and earning him a disappointed look from Dr Lynch.

"There's no need to be so defensive, Carrick. As study partners and more importantly, therapy friends, we need to learn how to share our..."

WAIT WHAT? *Therapy friends?*

I stand abruptly, my chair falling backwards and hitting the wooden floor causing Dr Lynch to jump a little in his seat.

"Goodness, Cynthia, whatever is the problem?" he asks, sliding his glasses back up the bridge of his nose with his forefinger, his kind hazel eyes brimming with concern where Carrick's are filled with vicious amusement.

Is he serious? What's my problem? My problem is that my father refuses to allow me to return home until I'm *fixed* and now I'm supposed to be vulnerable with these arseholes as my *therapy friends*? No. No way.

I reach for my pad, scrawling a message across it, but before I've even finished and can show it to Dr Lynch, Carrick snorts with disgust.

"Didn't you know? Not only do you get to study with us, we also get to share our deepest, darkest secrets with each other and fuck, you've made me want to hear yours!"

"Carrick, language!" Dr Lynch scolds, before turning his attention back to me. "Please, take a seat and let's discuss this further."

"Discuss further? She *can't* speak," Carrick points out unhelpfully.

"She has other ways of communicating. Don't you, Cynthia?"

When I don't respond, instead choosing to hide my angrily written words against my chest, Dr Lynch rests his hands on the table and waits. The silence that stretches between us is uncomfortable, even for me. Eventually, I release my grip on my notepad, pick up the chair and take a seat as if the world just didn't implode around me.

"You were saying?" he insists, giving me an encouraging

smile that I would appreciate if Carrick wasn't burning a hole in the side of my face.

No. I shake my head, forcing the muscles in my face to remain relaxed. I don't want to share my thoughts, at least not the ones I just wrote down in panic and anger. They'll make me appear weak. I can't be weak in front of Carrick. So instead of showing Dr Lynch what I actually wrote, I flip the page and write something else.

I thought that my father only agreed to one-to-one therapy sessions?

Dr Lynch reads my words, then meets my gaze. "Your father agreed to let experts take the lead on your care, that means allowing us to act accordingly based on our professional judgement. You will still have one-to-one sessions with me, but you will also be expected to take part in group therapy."

He won't be happy about this, I write, and for the first time I'm grateful that my father has a reputation.

Dr Lynch leans back in his chair, and says, "I've already had a long discussion with Mr O'Farrell. We are in agreement that group sessions are in your best interest. For too long your mutism has acted as a barrier between you and the world. Finding your voice, hearing you speak, that's your father's greatest wish, and I wholeheartedly believe that these young men will help you to do that."

"See, we're your saviours," Carrick gloats.

Despite all the sarcastic retorts rampaging through my head I refuse to react, deciding that from this moment on I'm not going to even acknowledge Carrick. The best way to deal with a person who uses their overwhelming personality and poor behaviour to get attention is to ignore them, so ignore him I will.

"They are passionate young men, with very..." Dr Lynch pauses, trying to articulate his thoughts whilst I wait for him to fill the gap. "...*Intriguing* personalities that I believe will help encourage you to find your voice."

Is this a joke? If I had a voice, my words would be lost to the terror of my heart squeezing my throat shut, as it is I remain outwardly calm. Arden has already threatened my life the minute I met him, and Lorcan insinuated that I owe him sexual favours because of his friendship with the arsehole and now I'm expected to share my trauma with these boys in group therapy sessions?

I'd prefer one on one sessions with you.

"It is, I'm afraid, non-negotiable," Dr Lynch replies after reading my statement, the kindness in his eyes turning to pity, and in that moment I see this for what it is.

He *knows*.

He knows that my father is a man you cannot say no to. He knows that these boys aren't kind, and I'd go as far as to say that my father requested I be placed with the most heinous people at the school because he believes that I'll be cured with cruelty and not kindness.

This is a farce. All of it.

This session. This school.

None of it is for my benefit.

This is about my dad wanting a *normal* child. This is about him needing me to be strong, and strength isn't a girl who cannot speak. That is not the O'Farrell way. Strength is a girl who finds her voice in order to put three troublesome boys in their place. What my dad has forgotten is that the last time he tried to put me in the path of three angry, messed-up boys, I made them my *friends*.

I guess, then, this is round two.

Though something tells me I will never be friends with Carrick, Lorcan or Arden. That their hatefulness wasn't built on abuse, twisting their goodness into darkness like Malik Brov's sons, but on something altogether different.

My anger is quickly replaced with a sense of impending doom, and it's only heightened when Lorcan and Arden step into the room, reeking of illicit sex and the distinct scent of marijuana.

They both have a lazy smile on their face, the whites of their eyes bloodshot. High on oxytocin and dopamine, they are oblivious to the tension in the room.

"So good of you to join us," Dr Lynch says, getting up from his seat and ushering them into the office.

Apart from wrinkling his nose, he doesn't acknowledge the glaringly obvious. Looks like Dr Lynch is good at turning a blind eye. Which is great for them, and terrible for me.

"We were helping Miss with a plumbing issue," Arden says, swallowing a smile as Carrick mimics a lewd sex act with his hands behind Dr Lynch's back.

"So Carrick told me. I'm glad you're putting your skills to work."

"Oh, we certainly made good use of them," Lorcan adds, smirking.

Bile rises up my throat at the gloating. I don't care who they've slept with, even though it's disgusting that someone in a position of authority can take advantage of two young men who're clearly emotionally unstable. What I care about is that I'm expected to have group therapy sessions with these arseholes because my father believes they'll anger me enough into speaking again.

Newsflash, I have zero control over my ability to speak. God knows I've tried over the years, but the sound won't come. I've resigned myself to the fact that I won't ever hear my voice again and no amount of bullishness from my father, and cruelty from whomever he puts in my path, will cure me. Nothing has helped me to find my voice.

Not the self-harm I've inflicted on myself over the years to try and coax out a cry of pain, or the copious amounts of medication forced into my system upon the advice of some quack my father's paid to drug me. I've seen numerous doctors and had hours upon hours of therapy, but all that time and money has been wasted. Not even the kindness and under-standing my beloved grandmother has showered me with over the years has helped.

Truth be known, if I could reach down my own throat and rip out my voice, I would.

I'd do it in a tattered heartbeat, with a cry of feral joy.

But I can't.

So I'm left with no voice, and evidently no say in my life either.

I may be able to communicate by writing words on paper, but nothing is more powerful than a voice being *heard*, and I may as well be writing in a foreign language for all the lack of understanding inflicted upon me over the years.

"So what did we miss?" Arden asks, sliding out a chair next to me, twisting it around and straddling the seat.

"Cyn throwing a hissy fit over the fact we're in group therapy together. She'd rather cut herself to shreds apparently," Carrick gloats.

My head snaps around as I glare at him and he smiles broadly. "There she is," he mutters.

I could kick myself for reacting, but I'm more concerned about how he knew that's what I wrote down before I decided against sharing that very personal information and wrote something else instead.

Carrick's gaze drops to the pad I'm holding. "Your marker pen bled through the page. It's not all that hard to read backwards. If you want to keep shit private, I'd use a pencil."

If I was able to speak, I'd be stunned into silence. His remark was cutting, but the advice was actually useful. I frown, uncertain of his intentions.

"What? It's just common sense, did you lose that as well as your voice?" he snips.

Back to being a prick again, then.

Lorcan feigns disappointment as he holds his hand over his chest and looks wide-eyed at me. "You're not keen on the idea of us being therapy friends? Why's that?"

The three of them laugh, and I draw on every last ounce of strength not to react or lash out like they so desperately want me to do.

"Actually, it's a valid question," Dr Lynch interscedes. "Would you care to elaborate, Cynthia?"

Isn't it obvious? I write as calmly as I possibly can. *This isn't for my benefit.*

Dr Lynch hesitates, then folds his hands in his lap and says, "I think it's important that you trust in the process. That's why you're here, isn't it?"

We both know that I'm here because I've been forced to be. I don't trust in this process. I don't trust these BOYS, I write, pushing my response into the centre of the table. I don't care if they read it.

"I wouldn't trust us either, but it looks like you've got no choice," Carrick says, his black eyes flickering with something I don't want to acknowledge right now.

Pity.

4

C arrick - present day

"I don't trust her," I say, leaning against the wall in our outhouse as Cyn sets up her ingredients and equipment on the huge metal table running through the centre of the space to make diamonds.

This is a trial run to check the equipment, the quality of the ingredients, and the environment. These are all key factors of the process according to Arden, who questioned Cyn in great detail on our journey back to the island together.

"You don't trust anyone," Lorcan points out, watching her closely as she places the leaves of several different plants that I've forgotten the name of into a glass beaker and pours high proof alcohol over them to extract the active chemical, forming the base of the drug. Later she'll slowly heat what's left over in acetone using a glass flask over a water bath. It will take time but eventually the liquid will crystallise, and voila, we have diamonds. Once the process has been honed, she'll start in earnest.

"I have every reason not to," I respond tightly.

Lorcan side-eyes me. He knows better than to bring up my past, so he doesn't. "Except me and Arden, of course."

"Hmm."

He knows I trust them both with my life, but that doesn't mean to say that their behaviour of late hasn't had me questioning their judgement.

"You're still pissed about what happened yesterday morning, aren't you?" he asks.

"Yeah," I mutter, scraping a hand over my face, biting back what I truly want to say.

"What?" Lorcan asks, dragging his gaze off of Cyn.

"You need me to spell it out for you, Lorcan?" I say, eying Arden as he studies her every movement. This isn't the first time we've watched her make diamonds, and if you ask me it's as boring as watching paint dry. I don't give a fuck how she does it, I only care about her getting it done and getting the fuck off our island.

"You're questioning us where Cyn is concerned, is that it?"

"You've forgotten what she's capable of," I hiss under my breath.

"I'm fully aware of what Cyn's capable of, as is Arden."

I scoff, pushing off from the wall. "And yet this morning you almost drank that shit she was brewing because she smiled at you. She's fucking with your head, so forgive me if I can't trust her intentions, or yours for that matter."

A muscle ticks in Lorcan's jaw as he looks at me and with a lowered voice says, "You saw that?"

"Yes, I saw."

"And now you don't trust me because Cyn is beginning to?"

"You think she trusts you? Come on, Lorcan. She *knows* who you are. She's manipulating you, just as much as you're manipulating her. Her childhood friends were murdered just days ago and we made that happen, and you think that smile was genuine? She fucking hates us, just like she always did."

Lorcan folds his arms across his chest. "Is this concern for my well-being or do I detect a hint of jealousy?"

"I'm not fucking jealous!" I hiss, hating how my pulse races when Cyn looks over at us both, disturbed by my outburst. Opposite her, Arden frowns.

"Take it outside. Cyn has work to do. She needs to concentrate and you're distracting her," he orders curtly, before wrapping his knuckles against the table and drawing Cyn's attention back to the task at hand.

Briefly she meets my gaze, her blank expression contrasts with the emotion behind her eyes, and in that moment I understand what she's trying to convey. She's warning me not to push her, just like she did yesterday morning, but doesn't she understand, that's all I ever *want* to do?

I want to push her into reacting. I want to push her into being loud, and I don't mean necessarily with her voice, though fuck knows I long to hear it. She's always been so quiet, so controlled, and yet I know there's more to her. I've witnessed it first-hand several times over the years, and this morning when I knocked the drink out of Lorcan's hand, I'd seen it once more.

I see it in her eyes now.

That part of her *excites* me. The wild, uninhibited part of her that only I've ever witnessed.

Over the years I've wanted to hurt her just so I could bring that other side of her to the surface and drag out the voice I'm convinced she's desperate to reveal. It's become an obsession, hearing her speak. I've done it too. I've hurt her. Over and over again. But each time she's bested me and her voice remains as mythological as the creature I've named her after.

"There's nothing to take outside," Lorcan replies, giving my shoulder a squeeze as he throws Arden a tight smile. "I'm going to stay, and Carrick is going to check the office to see if we've had any calls or emails from Soren about his order of diamonds."

"I am?" I roll my eyes. "Just tell me to leave, and I'll leave."

"Carrick," Arden says. "Leave."

"You don't have to tell me twice. I'm gone."

A couple of hours later, I hear Arden laughing at something Lorcan has said as I step out from the office into the hallway to greet them. Cyn is standing off to their right, heavy shadows painting the pale skin beneath her eyes. She's exhausted, and apparently neither of them have noticed.

"The Skull Brotherhood are chasing their shipment. They

want an expected delivery date," I say, leaning against the doorframe.

I shouldn't give a fuck that Cyn looks dead on her feet. I *don't* give a fuck, but if they want her to make the volume of drugs Soren has requested, then they need to at least make sure she's fit enough to do so. The sooner she fulfils her debt, the sooner we're free of her. Dragging my gaze away, I force myself to look at Arden who strolls towards me.

"Is that right?" he questions, his smile slipping from his face as he enters the office. "I'll call him and tell him they'll be ready when they're ready," he adds.

"He gave you shit, did he?" Lorcan asks, whilst behind me Arden picks up the phone and makes the call.

I cock a brow. "Not unless he wants the location of his hide-away shared with his enemies," I reply, flicking my gaze back to Cyn who sways on her feet. "You should sit down before you fall down."

She shakes her head, reaching for the wall as her palm rests against the panelled wood.

Lorcan whips his head around, takes one look at her and says, "When was the last time you ate?"

"You don't know when she ate last?" I ask, scowling, then straightening my features because why the fuck do I care?

"Do *you* know?" he throws back.

I don't. I assumed either him or Arden took care of it. "I'm not her fucking butler."

Cyn huffs out a breath, pushing off from the wall as she glares at us both, then with her nose in the air, like some stuck-up princess who's had the displeasure of interacting with the paupers of her kingdom, strides down the hall towards the kitchen. I stare after her, wondering how one withering look can make me want to punish her for daring to look at me with such disdain and then punish myself for allowing her to get to me.

"I guess she's going to rectify that herself," Lorcan replies, moving to follow her.

"A word," Arden calls from the office.

"He sounds pissed off," Lorcan says dryly.

"No shit." I reply just as dryly.

"A WORD!"

We both step inside the office as Arden looks between us. "Where's Cyn?"

"Kitchen. Carrick noticed she was looking a bit peaky. I surmised she needed to eat..."

Lorcan lets that statement hang in the air. I'm not sure what he's trying to achieve other than pissing Arden off for failing to notice that his most prized possession is on the verge of exhaustion. Arden cracks his neck, and if I didn't know any better, a flash of guilt crosses his face before he schools his face into a blank mask.

"Carrick, watch over her. Make sure she eats, rests, and doesn't do anything stupid."

"You want *me* to watch over her?"

"Did I stutter?" he retorts, daring me to object.

"I think Lorcan would be better equipped for the task, now that he's gaining her trust," I add, with more than a touch of sarcasm.

"I asked *you* to do it."

"I can go," Lorcan offers with a shrug like he isn't trying to get more alone time with Cyn.

Frankly he can have it, because every time I'm around her I switch between wanting to fuck her or kill her.

"I want Carrick to do it. He's the one who needs to make sure she doesn't go through with her threat. If he doesn't, then there'll be consequences."

"Consequences. Who for, me?"

Arden squeezes the bridge of his nose. "For *all* of us, brother."

"Point well made," Lorcan shrugs, dropping into the seat opposite Arden and picking up the letter opener on the desk, twisting it in his fingers. "But if he loses control, I get to take care of his mess."

I scoff. "I always knew you wanted to play hero."

"If Arden's her master and you're her tormentor, that really only leaves one role for me, brother," Lorcan shoots back, not bothering to deny it.

"Like I said this morning, she sees right through your act. Always has. She knows what to expect from me. At least I'm honest."

Arden leans back in his seat, watching me carefully. "Are you *sure* about that?"

What's that supposed to mean?

Instead of voicing that question, I turn on my heel, not bothering to respond. Arden might think he is Cyn's master puppeteer, but he isn't mine. I draw the line at being coerced into an altercation with him over a woman we've vowed to never let get between us again.

Stepping into the kitchen, I shake those memories aside, refusing to remember the time when we came to blows over the woman sitting at the table before me now. She might've been a girl back then and us mere boys on the cusp of manhood, but the feelings she provoked in us were powerful. There are many reasons I want her gone from our lives, but forcing a wedge between us is one of the main ones. She's only been here a short time and already I feel her edging her way between us once more.

"I'm to make sure you eat, though I see you've already taken care of that," I say, moving towards the table, a plate of sliced meat, a tub of butter and a loaf of bread resting on the surface.

She doesn't look up, instead she folds up a piece of paper that she was looking at and slides it into her recipe book, before picking up her sandwich and taking a bite. I don't bother to draw her into a conversation knowing that I'm the last person on the planet she'd ever want to willingly talk to.

Besides, the quiet suits me just fine. I've had a headache all day and it's beginning to get to the point where nothing but a dose of rum and sleep is going to cure it.

No more than five minutes later I feel Cyn watching me, the fine hairs on the back of my neck a warning to guard myself from her special brand of magic. I drag my gaze from the view out of the kitchen window and back to her.

"What?" I ask.

She chews on her lip, and I half expect her to get up and leave the room, but she surprises me by picking up her pencil and scribbling something down on her notepad, twisting it around for me to read. She still refuses to communicate with her voice, writing words on paper, and even those words are sparse. I see it as a challenge, getting her to speak. Hell, to even make a sound. One day we'll own her voice as well as everything else about her.

But she's stubborn.

She hasn't spoken a word for almost twenty years, ever since she witnessed her mother's murder as a small child. Fuck if it doesn't bother me that she still won't utter a sound to the men who she lost her virginity to when we were no more than eighteen.

It bothers me more than it should.

You have a headache.

"How do you...?" I ask, my voice trailing off as she starts to write her response before I've even finished the question.

Your eyes. They're glassy.

"That something you've learnt from your coven, *cailleach*?"

She narrows her eyes at me, not in a way that's angry but as though she's still assessing my symptoms. It takes her a moment to reply.

I don't have a coven. I just understand the human body and know how to treat illnesses using natural remedies. It's not magic, not in the way you think.

I read her words and snort. "I bet that's what you say to everyone before you curse them."

Unperturbed, she writes, *I can make something to soothe your headaches.*

"No."

I can help you.

"I don't need your help. I manage these headaches the same way I manage everything else."

By suffering, you mean? she writes, getting to her feet.

"I don't suffer, I just get on with it," I snap, pissed that she's looking at me like I'm some kind of martyr or worse, someone damaged.

She raises a brow, then pushes back away from the table and walks into the pantry. Glass chinks as she searches through the jars filled with different herbs, flower and plant matter all obtained for her in preparation of her arrival. Once Arden decided we'd call in her debt, he made sure she had everything she needed for her stay. A moment later she steps out with a jar of rosemary.

"Rosemary?"

She nods, placing the jar on the table and unscrewing the lid. Bringing it to her nose she breathes in, her eyes pressing shut in pleasure. I shift uncomfortably in my seat, getting the sudden urge to bend her flat over the table, lift up her skirt and bury my nose in her cunt, just so I can breathe in her scent in the same way.

"Fuck!" I mutter.

Her gaze snaps up and she blanches, slowly setting the jar on the table as she reads my expression. She must see something that she doesn't like because her gaze tracks to the kitchen door as though she's assessing how successful her escape might be if she needed to run.

She wouldn't get very far.

"I could tell you that you've nothing to fear and that I don't want to hurt you, but that would be a lie. I always have," I say, nothing if not honest. "If you run, I *will* catch you. Haven't I proven that every time in the past?"

Her cheeks flush a deep pink and I know she remembers all the times I caught her in our youth. It was always me who found her first. *Always.* I always let them believe they were the best hunters, they weren't.

She presses her palms against the surface of the table. Her pinky finger grazing the handle of a kitchen knife resting there. I can almost see the thoughts running through her head as she debates whether to snatch it up and lash out at me.

I wait, intrigued to see whether she'll give me a reason to hurt her, almost wishing she would put us both out of our misery and do what we both know she wants to do. Instead she reaches for her pad and pen, writing more than a sentence given the length of time it takes her to finish. I expect her to lash out, to berate me, scorn me, *curse* me with her words.

She doesn't.

I will make you an essential oil using rosemary. You can use it to rub onto your temples at the first sign of a headache. I can't help on this occasion as it will take at least four hours to make. For now I suggest you drink plenty of water and get some rest before it turns into a migraine.

When I look back up she waits for my response, her expression neutral, not a flicker of fear in her eyes. The urge to put it back there is intense.

"You can make what you want, but I'm not foolish enough to use it, *cailleach*."

Her gaze drops, and when she picks up the knife, my pulse

races sending a rush of blood to my dick. Fuck I want her to fight me so bad. I want her to draw blood.

I move to stand, rounding the table towards her. She doesn't turn to face me, waving the knife in front of her to warn me off like I expect her to. Instead, she takes a handful of rosemary from the glass jar and starts chopping it up.

"I said I don't want any," I repeat, edging closer, my fucking heart pounding in my chest as I imagine all the deviant things I want to do to her with that knife pressed against her throat.

I don't give a fuck about her earlier warning, or Arden's for that matter.

What I want at this moment is her fear. Then I want her to *fight*. Just like she always did when we were kids.

Still she ignores me as she sets the knife back on the table and grabs a pestle and mortar from the cabinet above the kitchen sink. When she places the chopped rosemary into the mortar and starts grinding the herb with the pestle, I decide that my patience has worn as thin as it can today and I grab her wrist, turning her around before she is even able to reach for the knife.

"I said I don't want any," I grind out through clenched teeth.

Her head slowly tilts backwards as she looks up at me, and when her misty grey eyes meet the black heat of mine, something close to electricity scatters up my spine, stringing me tighter than a coiled spring.

I know she hates me as much as I hate her, and yet this tingling sensation I feel whenever I'm close to her doesn't feel very much like hate.

It feels like something infinitely more dangerous for us both.

It feels like magic.

And in that moment, I recognise the blood pact at work, the thick, inky tendrils of the night we got so fucked-up on drugs, on each other, coiling around us and dragging me back to the biggest mistake we ever made. I can still smell the scent of her skin, feel the softness of her breath, see the curve of her spine as she arches beneath our lips, tongues and fingers. It's no longer a memory I've tried so hard to repress, but a reality I long to steep in.

I *should* push her away. I *should* put space between us.

I do neither of those things, and this time she doesn't try to escape.

This time she reaches up and presses her fingers against my temple, rubbing gentle circles over the taut skin there. For a moment I'm so caught off guard by her touch and the gentle concern emanating from her eyes, that I allow her wrist to slip from my grasp and her hands to massage my temple, easing the pain building inside my head. I allow her to give me comfort, which is something that I've only ever allowed my brothers to give me. And it's that sharp, abrasive thought that cuts through my trance-like state and brings me crashing back to reality.

"Get the fuck off me, *cailleach!*" I yell, pushing against her, and swiping at the invisible bond that taunts me every second of every fucking day. "I don't buy your act for one fucking minute."

She gives me a wide-eyed look, shock painting her features

a different shade of emotion. One I haven't seen in a long, long time. *Hurt.*

Not a physical hurt, but an emotional one.

My rejection hurts her and that in turn confuses me, because hurt has no place between two enemies, only hate, and I am filled to the brim with it.

"Don't ever touch me again," I warn, my voice a low rumble.

She nods almost imperceptibly, straightens her features and evens out her expression. Then without a single thought for her safety, she turns her back on me and walks away, just like she did that night in the grounds of Silver Oaks Institute right after Lorcan gave her her first kiss, I took her second and Arden stole her third.

5

Cyn - Fifteen years old

Surrounding Silver Oaks Institute there are fifty acres of grounds that the students can roam during their down-time, not that many of them take the opportunity. Most of the students keep to themselves, and in the three months that I've been here I've had very little interaction with anyone other than Arden, Lorcan and Carrick, who are constant thorns in my side with their snide comments and lewd behaviour.

So whenever I can, I escape into the small forest to the north of the grounds that borders the edge of the property. It has a plethora of plants, wildflowers and herbs that I can pick to my heart's content, as well as a pretty stream running through it. It's peaceful and a tonic for my restless spirit and broken heart, as well as a respite to the gathering storm that is the three boys who've become the bane of my existence.

I still have group therapy sessions with the bastards, and not a day goes by without one of them doing or saying something to try and hurt me. It only proves that I was right all along, that my father is trying to get me to use my voice to deal with those arseholes, and that Dr Lynch and Ms Weatherby are in on it too.

Well fuck them all.

Fuck my father for his *tough love*.

Fuck Ms Weatherby for turning a blind eye.

Fuck Dr Lynch for being complicit, for actively putting me in uncomfortable situations with the three boys under the guise of therapy.

And fuck Arden, Lorcan and Carrick. Fuck them most of all.

I don't understand what they gain from the situation. They don't know me. We have no history. We have nothing in common bar our attendance at Silver Oaks. I don't understand their hate. What purpose does it fill? Why do they want to hurt *me*?

Maybe it's because to them I'm just an easy target. I'm weak, voiceless.

I can't fight back with my words. I can't fight back physically. I can't fight back at all.

I'm at their mercy, and they have none.

Letting out a long, silent breath, I trudge across the frostbitten, grassy meadow towards the woods. It's nearing curfew but I don't care. After another tiresome solo session with Dr Lynch I need some time alone to clear my head. I need to think, and I need a plan if I'm going to survive my time here.

Stepping into the thicket, I take the path towards the stream that runs through the centre of the woods, all my worries falling away as I surround myself with nature.

Like my mother and grandmother, I have an affinity with the outdoors, with nature and the natural order of things. I have vague memories of my mum taking me on walks surrounding our family home back in Kilkenny, trailing through meadows filled with wildflowers as butterflies and bees lifted up into the scented air around us. She would pick flowers as we walked and tell me the Latin name for each one, explaining their healing properties. Then after her death, my grandmother would do the same until I became as knowledgeable as them both. Here in this space, away from the stresses of my life and the boys who are intent on hurting me, I feel peace, however fleeting that may be.

Stepping over a fallen log that's covered in a thick blanket of vibrant green moss, I walk down the bank of the stream and take a seat on a flat rock that juts out just above the trickling water. Dropping my bag beside me, I cross my legs and take a deep, shaky breath, allowing the scents of the forest to wash over me. The air is cleaner here, less clogged with the stench of cruelty and spite.

Shaking myself free of the dark cloud that I've been living under for the past month since I arrived here, I take out my leather-bound diary, opening it up to a fresh page and begin to write.

This diary holds the contents to all of my thoughts, as well as recipes for tinctures, ointments, herbal teas and lotions that I've gathered over time. Some are my mother's recipes, some my grandmother's and more recently, some are mine.

My father doesn't know that I've followed in my mother's footsteps, if he did I'm positive he'd try to stop me. My grandmother told me that he never believed in my mother's ability to heal with her tonics and lotions. He forbade her from practising, but she continued regardless.

I love that. I love that she refused to let him dull her glow.

My grandmother tells me that my mother fought hard right to the end against his bullish ways. That she challenged him every day. That she loved him despite his darkness. My father isn't a good man. He's gruff, difficult, violent towards his enemies and cold towards his loved ones, but according to my grandmother he loved my mother very much, she was the only person he ever showed any warmth to.

It wasn't always like that though. In the beginning they hated one another.

My father stole my mother from her family, his arch-enemies, the O'Briens, and he made her his. He did it out of spite and hatred, and honestly I don't think he ever expected to love her, but just like a wildflower that grows out of a barren field, their love blossomed.

She found a heart inside his chest and her love made it beat.

But that heart, and that love, died when she did.

I was a pale imitation in comparison to my mother, a duller version of her. If she was that single wildflower in a barren field, brightening everything with its beauty and vitality, then I was the solitary weed trying its best to survive in its shadows.

Over the years my father has tried everything to make me into my mother's image, but I don't have her stunning beauty, her charisma or her captivating voice. All I have is her affinity with nature, and that was something he only tolerated for her because he loved her so.

That tolerance, that love, doesn't extend to me.

I'm a burden... I write, the words blurring as the same old feelings of low worth and self-esteem rear their ugly heads. Nevertheless I continue to write in my diary, giving life to the thoughts inside my head and the silent words trapped inside my heart, because freeing them is better than letting them eat me alive.

I can't voice those thoughts aloud and let them release into the air, sharing them with someone else to ease my burden. All I can do is write them down, and purge my heart of the crushing darkness because I'm determined to try and grow something good out of something bad.

So for the next half an hour that's what I do. I purge my thoughts. I let go of the self-hatred. I rid myself of everything that's haunted me and all the bad feelings inside. It's cathartic, even if it's painful.

I'm a burden to my father, I scribble onto the page, determined to not let this cloud of self-hatred get the better of me. *I'm a reminder of everything he'd lost. I know he wished it were me who'd been shot that day. I know deep down that my father could have survived my death. After all, a child can be replaced with another, but for him nothing can ever replace the loss of my mother.*

She was one of a kind. She was the balm to his soul, the thrum in his veins and the centre of his universe. And the worst part about it all? I agree with him. She was irreplaceable. Special. A truly gifted individual. I can only hope that one day I'll be a fraction of the woman she once was.

For a moment I allow the bad thoughts and feelings to have life, acknowledging them, then I let them go. As I pack away my diary and pen, sliding them both into my bag, I remind myself that I am my mother's daughter. I am Cynthia O'Farrell and that means something.

I mean something.

Standing, I grab my bag and climb back up the mossy bank. It's getting dark, the sun is already slipping towards the horizon casting orange, pink and yellow across the forest floor as shadows creep into every crevice and crack.

I probably have about thirty minutes until curfew, and I consider making my way back to my room but the rebel in me doesn't want to obey the rules right now. I guess that part of my personality I can thank my father for. He never obeys the rules, and this evening I'm not going to either.

I venture deeper into the forest, climbing over fallen logs and traversing through overgrown shrubs, my fingers trailing over the rough bark of the tree, the sound of wildlife scurrying across the forest floor is comforting to me. As I walk, I gather grass and moss, mushrooms and bark, weeds and wildflowers, stuffing them into my bag. While I forage the forest for plant life that I'll use in my recipes. I lose myself in the feeling of freedom and peace it gives me.

That peace, however, is short-lived.

Seconds before they step out into my path, I sense them.

Their aura is as ugly and bleak as they are, suffocating the peace that I've worked so hard to surround myself with this past hour.

"Isn't it past your bedtime?" Lorcan says, stepping out from behind a huge oak tree as he grins at me, his smile as disingenuous as it is beautiful.

I side step him, knowing it's pointless to try and put some space between us, but do it anyway. He mirrors me, reaching for a strand of hair that has fallen free from my ponytail, his knuckles sweeping gently over my cheek.

"So pretty, and you don't even realise it," he says, the sincerity in his voice confusing me as he leans in and presses a chaste kiss against my lips before whispering, "You should run."

Before I'm even able to shake off the shock of his kiss and unravel his warning, a twig snaps behind him and I jump. Lorcan's expression darkens as Arden approaches, appearing to his right.

"What are you doing here?" Arden asks, a deep scowl forming between his brows as he looks between us both.

I hold my bag across my chest and stare at Arden, the unspoken leader of their trio, in the hope that the coolness of my gaze and the stubborn tilt of my chin will suffice as an answer.

None of your damn business.

"Have you been following us?"

This time it's Carrick who asks the question, and a shiver runs down my spine as he appears from behind a tree, camouflaged somewhat in his dark brown sweater and black jeans, the light from the sunset barely breaking through the shadows gathering in the forest behind them now.

Clutching my bag tighter against my chest, I shake my head, stepping into one of the last remaining pools of light. *No.*

"Liar," he accuses with a grin, and where Lorcan's smile is a beautiful display of kindness, however fake, Carrick's is a slash of dark intent as he stalks towards me. "You're just a pretty, little liar."

Lifting my nose in the air, I tip my head back and look up at him, standing my ground, refusing to be intimidated.

No, I repeat with another shake of my head.

"See, I don't believe you," he replies, gripping my shoulders and backing me up against the trunk of a tree, almost lifting me off my feet with the force of his hatred. Hatred that I don't understand. "Why are you following us?"

I flare my nostrils, my response an angry rush of breath as I push back against his chest and reach between us. He glares at me as I pull out my notepad and pen that I carry around with me everywhere I go. If he wants an answer I'll give him one.

It starts with *fuck* and ends with *off*.

Tutting, he restrains my arms once more, squeezing tightly as I struggle against him.

"No need to be rude," he snarls.

"Give her some space," Lorcan says, appearing behind Carrick, his silver-grey eyes meeting mine. In this light he looks almost ethereal, his pale skin glowing golden in the last ebbs of sunlight. "You got your answer."

I wish I could believe he's stepping in for my benefit, but I've become an expert at reading people and I know without any shadow of a doubt that Lorcan is as hateful as Carrick is, the falsity of his kindness is just his ammo. Of course Carrick ignores him, in fact he does the exact opposite and leans in closer, crushing his chest against mine and trapping my only way to communicate between us both.

"I think you're obsessed with us, aren't you, Cynthia?" he suggests, his hands sliding up my arms and creeping up my neck as his fingers curl into my hair. Leaning in close he breathes in, the tip of his nose dragging up my neck as he draws my scent into his lungs. "Hmm, you smell so good. I wonder if you taste as sweet."

Touch is as alien to me as respect for another person's boundaries is to Carrick, and I find myself caught in this battle between wanting to lean into the softness of his touch and rage against his total lack of regard for my feelings. In the end indignation wins out and I push against him, my notepad and pen discarded as I try and wriggle out of his hold.

"The more you struggle, the worse it will be," he warns, his lips pressing against the shell of my ear as his warm breath slides across my skin.

I can't help it, I shudder, and I don't even know at this point if it's out of fear or in lust. All I know is that I'm acutely aware of how his chest heaves against mine, how tall he is, how strong in comparison to how weak I am. If he wanted to hurt me, really hurt me, he could. I know it. He knows it, and the others know it.

Maybe that's why Arden replaces Lorcan's position behind him and says, "Now is not the time, Carrick."

"Why not?" he responds, his lips trailing heat across my

chilled skin before his mouth presses against mine in a kiss that stuns me. With eyes wide, I stare at him as he moves his mouth gently across mine, a low groan parting his lips before he says, "Don't tell me you haven't wanted to fuck her mouth with your tongue too."

"I said now is not the time!" Arden snaps, yanking Carrick off of me, the air chill against my heated skin.

Carrick holds up his hands, laughing as Arden shoves him away. "Hey, I was just fucking around. If you wanted to take her first kiss for yourself, you should've just said."

Lorcan snorts, slapping Carrick on the back. "You've got a death wish, mate."

"You call that a kiss?" Arden replies, a cocky glint in his amber eyes as he smirks at me.

No! I shake my head again, understanding what he wishes to do just before he does it.

Before I can even fight him off, Arden has me pushed back up against the rough bark, his lips on mine, his tongue breaking past my lips and licking into my mouth angrily as he pins my hips with his own and punishes me with his kiss.

God how he hurts me with his kiss.

He tastes of anger and vengeance, of bitterness and spite.

I try to push him away, but he wraps a hand around my throat, squeezing in warning, and despite the rush of anger, the indignation and the fear, my body betrays me. With hands that don't feel like mine, my fingers curl into his shirt, and I do something that shocks me to the core, I kiss him back.

I. Kiss. Him. Back.

He feels my body soften and his fingers uncurl just slightly around my throat, his pointer finger smoothing tiny circles on my neck as though he likes my reaction and wants to encourage more of it.

Then my brain catches up with my traitorous body, switching my reaction again.

This time I kiss him with as much venom as I can muster. I kiss him with the anger of a girl sick and tired of being underestimated in every way possible.

My teeth clash with his, my tongue sweeping against his own as I claw at him, pulling him closer not pushing him away. Then when he groans into my mouth, when he shows just how affected by my kiss he is, I strike, biting down on his bottom lip with a rush of anger, most of it directed at him, some of it directed at myself.

"Fuck!" he roars, shoving against me, swiping at his bloodied mouth with the back of his hand as he stumbles backwards, shock and the tiniest hint of respect flickering across his gaze.

Behind him Lorcan and Carrick look between us, their mouths agape as they stare at us both, and in that moment I become more than a voiceless girl, my actions speaking so much louder than words.

"You vicious little bitch," Carrick snarls, snapping out of his shock first as he steps towards me.

But I'm not done yet. With a warning glare on my face and Arden's kiss burning against my lips, I drop to the ground and grab my notepad and pen, scrawling my indignation across the page.

HOW DARE YOU!

My chest heaves as I stand, shoving my notebook under Arden's nose. I tap the page, fury painting my cheeks red. He looks from the page to my face and back again, silent.

So I write more words, determined to be heard.

You think you can intimidate me? You think you can scare me? You're just stupid, ignorant little boys. Try that again and I will make you suffer.

His eyes meet mine, and he says one word. "How?"

I blanch. *What?*

"How will you make us suffer, *Little Mouse*?" he asks, reading my reaction and interpreting it correctly.

Flipping over the page, I write my response.

I'll destroy all three of you before you ever destroy me.

He reads my words then tips his head back and laughs. He couldn't hurt me any more if he tried, because in his contempt I see my father, a man who looks at me and sees something lacking just like Arden does now.

"You and whose army...?" he asks, smirking as he licks his bloody lip. "If I want to taunt you, I will. If I want to kiss you, I will, and if I want to make you mine, I will!" His eyes flare dangerously, and behind him Carrick laughs. "But I will say this," he continues. "If you kiss me like that again, I'll make sure that when I eventually fuck you, you'll enjoy it."

Over my dead body! I write, my hands shaking so much the words are almost unintelligible.

"Don't tempt him," Lorcan says, a warning note to his voice, one I refuse to heed.

He'll kill you! I add, writing those words and knowing they're not true, because if my dad cared about me enough he would've done that already.

"Haven't you worked it out yet?" Arden asks, casting a sharp look at Lorcan before returning his attention back to me. "The only fucks your dad gives is getting you to speak, and guess who's tasked with that *honour*? I know for a fact he asked Dr Lynch to pair you up with the shittiest kid at this school. Guess what, now you've got three."

I shake my head even though I already know it's true. I worked that out for myself the first therapy session I was forced to attend with them. My fingers tighten around my pen, and this time I'm determined to keep my hand steady when I write, *I will never utter a word, not a sound. Not for you. Not for any of you.*

Arden reads my words, then with a sharp nod of his head he says, "Challenge accepted," before he steps aside and allows me to leave.

That night as I toss and turn in bed, the memory of their lips burning into my skin, I have no idea that those kisses would be the first of many. I have no idea that over the next few years more kisses would be stolen, whilst others will be given up in heated moments of passion and hate. I have no idea that I will tie myself to those hateful boys with every kiss, touch and moment of intimacy, marking me permanently.

Marking *them*.

6

A rden - present day

Rubbing my hand over the back of my neck, I attempt to ease the tension there. It's a month since we brought Cyn to our home and we've been taking turns watching over her as she works. Her presence is distracting, her countenance infuriating, her silence suffocating.

I don't even know why I'm so fucking attracted to her.

She's pretty, but not stunning.

Rail thin, not curvy.

Her grey eyes are more rolling fog than sparkling platinum.

Her hair is mousy-brown rather than deep mahogany.

She's a watercolour painting, muted and faded.

And yet...

She carries herself with a noble strength and courage that the deviant in me wants to break. She is gifted beyond anyone I've ever met, and could kill a man with her tinctures and potions should she wish. By now she could have easily slipped something into our drinks, or laced one of the joints we like to smoke. Hell, she could've poisoned us slowly, but she hasn't.

And that's as curious to me as her silence.

Cyn is a contradiction. An anomaly. A puzzle. Pandora's box.

And God help me, I want to crack her open and feast on all her secrets.

Needless to say, her being here is a challenge. Regardless, we're grown men, and it's not as if we haven't had years of experience dealing with her special kind of torture.

Striding towards my bedroom window, I lean against the frame and watch the wildness of the North Atlantic Ocean batter against the pebble beach a quarter mile from our home. Despite my window being shut, I can still feel the damp sea air working its way through the tiny cracks around the frame, but I'm used to the cold so it doesn't bother me. This island and this dark, creepy old monastery we call our home is our safe haven. This is where we can shed the personas we wear as the Deana-dhe and be ourselves.

Ironic then that the one person who knew us before we fully became the Deana-dhe, and could so easily pull back the veil, revealing the truth of who we are beneath the legends we've so carefully cultivated, is the very same girl who walks into view beneath my window now.

We always knew we'd bring her back to the island to fulfil her debt. In preparation we built the raised beds and planted some herbs and flowers that we thought might be useful to her. She's making use of them now, bending down to pull up handfuls of rosemary and sage, popping them into her wicker basket.

Truth be known, it wasn't easy to grow anything. Very little plant life survives on our rugged island aside from the hardiest of species, and most of what we originally planted died. Even during the warmer months of the year it's hardly ever sunny, and the air is always damp with mist rolling off the ocean that batters the island on a regular basis.

Nevertheless, after several failed attempts I'd researched what would grow, and we did our best. What we couldn't grow, I bought, stocking up the kitchen pantry with every imaginable dried herb, flower, plant, and fungi located around the globe. Carrick had asked me why I was bothering to obtain ingredients other than what Cyn needed to make the drug, and I'd given him some bullshit explanation about seeing whether she'd be able to come up with another drug we could sell on the black market.

It's not exactly a lie, but it sure as fuck isn't the whole truth either.

Cyn's an asset, and whilst I may not be a businessman in the true sense of the word, I know when something's valuable or in this case, someone. The Masks had known that too, that's why they had her holed up in their castle in Scotland making lotions and potions and fuck knows what else for their prisoners, the artists who once made up the show they dubbed The

Menagerie. Twelve artists who were stolen for their unique talents and stripped of their identities, given a number to answer to, and forced to perform in The Menagerie for rich men and women who'd buy their bodies afterwards.

Cyn was referred to as Thirteen.

She never performed in the show, but she took on another persona whilst living there, and I still haven't worked out if Cyn was complicit in The Masks' salacious ways or a prisoner suffering from Stockholm Syndrome herself. I suppose when all is said and done, it no longer matters. The Masks are dead and their prisoners set free.

Unlike Cyn who's gone from one cage to another.

Scraping a hand over my two day old stubble, I watch her place more cut herbs in the wicker basket, the wind blowing her hair wildly about her head, and ask myself whether it's wrong that I want to keep her past her fulfilment of the debt. The only response I can come up with is *yes*, of course it fucking is. But the real question, and the only one that matters, is do I give a fuck?

The answer to that is an emphatic no.

Despite that, I know that keeping her here will complicate matters between the four of us. Carrick can barely stand being in the same room as her. Lorcan seeks her attention just like he always did, and me...? When it comes to my feelings towards Cyn, complicated is an understatement.

But irrespective of the fucked-up way I both want to own everything about her and rid myself of this blood pact she's cursed us with, she's an asset that we'd be a fool to let go of.

And I'm not a fool.

So I tuck away my complicated emotions towards the woman who's been a thorn in my side since the first day we met, and remind myself that I'm doing the right thing for us. At the end of the day, our brotherhood is all I give a fuck about. We can overcome some short-term discomfort for long-term gain. We're the fucking Deana-dhe for shit's sake.

Gripping the window ledge, my breath mists up the glass as I continue to watch Cyn at work. Despite her recent loss, she's surprisingly stoic. I don't know why I imagined her to be an emotional mess, she's never once given me a reason in the past to believe she's anything other than mentally strong, but I had at least expected her to be a little more forlorn than she is. The Masks were her friends, and despite their abominable behaviour their death would be a blow, wouldn't it?

Then again, they were fucking psychopaths, so perhaps her relationship with them was as hollow as the hallways of this monastery. Hallways that now echo with the familiar sound of Carrick's harsh steps as he strides towards my bedroom.

"What're you looking at?" Carrick asks as he pushes open my bedroom door, not bothering to knock.

I keep my gaze fixed on Cyn, answering his question with one of my own. "I thought it was your day to watch over her," I say, twisting to grab my thick woollen jumper from my dresser by the window.

"Lorcan's taken over so I could come here to speak with you. Pretty sure he'd be happy to do it full time. He's got a leaky dick for her."

Shoving my arms into the jumper and pulling it on over my

head, I lean back against the window ledge and fold my arms across my chest. "And today she's your responsibility."

"You think I can't handle her?"

I level my gaze at him. "Can you?"

"Always have, haven't I?"

"That's debatable," I mutter, knowing full well he's never been able to handle himself around Cyn, which begs the question why I've given him equal responsibility of watching over her. "So what did you want to speak to me about?"

"You," he replies, casting his gaze to my desk nestled in the corner of the room. On top of it are numerous sketches I've drawn over the past month since Cyn's arrival.

"What about me?" I ask, striding over to the desk and gathering the pen and ink drawings into a pile.

"You're getting visions again?" he asks carefully, his black eyes following my every move.

"No. I've not had one for a long time. I was just drawing."

"Arden..." Carrick begins, his voice filled with concern. "She's fucking with your head."

I snap my gaze up to meet his. "This has nothing to do with Cyn."

"Bullshit," he argues, reaching for the drawings.

I don't bother to stop him, I've got nothing to hide. He looks at my sketches. Some have been drawn in a hurry, the harsh lines almost angry, others I've taken my time with, trying in vain to purge myself of these uncomfortable feelings.

"They're all of *her*," Carrick accuses, snapping his gaze up to meet mine.

"And?"

"And you just denied that she was fucking with your head. What the hell is this, if not her doing exactly that?"

"They're sketches. That's all."

Carrick reaches for me, squeezing my shoulder. "Brother, this is me you're talking to."

"She is no more bothering me than she's bothering you."

"So a lot then?" he says, scowling now.

I lift my hand and mirror him, squeezing his shoulder. "I've got it under control, and I need you to keep yourself under control too. Can you do that?"

He nods sharply.

"Good."

Sliding my palm along his shoulder, I grip the back of his neck and step closer, bringing his forehead to mine. "I won't allow her to come between us again. Understand?"

Carrick's nostrils flare. "Don't you feel it?" he asks, and I know exactly what he's talking about.

The blood pact.

"I feel it."

"Even after all this time, it's still as powerful as it ever was," he admits, reaching up to grasp the back of my head, his whisky-coated breath sliding across my skin. "I want to be free of it."

"We'll find a way."

"How? You remember what that old crone said. Nothing can break it except–"

"Out of the question," I reply, my fingers gripping his head tighter, remembering only too well what that old woman had said the night we snuck out of Silver Oaks and visited the circus in town with the scent of Cyn on our skin, and her virginal blood thrumming in our veins.

"Then we're cursed forever, brother. Can you live with that?"

"I said we'll find a way."

His hand slides around to the front of my throat, folding over the butterfly tattoo that sits there. It's an exact replica of my father's tattoo, the one that's now wrapped around the handle of the knife that's cradled in a velvet box and tucked away in my wardrobe. He and Lorcan have the same one too, a black winged butterfly with two skulls perfectly inked onto each wing. They've been tattooed in such a way that it looks like a real butterfly perched on our necks.

"I want her," he says, his voice darkening with a need that makes my pulse throb beneath his fingers.

"I know."

"I don't *want* to want her," he grinds out, his thumb rubbing in circles over my pulse.

"I know that too."

"It's like a sickness, Arden. I feel the bond like a knot in my stomach. It churns inside of me, growing bigger every day she's here. I want her so fucking badly, and I hate it. I hate feeling like this."

"I know. I *know*," I repeat, understanding him so completely.

"The way she smelt, the feel of her skin beneath my hand, the way her eyes glazed over with lust when we fucked her, the story her body told us that her silence tried to keep hidden. It kills me to want someone I loathe. It fucking kills me."

"Stay strong, brother. I'll find a way to end this torment," I reply.

He nods, choking on the pain, the lust, desire and hate, and the wild need to fuck the one woman we can't, we *shouldn't*. "For you. For Lorcan. I'll do it," he promises, hauling me against his chest, and crushing me against him in a brutal hug.

I can feel the stiffness of his cock, like I imagine he can feel the hard length of mine, our bodies betraying us both to thoughts of a woman we vowed we'd never allow to get between us again. I'm not embarrassed by my erection. It's not as if we haven't seen each other with a hardened dick. Over the years we've shared women, and very occasionally indulged in each other, but knowing it's Cyn who's caused this physical reaction is the part that's so fucking difficult to swallow.

"But it hurts. It fucking hurts, Arden," he breathes into my neck, his words a truth that resonates with my own. "I could deal with it when she was living so far away from us..." he croaks. "I could relieve myself with other women, distract myself with work, but her being here, within reach, taunting me with her fucking silence..."

The crack in his voice undoes me.

Carrick never shows vulnerability. *Never.*

He's unravelling.

Fuck.

"Brother," I murmur.

He hauls me closer, his teeth latching onto the tender skin of my neck, and I groan. I know it isn't me he wants, this is the need to let go of some of the tension. The sheer fact he's grasping at me like a man losing his mind forces me to rethink everything. It has me questioning my decision to bring her here, of even agreeing to the debt in the first place.

Making a decision, I step out of Carrick's arms, forcing myself to be the leader he needs right now. "Bring her to me in the den. Lorcan too. There are things I wish to discuss."

"Now?"

"Right now."

By the time Lorcan, Carrick and Cyn enter the den, I've gotten a hold of myself enough to be able to handle being in the same room as her. It takes a great deal of self-control not to act on my desires, despite it beginning to unravel, fraying like the worn rug beneath our feet. But I *have* to keep reminding myself that all this discomfort is worth the outcome. The drugs she'll produce for us will secure our future. Right now, I have to find a way to balance that need and the welfare of my brothers.

Lorcan enters the den first, his white-blonde hair in disarray from the wind that's howling across the island bringing a bank of dark grey clouds and the threat of rain.

"Arden?" he asks, folding himself into the armchair that sits opposite mine, holding my gaze.

"There are things that need to be said," I reply, my gaze trailing to Cyn as she carries in the wicker basket, her shoulders wrapped in a thick brown shawl, her cheeks ruddy with cold.

"Fair enough," Lorcan responds, the question in his eyes remaining unanswered for now.

"Sit here by the fire," I urge Cyn, determined to prove to

myself that I can and will control myself around her. I can even be pleasant, no matter how much it pains me.

She nods, dropping the wicker basket by the door and settles on the low stool situated just in front of the fire. The flames are low, giving off enough heat to warm her up, but not enough to make her too uncomfortable. I can smell the ocean on her, and refrain from dragging her onto my lap and breathing in the scent I love the most in the world.

"Carrick," I say, flicking my gaze to the only remaining seat.

His eyes narrow as he steps into the den, drinking in the curve of Cyn's neck and the delicate slope of her shoulders hidden beneath an unflattering shapeless t-shirt and skirt.

I know what she tries to hide, but she forgets we've seen her naked when we took her virginity and sealed our bond with her virginal blood, high on the drug we've brought her here to make.

Swallowing hard, Carrick sits opposite Cyn, and I can't help but notice how her body stiffens a little in his presence.

"Let's get this over with," he says tightly.

"We all know why Cyn is here, and that is to fulfil her debt," I begin, meeting Cyn's gaze as she glances over at me.

Something flickers in her eyes, and I know she has something to say before she reaches into the front pocket of her pinafore dress and pulls out her pad and pencil. She writes quickly, then holds the pad up to me to read.

Once I have the process perfected it shouldn't take me longer than five months to complete the order.

I jerk my chin so that she understands she should show her words to Lorcan and Carrick.

"That's longer than I thought," Lorcan remarks, though out of the three of us he seems the least bothered by it.

"That's too long," Carrick adds, barely glancing at the page. "Soren is expecting a delivery much sooner."

Cyn shakes her head, dropping her gaze and writing some more, showing it to him.

Carrick reads her response, then snorts, folding his arms across his chest and leaning back in his seat as he glares at her.

"I don't much care. I'm sure you can mix up some tincture to keep you awake, right?"

"Cyn?" I ask, and she shows me her notepad.

I am one person, and there is only so much I can do in a day. Providing I am left to work I can get the full amount completed in five months.

I understand what she means without her needing to spell it out to me.

"That's why I've called this meeting," I explain as Lorcan leans forward in his seat and takes Cyn's notepad, reading her words then passing them to Carrick who chucks the pad on the floor by her feet.

She keeps her eyes on me, her body twisted to the side as she waits for me to continue, but I can tell that Carrick's disregard for her words and the notepad she uses to write them on has angered her. There's a rigidness to her spine and a pinched look around her eyes as though she's on the cusp of letting rip. I give her a moment, hoping that she'll reveal her emotions, but like always she forces herself not to react. Her control is envious.

"You're adept at herbology. Gifted. You understand things

that no one else does," I begin, swallowing back the bile that burns my throat and forcing myself to ask the question. "It is no secret that we want you, Cyn. So, I am asking you whether there is something you can provide us with to control our desires–"

"You're joking?!" Carrick interrupts, rising from his feet in a fit of anger. "Tell me you're not asking this *cailleach* to drug us?! Have you lost your damn mind?"

Lorcan leans forward in his seat, calmer by far than Carrick but disturbed by my suggestion nevertheless. "Arden, Carrick's got a point. It's not right."

"I need to ensure Cyn fulfils her debt. We need to find a way to live together until she's made enough diamonds and can leave," I say, keeping my voice calm despite knowing that I am lying to my brothers.

If this works, she'll never have to leave. We can keep her without risking our brotherhood. The three of us will no longer desire her and we can benefit from her skills, reaping the reward from the sale of diamonds. It's the only way to keep us all happy. Well, except for Cyn, of course.

"This is insane," he argues.

"Sit down, Carrick."

Gritting his teeth, Carrick's fingers curl into fists as he tries to control his temper and his lust, both of which are aimed squarely at Cyn. The way he's looking at her, the intensity of his gaze is potent and exactly the reason I have to find a work-around to the mess we made and spin it to our advantage.

"Carrick, sit down," I order.

With one long shaky exhale of breath, he sits back down.

Cyn drags her gaze from Carrick, gathering her shawl

tighter around her shoulders as she chews on her lip, a sign she wishes to talk.

"Use your words, Cyn," I urge, repeating what Dr Lynch used to say so often to her when we were kids. For whatever reason she seems frozen, unable to do anything bar stare at her notepad.

Standing, I take two steps towards her, feeling the pull between us like a butcher's hook in my sternum, dragging me towards her, every step excruciating. I stop in front of Cyn, her head level with my crotch. Sinful thoughts of her unzipping my fly and sucking me off cascade in my mind, but I push them away roughly.

"Cyn, can you do what I ask?"

A heavy sigh releases from her lips.

"Cyn?" I repeat.

Her shoulders turn inwards as her head drops and she writes something on her notepad, then slowly lifting her head, she makes eye contact with me. A brief flicker of emotion passes behind her eyes before she offers up her response. Taking the notepad from her, I read it out loud so Carrick and Lorcan can hear.

Yes, I can do it.

7

Cyn - fifteen years old

"I'm just popping out for a cigarette, Cynthia," Mr Rancliff, the Science teacher, says.

He stops by my table, briefly watching me place the chopped up valerian root in a clean sterilised jar before pouring over the required amount of alcohol for the tincture I'm making. "Make sure you lock away the vodka in the store cupboard if I'm not back before you've finished. You've got the spare key, yes?"

I nod, giving him a small smile before turning my attention back to the task at hand. I like Mr Rancliff, he's about the only adult here that I actually respect. He's genuinely interested in my experiments and has allowed me use of the lab ever since he caught me smoking behind the greenhouse a few days after my arrival. That day, instead of reporting me to Ms Weatherby, he asked for a toke of my joint, expecting cannabis. What he got was a mixture of lavender, mugwort and raspberry leaf. None of which is illegal to smoke but when combined aids relaxation, easing anxiety and stress. We'd shared the joint, smoking in silence, and afterwards he'd asked if I would supply him with more. I'd agreed on the proviso I could access the science lab when it wasn't in use.

I'm pretty sure he'd be fired if Ms Weatherby found out about our agreement, but it's not as if I can tell anyone. Nor would I. Mr Rancliff has become my friend and this lab is my safe haven, a place of comfort and safety, a place I can hide within. It's respite from Dr Lynch and his incessant desire to get me to talk, from the weight of my father's wishes to make me normal, and from *them*.

Arden, Lorcan and Carrick.

My hand trembles as I recall our interaction in the forest a couple of weeks ago, and I have to press my palms on top of the workbench to stop them from shaking.

They'd kissed me.

And each kiss had been as different as day, night, and a total eclipse.

Lorcan's was a brief brushing of lips against mine, featherlight, tentative, chaste. Almost like a greeting, a door opening in welcome, dawn on a new day. It was confusing to say the least.

Carrick's was gentle, yes, but there was intent behind it, in the energy leaking from him as he held back something dark and ominous. It had felt like the calm before a violent thunderstorm under a midnight sky, one that had every intention of striking me down had Arden not stopped him.

And Arden's kiss? It was overwhelming. It was intense. It was passionate. It was a total blackout, sucking the light from me and encouraging something else to bloom.

It woke something up.

That quiet, obedient part of me was shoved aside and in her place someone with a backbone was born. I may not have said a word, but I made sure I was heard.

And it's left me wondering how one kiss can be so powerful?

I've been asking myself that question over and over again, whilst simultaneously doing everything in my power to avoid bumping into them outside of our designated therapy and study sessions. Luckily for me, on the two occasions I've happened to be in their company since our meeting in the forest, they were preoccupied. Apart from a few crass comments and a handful of jibes they'd let me be.

Maybe they've already tired of me?

Then I remember what Arden had said, and I know that's wishful thinking.

Dragging in a deep, calming breath, I focus on the liquid in front of me. The tincture this will eventually produce will help to combat my insomnia and top up my depleting supplies. Sleeping isn't easy when all you dream about is the brutal murder of your mother and the last words she uttered to you as the life ebbed from her eyes.

"Hush now, stay quiet," she'd said.

She hadn't told me she loved me, she hadn't said goodbye. She'd used her last words to try and protect me. She'd told me to stay quiet.

So that's what I did.

From that moment onwards I didn't utter a sound.

I played dead as angry men with guns fought outside of the room.

I didn't scream.

I didn't cry.

I didn't beg for her to wake up.

I simply closed my eyes and hung onto her corpse, silent, wishing I were dead too.

When my father finally found me covered in my mother's blood, practically catatonic, he'd assumed I was dead, and in that moment of wild grief as he hauled my mother against his chest, crying out her name over and over again, I saw the truth of his heart.

He didn't love me, not the same fierce way he loved my mother.

He didn't even check to see if I was breathing.

It was my uncle Jack that realised I was alive when he entered the room some time later. It was his arms I was carried in, his home I was taken to in the aftermath, and his estate I lived in with my grandmother for six months afterwards.

My father visited me once during that time, two days after my mother's funeral, to bring me the gold chain that I wear wrapped around my neck now.

He barely spoke.

I didn't say a word.

It was another month following my mother's death that he finally realised I'd lost my voice the same day we lost my mother.

He's been trying to get me to speak ever since.

Behind me the door to the lab slams open and I jump, dragged from my morbid thoughts back into the present. A quick glance over my shoulder tells me that my respite is over.

"So this is where you've been hiding?" Arden says as he steps into the room, Lorcan behind him.

Reaching for the jar, I screw on the lid, internally cursing them both for disturbing me. Then I gather up my recipe book and muslin bags filled with herbs and place them in my rucksack, ignoring them both.

"I asked you a question, Cynthia," Arden says, his warm breath scattering across the back of my neck as he steps close, with no regard for my personal space. "Answer me."

I don't answer him. I'm too distracted by the way he presses his chest against my back, trapping me between his body and the worktop. A massive part of me wants to elbow him in the stomach and shove him away from me, the other part knows that if I did, I'd make this ten times worse. So I pick up my pencil and answer him.

I'm not hiding.

He laughs. "I don't believe you."

Believe what you want. I'm working.

"On what?" Lorcan asks, stepping up beside us both and peering down at my pad.

None of your business.

I regret my snappy response the instant I've written it.

"That's where you're wrong. This *is* our business. You're our business," Arden says, reaching over me and into my rucksack, pulling out the muslin bags. I try to grab them from him but he holds them above his head, dangling them out of reach.

"What are you making, Cynthia?" he asks as Lorcan walks around the workbench and grabs the beaker filled with valerian root and vodka, and takes a sniff.

"What the fuck is this?" he asks.

My eyes flick to the clear glass bottle labelled *alcohol* and Lorcan notices, snatching it up. Unscrewing the cap he takes another sniff then grins. "You've been holding out on us. I'm pretty sure this is vodka," he says, placing the bottle to his lips and taking a swig without even bothering to check if he's right. What an idiot. That's seventy percent proof vodka. More than a few shots and it's stomach pumping territory.

Behind me Arden presses his lips to my ears. "What are you making, Cynthia?" he repeats slowly, his voice curling around the words like smoke from the end of a lit cigarette.

Distracted by Lorcan as he takes another mouthful, I don't respond to Arden's question as quickly as he'd like, and that only serves to annoy him further

"Answer me!" he demands, reaching around and grasping my chin, forcing me to look up at him.

My teeth clamp together, fiery bolts of rage boiling my blood. How dare he come in here and disturb my peace! How dare he lay a hand on me! How dare Lorcan risk my agreement with Mr Rancliff by guzzling back the vodka with every intention of getting shitfaced.

Twisting my body in his hold, I shove against Arden's chest

with all my strength, but whilst he stumbles a little, dragging me with him, he doesn't let me go.

A dark smile spreads across his face like the moon eclipsing the sun. "Do you think just because we haven't paid you much attention the last few sessions with Dr Lynch that we'd forgotten the challenge you'd laid down for us, huh? Because we haven't," he sneers, gripping my upper arm with one hand as he yanks on my ponytail with the other. "Tell me what you're making and I might let you go."

My chest heaves as I blink up at him, forcing the stinging tears away. I will not cry. I refuse. Instead, I dare him to do his worst, setting my jaw in a stubborn line and glare up at him.

"Tell. Me!" he insists.

"Arden, she needs her pad and pen. She can't answer you without them," Lorcan says, stepping into my peripheral vision, his voice neutral, almost bored sounding.

"She *can* tell me by using her goddamn words," he snarls.

"Arden–"

"Give me the vodka!" Arden snaps, glaring at Lorcan who lets out a sharp breath.

"Why?" Lorcan asks, his question more curious than concerned, the arsehole.

"Hold her arms. Let's see if getting her drunk will help loosen up her vocal chords."

The sharp laugh that seeps from Lorcan's lips is as devious as the look in Arden's eyes as I struggle in their hold. But it's no use, I'm no match for the pair of them.

With my arms secured behind my back by Lorcan, Arden is

free to grab the bottle of vodka. He presses it roughly against my lips.

"Open up, Cynthia."

In response I clamp my lips tighter together and turn my head away. *No!*

Gripping my jaw with his fingers, Arden twists my head back around to face him, then he opens his mouth and pours in a long glug of liquid, a villainous glint in his eyes as he places the bottle on the workbench behind us. I realise in horror what he's about to do and buck against Lorcan's hold.

"You wicked bastard," Lorcan says, a smile in his voice as he grips me tighter.

God, how I wish Mr Rancliff would walk back in and end this horror, but he doesn't, and as Arden reaches up to pinch my nose shut, all I can do is hope that I can hold my breath long enough for him to return.

I manage thirty seconds before I open my mouth on a gasp.

Arden doesn't waste a moment as he lays his mouth over mine and dribbles the burning vodka into my mouth, forcing it shut the moment I've taken the liquid from him.

I have no choice but to swallow.

The burn down my gullet is as barbaric as the tears streaming from my eyes, and I gasp for air, choking on the taste, wanting to throw up from the humiliation, wishing I could scream.

"What are you making, Cynthia?" he repeats.

Again I twist my head away and clamp my jaw shut. It's futile, I know, but I do it out of sheer stubbornness. I will not make this easy for him.

Arden smirks, takes another mouthful, then repeats the action, but this time as he forces me to swallow the vodka he follows the liquid with his tongue. His kiss chases the burn as his lips press angrily against mine.

I don't have time to even comprehend the kiss, let alone retaliate before the sound of someone clearing their throat puts an end to it. Lorcan reacts first, dropping my arms and hissing at Arden.

"Let her go," he warns.

But Arden takes his time, drawing my bottom lip gently between his teeth before stepping back and turning his attention to Mr Rancliffe. "Afternoon, Sir, are you good?"

I wait for Mr Rancliffe to shout, to defend my honour because it's clear I'm a victim here, but he doesn't. He simply looks at me and says, "I'm closing the lab."

A breath catches in my throat as I try to fight the betrayal. Why does every adult in this institution insist on turning a blind eye when it comes to these boys? Can't he see what's happened here?

"Cynthia," he continues. "Gather your things and leave."

"Yes, *Little Mouse*, leave. Mr Rancliffe and I have things to discuss," Arden says, swiping his thumb against the corner of his mouth and grinning, his amber eyes molten.

I stare back at Mr Rancliffe, shocked, embarrassed, angry, *hurt*. Why isn't he doing something? Why is he just standing there avoiding eye contact with me? I was beginning to trust him, and his blatant disregard for what's happened is disheartening.

But he just sighs. "Leave, Cynthia. Go back to your room."

The following day when I wake up, news of Mr Rancliffe's unexpected resignation is all the other students are talking about. Gossip is rife as I enter the cafeteria for breakfast. Most of the students think he was caught pilfering from the lab, others said he was a pervert preying on the female staff, but as I look over at Arden, Lorcan and Carrick sitting in their usual spot two tables over, I know his sudden departure two months before he was due to retire has everything to do with them and a whole lot more to do with me.

8

L orcan - Present day

Throwing back the covers on my bed, I blow out an aggravated breath and sit up, scraping a hand over my face. It's no use, I can't sleep.

Just like every night for as long as I can remember it's been the same. It takes me forever to drift off, and if I eventually manage to sleep I wake up again no more than a few hours later. I've been living off four hours of sleep a night for the past fifteen years. But tonight there'll be no sleeping at all. Not after what Cyn has agreed to do.

"Fuck," I mutter, pressing my bare feet against the hard-wood floor as I look out of the window and into the pitch black that greets me. If it weren't for the pendulous moon, hanging in the sky like a bad omen, and the small amount of light from the embers in the fire, I wouldn't be able to see a thing.

Ignoring the cold as it wraps around my naked body and snatches at the residual heat from the fire, I pull on my sweat-pants and t-shirt, shoving my feet into a pair of thick black socks. There's a bottle of whisky with my name on it, and I intend on drinking enough so that I can pass out and forget about Arden's plans to numb us of our attraction to Cyn. I'll wake up with a hangover from hell but at this point I'll take that in exchange for a few hours of respite.

Stepping out into the darkened hallway, lit only by the light from my mobile, I walk past Arden's room, stopping briefly to peer inside. He's lying face down on his bed, the pillow bunched up beneath his cheek, the duvet cover low on his back, revealing his intricate tattoo. We all have several, but Arden has the biggest. A huge butterfly covers the top half of his back and beneath it a field of wildflowers. It's a beautiful tattoo that reminds me of home. Not the monastery we live in now, but the fields that surrounded our village where we grew up.

Lingering in the doorway, I watch Arden as he snores gently, envying his ability to switch off. Of the three of us, he's never had any difficulty sleeping, but that probably has more to do with his gift than it does anything else. His body has no choice but to shut down when his mind wants to show him things yet to unfold. I'm not sure what's worse, not being able to sleep or seeing things in your dreams that you've no business witness-ing. What I do know is that it's a burden, a heavy one and some-times he's barely able to stand the weight of it.

Slipping past his room I head further along the hallway, passing Carrick's bedroom. He's fast asleep too, except where Arden was peaceful in his sleep, Carrick is thrashing around, the covers twisted between his legs, his fingers clenched and his face screwed up in agony. I know better than to enter the room to try and wake him, learning early on in our friendship that waking Carrick up in the midst of a nightmare is as bad as pestering him about his attraction to Cyn. Both would end with a split lip and a black eye.

Retreating, I cross the hallway stopping outside of Cyn's bedroom. The door is no longer hanging from the frame, but has been removed entirely. Perhaps it's foolish to give her the freedom of an open doorway or perhaps she's foolish for not insisting that we put the door back up. Either way, Cyn is as vulnerable as she ever was when it comes to us.

Knowing I shouldn't, but doing it anyway, I step into her bedroom, the urge to look upon her sleeping form forcing my feet to move. My breath is snatched from my chest as the soft glow from her table lamp illuminates her in a warm golden light. She's lying on her back, her hair loose across her pillow, her lips slightly parted as she breathes, her dark lashes fluttering against her cheeks. She looks at peace, unafraid, and I can't help but step closer, drawn to her understated beauty and quiet calm.

Physically, there's a fragility about her, something almost breakable. I see it in the stark curve of her collarbone and the fluttering pulse in her neck, her slender fingers and delicate wrists.

With age, she has lost the fuller cheeks of youth that I recall so well, her cheekbones are now a defined slope beneath her skin. Delicate lines crease around the corner of her eyes telling a story of a life filled with smiles, if not exactly laughter.

That bothers me. It bothers me to know that The Masks were the ones to etch those lines into her skin, men who shouldn't be able to draw out anything other than screams from their victims, and yet, those lines tell a story that we were never a part of. She's lived this other life with The Masks, and in the midst of that she'd found happiness.

It seems inconceivable to me, and I have the sudden urge to erase them from her memories, to give her new ones where I'm responsible for making her smile.

Me.

Lorcan Sheehan, one third of the Deana-dhe, a living God who walks amongst mortal men.

Except I'm not a fucking God. None of us are.

We're an urban myth, a far-fetched story made real by fearful men and women. All those whispered stories, the rumours uttered in dingy back street bars, private clubs, gambling dens and gilded ballrooms have served us well over the years. Our reputation precedes us, and all we need to do is play up to those stories any time we're in public. If people want to believe I'm an immortal man who sucks blood to survive, then so be it. If that's how they choose to interpret my unusual colouring, likening me to a mythical creature, I'm not about to correct them. It's manipulation at its finest.

But Cyn, she knew us before we stepped into those personas. She saw the beginning of our evolution, had a hand in shaping us into the men we became. That's part of the reason why she's so dangerous for us. She can strip back the legends we've become and lay bare the men we are with a few well placed stories from our childhood.

Yet she doesn't.

In all the years we've known her, she's never once revealed our secret, that we are just *human*.

I used to think it was because she was afraid of the repercussions, but now I believe it's because she understands what it means to hide behind what the world perceives you to be. She's the daughter of a powerful man and a brutally murdered mother. She's the tragic woman who exists in a state of quiet, fading into the background. Someone not worth giving your attention or your time. A person to pity.

But we know different. *I* know different.

And I want her, the woman she is, not the person everyone sees.

I don't care about the fucking blood pact, or the fact she never belonged to us.

I want her for as long as I can have her.

Fuck knows I don't deserve Cyn. I spent my youth hurting her alongside my brothers. I played with her emotions, was kind to her one minute, cruel the next. Carrick thinks the glimpses of kindness I afforded her when we were kids was an act, and whilst it might've started out that way, I soon realised that I didn't have the same desire to hurt her as them. I preferred the smile on her face to the fear in her eyes.

I still do.

So Arden's suggestion to allow Cyn to drug us, to sedate our attraction, is abhorrent to me. Why the fuck would I agree to that? Sure, I want to fuck her, but I don't *want* to hurt her and that marks me different from Arden and Carrick. I guess it always has.

Shit, if my brothers knew the depth of my feelings for her, they'd be questioning my sanity. How could I want the one person who almost broke us, who in some way had a hand at making us into the men we are today? Three men who are revered and despised in equal measure. The murder of Arden's father might have birthed us, but it was Cyn who shaped us, and it happened over time, way before that night we enjoyed each other's bodies when we were eighteen.

Shifting in her sleep, Cyn rolls onto her side, the cover falling off her shoulders and revealing an expanse of flesh that I haven't seen in years but have daydreamed about for just as long. The urge to run my lips across her bare shoulder is a powerful one, and I find myself stepping closer to her bed, my fingers held only centimetres above her skin. On the tip of her right shoulder is a beauty spot the size of a penny and almost as perfectly round. Seeing it again has me remembering so clearly the taste of it beneath my tongue.

Without hesitation, and with a large dose of foolishness, I lean over Cyn and press a soft kiss against her shoulder, savouring the warmth of her skin beneath my lips and the tingle in my balls as my body wakes the fuck up. When my tongue peeps through my parted lips and licks her beauty mark, I know I've overstepped, and I force myself to stand, to take a step back.

With one last lingering look, I twist on my heel and head

downstairs towards the den, to grab a bottle of whisky and sink into oblivion.

I'm a quarter of a way through a bottle when I sense someone stepping into the den behind me. Assuming it's either Arden or Carrick, I take another swig of the burning liquid and wait for my body to fall into a drunken stupor.

"Go back to bed," I murmur, watching the flames dance in the hearth.

The silence that follows, and the delicate scent of wild-flowers lingering in the air, tell me it's neither of my brothers, but Cyn who has stepped into the room.

I don't turn around, not because I fear the room will spin, but because I've done nothing but sit here and recall all the times I kissed her during the years we spent together at Silver Oaks Institute, and I don't want her to see the truth of that on my face.

I've sat here for the past hour remembering every single kiss leading up to that night I finally slipped inside of her, savouring the moment she'd reached up and trailed her fingertips delicately over my back as I fucked her.

Arden might've entered her first, taking her virginity, and Carrick might've given her more orgasms than either of us combined, but it was me who witnessed the surrender in her eyes when she'd given herself up to us. I'd known then with absolute certainty that whilst she may never be ours outside of that night, she will always, *always* be mine.

Cyn takes a seat on the footstool facing the fire, placing her notepad and pen in her lap before holding up her palms to warm them. It strikes me as strange that she didn't take the seat opposite mine and therefore sit further away, but I don't question it.

Lifting the bottle I down another mouthful, relishing the burn and enjoying the warm feeling that spreads outwards from my stomach, watching her as she picks up her pencil and writes something in her notepad, before twisting around to face me, the light from the fire painting her in warmth.

Having trouble sleeping?

"Yes."

She waits as though expecting more of a response, but what else is there to say? I'm an insomniac, there really isn't much more to it than that.

Her eyes drop back down to her pad as she contemplates what to write next, and I watch her hold her pencil hesitantly over the paper.

Do you remember that time back at Silver Oaks when you and Arden found me in the science lab and you wanted to know what I was making?

"I remember," I reply.

How can I forget? Arden had forced her to drink vodka from his lips because she'd refused to tell us what she was making. I'd been so fucking jealous that it wasn't me filling her mouth, and so angry at the fucked-up way he was treating her despite how I'd acted, that I'd wanted to punch him. I might've had Mr Rancliffe not walked back into the lab.

She nods, then writes some more. *I was making a tonic to help aid sleep because I don't sleep well either.*

"Why?" I ask, shifting in my seat as the shawl wrapped around her shoulders slips a little lower. My gaze is drawn to the beauty spot on her shoulder that I had kissed. Taking another shot of whisky, I ignore the stirring in my pants and wait for her reply.

I'm haunted by my mother's murder.

Of course she is, what a stupid fucking question. It takes me a moment to respond, and the silence that follows is filled by the crackling logs in the fire and the harsh note of tragedy ringing in the air. "So your tonic works, does it?" I eventually ask.

She gives me a withering look and I force myself not to smile.

Yes. Would you like some?

I consider her offer. I'm not like Carrick, I don't distrust her, but I'm enjoying her company way too much to want to sleep right now. "Can we talk for a while?" I ask instead.

What do you want to talk about? she replies, her cursive as neat and controlled as she is.

There's a wariness to it, and an edge of caution. If I'd thought she was beginning to trust me, then I was wrong. She no more trusts me than Carrick does her, which begs the question why she's sitting here talking to me now.

"Are you ever planning on doing anything about the man who murdered your mother?"

After she's gotten over the shock of such a blunt question she heaves out a breath and replies.

I'm waiting for the right moment. I've been a little busy.

"You're free of The Masks now," I point out, knowing that she was living with them in their castle for at least a year before we arrived and took her from them, after seeking our revenge, of course.

And now I'm here. There's not been much chance to seek vengeance.

"I didn't think vengeance was part of your vocabulary," I say, curious at the lack of emotion in her response.

The Masks were her childhood friends, their recent death and the circumstances surrounding it must be traumatic, and yet she's acting like it never happened at all. If I hadn't seen their dead bodies with my own eyes, I might've thought the same. Her eyes meet mine and a hint of a smile creases the lines beside them.

What makes you say that?

"You haven't killed us..." I say, leaning forward in my seat, placing the bottle of whisky at my feet. "Why, Cyn? After everything we've done. After what we've put you through. Why?"

It's a question that has been bothering me, and I guess now is as good an opportunity as any to find out.

There's always time.

I laugh at her response despite the fact she's not smiling. Call it stupidity, call it a hunch, but I know Cyn would never willingly hurt us despite her threats. She has every right to, of course. But she won't. It isn't in her nature. She's a healer, not a murderer. I believe that strongly. The same can't be said for Carrick though.

"Carrick thinks you'll kill us," I remark, a statement of fact we're both aware of. Cyn's brows crease and I can't for the life of me interpret the look in her eyes.

And you don't?

"I think you could, easily. Hell, this potion, or whatever it is Arden wants you to make to *cure* us of our desire for you," I say, barking out a laugh, "Would be the perfect opportunity to do so. Not sure what he's thinking in all honesty. Carrick won't take it because he doesn't trust you not to kill him, and I won't because I don't want to stop feeling this way. My attraction to you isn't a sickness that can be cured, or a desire that can be put out. You asked us not to hurt you and I won't. I give you my word."

Her head snaps up at my confession, and I know she's questioning my honesty as she stares at me. I let her look. I allow her the time to study me, to uncover the truth because I'm not lying.

After long minutes where my dick grows impossibly hard from her attention, Cyn wraps her shawl tighter around her shoulders and stands. Whatever hope I had of spending the next few hours with her disintegrating with every passing moment.

"Cyn, why are you really here?" I ask before she can leave the room.

To fulfil my debt, of course, she responds quickly, almost too quickly.

I nod, studying her as closely as she just studied me, trying to find the truth of her heart buried beneath the carefully placed walls she's erected around it. She's gotten good at hiding.

"But why come to *us* in the first place? You knew the price would be a high one. Why risk it, knowing who we are and how we've treated you in the past?"

Because you were the only ones who could find out who was responsible for killing my mother, she writes.

"Was it worth it?"

She licks her lips, and I catch a glimpse of uncertainty in her eyes before she shuts it down.

I don't know yet.

9

Cyn - Aged Sixteen

Traipsing across the courtyard from the building that houses the dorm rooms, I enter the tiny chapel, pushing open the heavy wooden door and entering the space. It's a beautiful chapel with a large, stained glass window depicting the Virgin Mary. Sunlight passes through the multicoloured glass, painting the stone floor and rows of wooden pews in kaleidoscopic light. Incense burns at the altar, white smoke drifting up into the air. The scent is sweet, comforting somehow, and I breathe in deeply as I stride over to the empty confessional booth.

Aside from Sunday services where all students are required

to attend Mass led by Father Brian, the chapel is always empty.
I've never once met another student on my visits, but that
doesn't surprise me much. If the other students' families are
anything like mine, religion has been shoved down their
throats since they were babies and the last thing they want to
do is spend any more time under the omnipresent eye of a God
they're not even sure they believe in.

My family are Catholic, and attending Mass was a regular
occurrence growing up. My father is religious when it suits him,
but he's not a God-fearing man, or a pious one. He lives by his
own rules, always has.

And me?

I find it hard to believe in something that is supposed to be
all-powerful, but chose not to protect my kind, selfless mother
from a violent death, taking her from me. Which begs the question why I'm sitting in the confessional booth, with the thick
velvet curtain pulled shut, writing my confession onto the pad
I'm holding in front of me. A confession that will never be read
by Father Brian or anyone else for that matter.

And the worst part? It isn't just my absurd need to confess
my sins that has brought me here, but loneliness too. Two days
ago I turned sixteen and I've had no contact from my father or
from my grandmother. Nothing.

That stings.

So here I am, finding something... Comfort, I suppose, in
the familiar surroundings of a church and a God I don't
believe in.

Forgive me Father for I have sinned, I write, my pencil
hovering over the stark white paper of my pad just waiting for

all my ugly secrets to dirty it up. *A week ago, Arden kissed me again...*

Drawing my bottom lip between my teeth, I hesitate, finding it hard to write the truth of my confession, not because I fear punishment from God but because I'm afraid of my own feelings.

I liked it, I eventually admit. *I liked the way his body pressed against mine. How Lorcan held me captive, and made me helpless. I liked the way Arden's tongue probed my mouth, in search of something only I could give him. Yet I hate him. I hate them. I don't understand why I enjoyed their kisses given from mouths that have hurt me with cruel words. All I know is that I want them to do it again.*

My confession spills out of the pristine page like black ink in water, a confession fit for several repetitions of 'Our Fathers' or maybe even a penance or two.

I stare at my confession and the deepest darkest secrets held inside of me, utterly confused.

Why can't I stop thinking about the three of them despite hating them? Why do they scare me and excite me at the same time? But more importantly, when will they kiss me again?

My silent questions are answered by the sound of the heavy wooden door to the chapel opening and footsteps striding across the stone floor of the nave. I remain seated, a sudden chill passing over my skin, a familiar feeling that sets my teeth on edge.

I don't know how I know it's one of them, all I know is that it is.

Long seconds pass and I hear nothing but my own slow breath releasing from my lips. It's too loud and I cringe, my heart pounding in my ears, my skin prickling. Reaching out, my fingertips graze the edge of the velvet curtain and ever so slowly I pull it to one side, peering through the gap. My gaze falls on a tall figure with wide shoulders and a slim waist, standing in the multicoloured light from the stained glass window. His face is hidden by the black hood of his sweatshirt, his head lowered to the floor.

Is he praying?

I can't tell if it's Arden, Lorcan or Carrick, but I know without a shadow of a doubt it's one of the three. They have this aura that follows them everywhere they go, a darkness that can't be contained beneath human skin. Sometimes when I dream about them at night, they're nothing more than shadows, creatures made up of sinful thoughts and cruel intentions, inky fingers and trailing smoke. Always watching me, calling my name, ordering me to speak.

But I won't, not for them.

Not ever.

But you will kiss them, my inner voice goads me.

Ignoring it I sit forward, transfixed by the hooded figure as he stands, head bowed, hands tucked into the pocket of his jeans. Minutes pass by and then, slowly, he lifts his head, his hands rising to push back the hood of his jumper and as he does so, thick brown hair flops over his forehead.

It's *Carrick*, and I watch entranced as he begins to sing.

My breath is snatched from my lungs and my skin covers in a rash of goosebumps as a familiar Gaelic song, *Mo Ghile Maer*, fills every available inch of the chapel, including the deep, bottomless ache in my chest. I haven't heard anyone sing this song since my mother was alive, and I can't help but feel that this is somehow a message from her, but what is she trying to tell me?

All I know is that if fallen angels could sing, I'm certain they'd sound like him. Carrick's voice is haunting, melancholy, otherworldly, wistful and utterly *moving*. Unbidden tears spring to my eyes and my mouth opens in a silent gasp. I have never, ever, felt something so spiritually as I have in this moment. It's like he's reached into my heart and tethered himself to my soul with every note that releases from his lips. I'm enraptured, caught in the snare of his emotion, and if I wasn't sitting down I'd fall to my knees.

My heart aches. My eyes sting. My soul cries for him.

I cry for him.

Tears stream down my face for whatever heartache, whatever trauma he's been through to make him sing like this, so *broken* like this.

Without thinking it through, I get to my feet on shaky legs, and pull back the curtain still clutching my notepad and pencil. Like a butterfly drawn to the sweet scent of a wildflower, I move towards him, trembling, feeling more fragile than I have in a very, very long time.

His eyes are shut, his body relaxed as he sings, and I take the opportunity to study him. Without the permanent scowl on his face and the tension in his jaw, he's more angelic than devilish. Right now, the curtain has been drawn back, and I can see a glimpse of the boy beneath the wickedness he carries so well.

When I'm a few steps away from him, I stand still, my face wet with tears, my heart aching for him, for the memory of my mother and the love she showered me with. I want to touch him, to pull him into my arms and tell him that whatever it is that haunts him has no place in a heart so gifted, so full of passion. I want to tell him that we can start over, that I can be a friend and not his enemy if only he'd open himself up to the possibility of it.

When the last note releases from his lips, I can't help but shudder, reacting physically to a connection I can't quite understand.

Then he opens his eyes, and the connection I felt is immediately severed, the harsh slash of a knife slicing through the tentative hand of friendship that he had no idea I was about to offer.

"What the fuck are you doing here?" he snarls, his black eyes fierce in his anger as he rounds on me, his cheeks flushed pink as though ashamed of his gift, embarrassed by it.

I want to tell him that his voice is the most beautiful thing I've ever heard. I want to tell him that it's an instrument he should never hide away, that he should share with the world, that it moved me, but the way he's glaring at me sends a warning slashing down my spine, and I say nothing.

"What the fuck are you doing here?!" he repeats, nostrils flaring, the force of his anger like a sucker punch to my stomach. I stumble backwards, holding onto the wooden pew to right myself.

"Well?"

My fingers shake as I write my response, making the words barely legible. *I come here sometimes. It's peaceful.*

"Liar!"

I shake my head, holding my hands up in surrender. It might not be the entire truth but it's the best I can give him. How can I tell him that I come here to confess my sins to a God I don't believe in about feelings I have no business feeling, let alone acknowledging? How can I tell him that I'm lonely, that I ache for my mother's love?

"You're following me," he accuses, stepping forward as I stumble back. "First the forest, now here. What the fuck do you want?"

Is he insane? If anything he's following *me*.

"Always creeping around like a petrified little mouse, like fucking vermin! What do you want?"

I don't want anything from you! I write, my own anger harsh as I raise my voice with bold lines and gritted teeth. I'll give him vermin, the bastard.

"No?" he laughs then, and it's bitter, full of sticks and stones and words just waiting to hurt me. "You're nothing but a pretty little liar!"

I DON'T WANT ANYTHING, I repeat, holding the pad up in clenched fingers, shaking it at him.

"You want my pain though, don't you?" he accuses, glaring at me. "I see the tears barely drying on your face, but they're not yours to fucking cry! This is *my* pain. No one else's. Not yours. Not Dr Lynch's. Not even Arden and Lorcan's but MINE!"

I'm shaking now, every single cell inside my body is telling me to run. His anger, his pain, it's alive, and it wants to annihilate me. Nothing I could do or say will temper the flood of his rage.

Despite knowing that, I feel the need to hurt him with my words as much as he tries to hurt me with his.

Grabbing my pencil tightly, I write, *You might have a beautiful voice but it's nothing but a lie. You don't have the power to heal someone with it, not when your heart is so ugly!*

A slow, dangerous smile pulls up his lips. "You're right, I don't. All I want to do is *ruin* you. I want to ruin you in this fucking place under the watchful eye of *God*," he spits.

Then he lunges for me.

On instinct I throw my notepad and pen at him, then turn on my heel and run.

I don't think about my confession. I don't think about how only moments ago I was enraptured by him, by his voice that brought me to tears.

All I think about is getting away from him.

Why I thought that'd be possible I don't know, because by the time I reach the end of the aisle and hook a right, heading towards the entrance to the chapel and my only escape, he's already standing there gripping my confession in his hand.

"Forgive me Father, for I have sinned..." he begins, leaning back against the door as he reads, his lyrical voice making a mockery of my deepest secrets.

I slam to a halt as if I've hit an invisible brick wall, my eyes stinging with fresh tears that I refuse to cry. The way he mimics my voice, a voice he's never heard, nor will ever hear, threatens my resolve to stay strong in his presence.

When he finishes, he lifts his gaze to meet mine and smiles in a way that splits my chest open. I'm shaking so hard with humiliation, with rage, with sadness, that I don't know whether to fall to my knees and hope the ground swallows me up or throw myself at him and gouge his eyes out.

In the end that decision is taken away from me when he says, "And what about *my* kiss, Cynthia? Don't you crave that too?"

He doesn't bother to wait for my response before he closes the gap between us, catching my wrist before I can take off and run again.

"Don't!" he demands, yanking me back against his chest, his arm wrapping around my back as he pins me in place. "If you run, I'll only chase you."

I struggle against his hold, lashing out at him with my free hand but he grabs that wrist too and spins me on my feet forcing me back against the wooden door. I try to kick out at him, but he pins my body with his, holding me in place.

"It hurts, doesn't it?" he whispers, his lips brushing the shell of my ear, my nose pressed against the crook of his neck, "Having someone bear witness to the parts of you that you wish to keep secret."

He's so close that I can't help but draw his scent into my lungs. He smells like cigarette smoke and rainfall, worn leather and calla lilies. I can't deny it, there's a part of me that wants to surrender to the sadness and the melancholy that he's buried beneath his anger and self-righteousness, but the other part of me wants to fight back, to hurt him as much as he hurts me.

That part wins.

Slowly, I drag the tip of my nose against the throbbing pulse in his neck, my lips brushing against his skin, my tongue snaking out to taste his bitterness, teeth scraping against his collar bone.

"What are you doing?" he asks, his breath hot and heavy, his body hard against mine.

I answer by biting down. Hard.

He roars in my ear, his body jerking, but he doesn't let me go. If anything he holds on tighter.

"Fuck!" he hisses. "Fuck. Fuck. Fuck."

I've pierced his skin with my teeth, his blood trickling into my mouth.

I should let go.

I don't.

I *taste* him.

God, help me. I taste him.

I don't know what possesses me. All I know is that I'm standing in a church sucking his blood like a creature of the night, and despite how disgusting that sounds, I don't hate it.

I don't hate it at all.

"Fuck, Cynthia..." he groans, the sound of his voice is so far removed from what it was moments ago that a different kind of feeling bubbles in my chest. I don't know how else to describe it other than *darkness*. There's something about Carrick that brings out the worst in me. Something dangerous.

He shifts against me, groaning as I lick at the blood that trickles into my mouth, swallowing the metallic taste of his very essence. Somewhere in the back of my head a tiny voice is telling me to stop, that this is wrong, this is a place of worship, of holiness and light, but I ignore it.

"So she does bite. I did wonder," he murmurs as he releases

my wrists, his hands sliding up my arms and grasping the back of my head.

Long fingers curl into my hair and I expect him to forcefully pull me off of him, but he just holds me in place, arching his neck so I can get better access.

"Fuck, don't stop."

So I don't stop, and as time passes, what started out as this need to hurt him turns into wanting to hear him groan beneath my touch. There's a power in his submission that I haven't felt before. It's addicting.

Had Father Brian not stepped out from behind the pulpit like some kind of apparition, I'm not sure when we would've separated. But his presence is like a bucket of ice cold water over me and I pull my teeth from Carrick's skin, shoving him forcefully away.

When my gaze meets Father Brian's, he takes one look at my blood-stained teeth and Carrick's hand pressed against his neck and crosses himself.

"Lord have mercy on your souls!" he exclaims.

And honestly, I couldn't have agreed with him more.

10

Carrick - present day

"I won't fucking do it!" I snap, staring at the tiny bottle of dark green liquid that Arden places on the table between us a week after our discussion in the den. Lorcan snatches it up, holding the bottle up to the light, studying it. Next to him Cyn watches us argue as she slowly chews on a piece of cooked beef, her expression neutral despite the colour defusing her cheeks.

"Carrick, it's the only sensible option. You know that."

"The fuck I do," I respond.

"This is happening."

"No," I insist, fucked-off that Arden thinks another one of

Cyn's potions is the answer to our problems. Everything she makes leads to fucking chaos.

Chaos or *death*.

"I watched Cyn make this. As far as I can tell, there isn't anything in it that could be harmful," he says leaning forward, his elbows resting on the table.

"So now you're an expert in herbology?"

"I've studied some things," he argues, glancing over at Cyn who rests her knife and fork on her plate, her food half eaten. She should really eat more. The last thing we need is her getting sickly and being here for longer than necessary. "Verbena is safe."

"*Safe*?" I scoff, shaking my head at him.

"Yes, safe."

Out of the corner of my eye I watch Cyn scribble something onto her notepad before she reaches into the pocket of her pinafore dress and pulls out a small hessian bag affixed to a long length of leather. She slides both the pad and the hessian bag across the table towards me.

"What's this?" I ask, glancing from her face to the pad.

This contains witch hazel that has been blessed under a new moon. It will guard your heart and cool the passions. If you do not trust what I've made, wear this around your neck as an alternative.

I frown, picking up the necklace. "You expect me to believe that this will work?" I ask, passing the pad to Arden who reads her words and then pushes it across the table to Lorcan. "That you haven't laced it with poison?"

She shrugs, taking the pad back from Lorcan and scribbling down something else. Holding it up for each of us to read.

If you refuse to trust me, then this is the only alternative. It must be worn around me at all times and under no circumstances should you get it wet.

Reaching into her pocket she pulls out two more necklaces, handing one to Lorcan then Arden. They each take it from her.

"Is this as potent as the tincture?" Arden asks.

I don't know for certain. What I do know is that this particular item needed a spell in order for it to work, and that spell wasn't cast by me, she writes.

"Who the fuck was it cast by, if not you?" I ask, reaching up to run my fingers over the scar at the base of my neck caused by her teeth all those years ago. It's covered now by a tattoo, but just because you can't see it, doesn't mean it didn't happen.

Cyn flinches, and I can tell by the way heat flashes up the column of her neck that she remembers that moment between us in the chapel at Silver Oaks as much as I do.

Fuck, how can I forget?

It was the most humiliating and the most exhilarating moment of my life.

Do you remember the old woman at the circus? she writes, her question throwing me a moment.

"What about her?" Arden asks, cutting in, a muscle in his jaw flexing as he grits his teeth. Of course he remembers her. We all do. She was the old crone we sought out after making the blood pact and taking Cyn's virginity.

A week after that day we snuck out to the circus, I went back to see her. I begged her to help me undo the blood pact. She couldn't. But she did give me these. I never got a chance to give them to you.

"Yet you kept them all this time?" Lorcan asks, watching her curiously.

She nods. *I knew one day they'd be needed.*

"Will they work?" Arden asks.

I don't know. She promised me that they would. But I have no way of knowing for certain, she repeats, eying me. *My work is based on knowledge of the human body, herbology and science. Which in and off itself is a kind of magic, just not the kind of magic you think I'm capable of.*

"And yet you managed to curse us with a blood pact," I point out, a statement that is ignored by everyone as Arden takes the bottle from Lorcan, unscrews the cap and squeezes the pipette, placing three drops beneath his tongue.

"Then I'm not taking any chances," he says, washing the taste away with a mouthful of Guinness.

"You're a fucking eejit!" I exclaim, scowling at him.

"I've never once acted the fool, and I'm not about to start now. Cyn has proved time and again that she is adept at her work. I trust her in this," he says calmly.

"You trust the woman who's spent over a year living with The Masks, who was friends with those fucking deviants growing up? Men we had a hand at killing!" I argue.

Cyn shifts in her seat, her spine snapping straight at talk of her childhood friends. Out of the corner of my eye I see her scribbling something down on her pad, but this time I have zero interest in what she wants to say. When I refuse to look at her words, she passes the pad to Lorcan, who takes it from her and reads.

"You think you've passed judgement, Carrick? Need I remind you how you treated me at Silver Oaks?"

Lorcan eyes me. "She's got a point."

"That's different."

Cyn takes the pad back from Lorcan.

How? she writes.

"I didn't brainwash you into thinking you were safe with me," I begin, hating the fact I'm letting her get to me, but being unable to do a damn thing about it. "I didn't build you a cage and tell you it was a palace. I didn't make you perform for men and women then sell you off to the highest bidder so they could use you to fulfil their fucked-up fantasies. I didn't fuck up your head so badly that you thought your prison was actually your home, and I sure as fuck didn't strip you of your name and replace it with a number like a prized cow."

Cyn swallows hard, and I see how she forces the anger I know she feels towards me deep, deep down. It irritates me more than it should because I want her anger, I crave it.

Dropping her gaze to her notepad, her fingers shake a little as she writes. Eventually she pushes the pad across the table.

I chose to be Thirteen and live with The Masks. I chose to become a number because I didn't want to be Cynthia O'Farrell a moment longer. At Ardelby Castle I could be me, not the mute girl, not Niall's daughter, not the woman who witnessed her mother's death as a child, not a victim. Jakub, Leon and Konrad let me be who I am. They never hurt me. Not once. Can you say the same?

Slowly I lift my eyes to meet hers. "Then you were fortunate. The other Numbers, they weren't so lucky."

This time Cyn doesn't respond, she simply folds her hands

into her lap and stares at a spot over my shoulder, checking out of the conversation altogether like she's prone to do.

"That's enough talk of The Masks. They're dead and no longer a problem," Arden says, cutting the tension in the room with the sharp snap of his fingers.

"So how are you feeling?" Lorcan asks Arden, trying in his own way to ease the building tension between us all.

"Fine. I'm assuming it'll take a little time to work?"

Cyn nods.

"And you? Are you going to drink it?" I ask, firing my question at Lorcan who's staring at the bottle with a frown.

He fingers the small hessian bag, settling his gaze on me. "I don't need the tincture to keep me in check. However, I will wear the necklace if it makes you feel safer," he says, directing the second half of his statement at Cyn as he ties the necklace around his neck, tucking the hessian bag beneath his jumper.

She acknowledges him with a dip of her head before letting her gaze fall back on me. Her easy acceptance angers me. I scoff, rolling my eyes.

"Don't be a fool, Cyn. Lorcan wants to fuck you as much as the rest of us, and if you think for one second he won't take that damn necklace off the minute he's alone then *you're* a fool."

"This isn't about me," Lorcan says, swiping a hand through his hair. "This is about getting the job done. Cyn needs to feel safe in order to fulfil her debt. We need her to fulfil her debt in order to supply Soren. Like it or not, something has to give. So either wear the damn necklace or take a couple of the drops, but for love of our fucking brotherhood, stop making this more difficult than it needs to be!"

"*Me* making it more difficult?" I bite out the words, before pushing back the chair and standing. "I'm not the one who cursed us with a blood pact binding us to them forever, and I'm not the one who has the gall to complain about the consequences of that."

"Carrick, we talked about this," Arden begins, but I cut him off.

"No. You made a decision for us. One I haven't and will not agree to." Seething I turn my attention fully to Cyn. "You made your damn bed, now you lie in it. Don't do anything to piss me off, and for fuck sake don't run, because you know better than anyone what will happen when I catch you."

Then I stride from the room, leaving the discarded hessian bag on the dining room table and cursing everyone under this roof.

11

Cyn - Aged sixteen

Drying my face off with a towel, I pop it back on the handrail in my bathroom then grab my cup of chamomile tea from my desk in the corner of my bedroom, and climb onto my bed, more than ready to sleep.

It's been a long day and I'm hoping that the lavender cigarette I finished smoking a few minutes ago, combined with the herbal tea, will help me drift off. Failing that, I have my sleep tonic to fall back on. I don't like to use it every night as it causes me to go into a really deep sleep and the grogginess can linger a little the next day, but if I need it, I'll take it.

As I make myself comfortable, I make a mental note to

experiment a little more with different quantities of herbs to get the perfect sleep tonic, then take a sip of my tea reflecting on my day. As days go, today wasn't horrendous. Arden, Lorcan and Carrick were nowhere to be seen, which is always a bonus, and a couple of girls in my Maths class even smiled at me.

I'm not about to instigate a friendship or anything, but admittedly it felt good to be seen by people other than my tormentors, who've been giving me a wide berth ever since Father Brian caught me and Carrick in the chapel doing something we shouldn't.

Our penance was decided after he frogmarched us both into Ms Weatherby's office. Carrick got a week in solitary confinement for taking advantage of such a *vulnerable* girl, and I got the same amount of time in the science lab stripped away, but only because my father came to my aid. I'm not sure what he said to persuade Ms Weatherby, but I'm guessing it was either a threat to her safety or a large donation to the school.

Either way, later that evening my father sent me a one line email that said; *Next time go for the jugular, it's messy but effective.*

I guess that was his way of letting me know he hadn't abandoned me completely. Which is just as well, as I was beginning to feel like an orphan. It's been months since I've been home, and it doesn't look like he's going to send for me any time soon. So like it or not, I have to try to survive here. Biting Carrick was me trying to do that. At least that's what I keep telling myself over and over again. It was just survival. Nothing more.

Heaving out a sigh, I place what's left of my tea on my bedside table, turn off the lamp and scoot under the covers trying to get comfortable. Whilst my body feels relaxed, my mind is wide awake. I try not to fall into the trap of checking my watch every ten minutes to see how much time has passed and then stress about how little sleep I'll be getting. When an hour passes, I give up trying to fall asleep under my own steam and reach for my sleep tonic, placing a few drops beneath my tongue, then allow my mind to wander.

Like always of late, my thoughts take me to the three boys who've turned my world upside down and me inside out. Yesterday Carrick was let out of solitary, and I'd expected some kind of retribution, but so far... *nothing.*

Maybe my father sent them a message too?

I really, really hope so.

Or maybe they're done with me.

In the chapel I'd stepped out of my comfort zone and done something I never ever thought I'd be capable of. I don't ever intentionally hurt anyone, but I chose to hurt Carrick. I can't even say I did it in self-defence because at that point all he was really doing was keeping me from leaving. I bit him because I was angry. I didn't let go because he asked me not to, and I tasted him because he liked it. Because *I* liked it.

And it's that memory of Carrick's body pressed against mine, his groans filling my ears, that finally drags me into a deep, restless sleep.

Inky darkness filters into my subconscious mind, as hands made of smoke and mist trail over my skin like a soft caress. It feels like fog rolling over a darkened moor, reeds trailing against the still waters of a bottomless lake.

It feels like a butterfly's wing quivering in the moonlight.

It feels so real that I can't help but lean into its touch, reacting in a way that's unfamiliar yet pleasurable. Warmth blooms beneath my skin, and I find myself drawn to a darkness that is no more evil than the pitch black of night. It feels familiar somehow, and perhaps there's a small part of me that's afraid, but the other part? That part wants to receive whatever it's trying to imbue with its touch.

Pleasure, comfort, desire, need... *magic*.

I bask in the feeling, knowing that I'm safe, that this is a dream brought on by my powerful sleep tonic. In my mind's eye I can see the darkness swirl and dissipate as though it's trying and failing to become solid. Black and grey intertwine as it ebbs and flows around me.

Touching, caressing, stroking over my skin.

There's safety in its arms, this darkness.

And then, just like that, something changes.

There's a shift in the air as though the smoke wants to crawl into my nose and mouth, my ears and eyes, my pores, to deny me of oxygen. As though it wants to suffocate me.

The hairs on the back of my neck rise as the darkness thickens, evolving, becoming solid. It's no longer featherlight. The tendrils of smoke turn into fingers then hands, sliding down my arms, reaching across my stomach, trailing beneath the curve of my rib cage.

Searching. Touching. Exploring.

Fingers roam, palms press, hands squeeze.

My body is aflame. A fire chasing over my flesh.

Darkness is replaced with fire. Burning, scorching, annihilating.

I hear voices and fight towards consciousness, swimming up against the dark ocean of my dreams towards the moonlight beckoning me to the surface, trying to understand the whispered words, the muttered phrases, the angry threat of something I don't understand.

Then goosebumps spread out over my skin, my subconscious mind whispering a cautionary tale, one I refuse to believe.

This is real. This is real. Wake up. Wake up.

WAKE UP!

I struggle to rise from beneath the power of my sleep tonic, fighting to regain consciousness as that voice inside my head shouts over and over again to *wake the hell up*. But my body is heavy, relaxed, not my own, and with every passing second the gentle becomes bruising, the caresses antagonistic. The darkness is no longer a wisp of smoke but a heavy hand and squeezing fingers, morphing from a pleasant dream into a living nightmare.

Then the veil of darkness is lifted and they're everywhere. Hands on my hips, pressing my shoulders into the bed, holding my ankles. There are too many hands, all over me. Fingernails digging into my flesh, roughness sliding around my chest, binding me tightly.

No! I push outwards, flailing against the monster trying to hurt me, grasping at wakefulness, trying to claw back towards consciousness.

Something is wrong.

Something is terribly, terribly wrong.

"Keep her still!" a familiar voice hisses, the darkness no longer a friend, but foe.

One that I recognise.

Arden.

"Then hurry up tying the rope," Carrick snaps back, and my heart plummets deep into my stomach.

Rope?

No. No. No. No. No!

My eyes snap open, and I blink back the harsh light aimed at my face.

No please.

My enemies. They're here. In my room.

I try to sit up but my arms are caged against my body, wrapped tightly in rope.

They've tied me up.

They've. Tied. Me. Up!

I kick out with my legs, but Carrick has my ankles gripped in his strong hands, pinning me down.

"There's no point in fighting us. You won't win," Carrick says, releasing my legs as he steps backwards.

I lash out, kicking at him, but he moves back out of reach, laughing.

His fucking laugh scores me open and I gag. I turn on my side, gagging. Wanting to be sick. Wanting to throw up all over them. Wanting to get them to leave me alone.

Please, just leave me alone.

"Arden, maybe we should let her go..." Lorcan says, as I

heave and cough, tears burning my eyes, blazing trails of hurt down my cheeks.

"No," he snaps, crouching down in front of me, his amber eyes reflecting my fear back at me. "Not unless she begs us to."

"Arden!" Lorcan persists, but I can't even look at him.

I can't look at the boy whose voice carries pity and regret, sympathy and kindness but does *nothing* to intervene. Words mean nothing, but his lack of action speaks volumes.

I hate him for his cowardice as much as I hate Arden for his cold detachment and Carrick for his blazing hatred.

Arden leans closer, his fingertip swiping at an escaped tear and says, "Beg."

My mouth opens and something pitiful rises up in my chest.

It's nothing more than a drop of rain splashing against a petal. No louder than long grass blowing in the breeze or a ladybird walking across a leaf.

It barely exists. It's not strong enough to make a difference, to make them hear.

But oh how I want to scream. I want to curse them with words, rip them to shreds with my anger. But nothing comes. Nothing.

Silence betrays me once again.

It betrays me as they drag me to my feet and march me out of my bedroom. My voice remains stubbornly silent as they haul me along the corridor, down the stone steps and usher me out into the night. It doesn't make a sound as they pull me into the forest over sharp stones and stinging nettles. It refuses to make a peep as they tie me to a tree trunk, light a fire and welcome half of the school to a party I haven't been invited to as a guest, but as a victim of their abuse.

I don't whimper. I don't scream or curse. I don't shout or rage.

I remain silent.

I remain silent as they seek their revenge.

I remain mute as Carrick uses a marker pen to write hateful words across my cheeks.

"Witch. *Cailleach*," he says, saying them out loud as he writes before stepping back and passing the pen to Arden who takes it from him.

"You hurt one of us. We hurt you," Arden says, his amber eyes flickering with a fire so intense I turn my face away from it. "Carrick was sent to solitary confinement, probed and fucking prodded as they tried to break him all because *you* bit him. He suffered because you're the daughter of a powerful man and he's no more than an orphaned boy of a drunken son-of-a-bitch. This is your penance. This is for the sins you've committed on my friend."

As tears cascade down my cheeks, Arden drops to his knees, grips my thigh and writes the word *enemy* across my skin. Then he stands and chucks the pen to the nearest person to him. It's one of the girls who smiled at me earlier today, that smile stretching into a sneer as she steps up and presses her abuse into my skin too.

The crowd laughs. Drinks are passed around. Music is played. People get drunk and with it, lose their inhibitions and any sense of right and wrong.

One by one they step up in front of me, ripping at my

pyjamas so they can mark my flesh with words I'll never be able to speak, until finally I'm naked and shivering, my body covered in layers of black pen. Words smudged. Pain bleeding into my skin.

My head drops, my eyes streaming silent tears as my heart thumps a defeated beat, and all I can think of is why it wasn't me who died that day instead of my mum.

"Don't cry," a soft voice says.

A voice I know only too well.

Lorcan.

A gentle finger lifts my chin, a thumb swiping at the tears cascading down my cheeks.

I stare at him, my lips wobbling, my throat tight, my heart breaking.

Why? I silently ask.

He heaves out a sigh, then he starts to untie me.

Carrick comes over, his face a mask of pure rage. "What do you think you're doing?" he asks, dropping an empty bottle of beer to the forest floor and glaring at his friend.

"What does it look like?"

"It looks like you're stopping our fun," he scoffs.

"Do you want another stint in solitary?" Lorcan asks, easing the rope from me then pulling off his woollen coat and putting it over my shoulders.

I slide my arms inside and wrap it tightly around me, the hem falling to my knees, long enough to cover up my nakedness, but not my humiliation. That still burns brightly on my cheeks, and drips from my lashes like jewelled starlight.

Arden slips from the group of drunken students, striding

over to us. "What's this?" he demands, casting a cursory glance over me. Despite the flames in his eyes, he's nothing but cold, callous.

"This is me saving our arses," Lorcan retorts, side-eying me.

"Saving us?" Carrick snaps. "Looks like you're siding with *her*!"

"I'm doing no such thing. You know what happens in solitary. Do you really want to go back there?" he counters.

"I don't honestly care. Her humiliation is worth it. She fucking bit me and what happened to her? *Nothing*," Carrick retorts, his lips pulling back over his teeth as he glares at me.

That's not how it played out and he knows it, but I don't react. Instead, I press my eyes shut, gathering what little I have left of my dignity and walk off, ignoring the whistles and catcalls from the partygoers. I don't care to listen to their argument or their excuses. I just want to scrub this night off me and sleep.

"Wait up!" Lorcan shouts, catching up with me as I head towards the faint lights from the dormitories that I can see between the treeline up ahead. He takes my elbow as I stumble over a log, but I pull my arm away, flinching from his touch.

"Let me help you."

I just tuck my chin to my chest and keep walking, ignoring the sharp scratch of twigs and stones beneath my feet.

"It went too far," he says, and I can feel the heat of his stare as he stays in stride with me. "It went too far, Cynthia."

Is that supposed to be an apology? Am I supposed to feel grateful that he's acknowledged what they've done? How about a real apology? Scratch that, how about never doing it in the first place?

Anger like nothing else takes over and I stop in my tracks, the distant laughter and chatter from the students still partying a reminder of the humiliation I've suffered tonight.

I round on him, pushing against his chest with everything I have. He stumbles, his back hitting the rough bark of a tree. Then I slap him, hard. His head whips to the side, the sound of my palm meeting his cheek, a thundercrack that sends birds sleeping in the canopy above squawking into the sky. My palm stings from the contact, my whole body shaking as he slowly turns his head back around. I expect him to lunge for me, to react to my slap.

He doesn't, he simply nods. "I deserved that. I deserve so much more than that."

Then taking two steps towards me, he ducks down and lifts me off my feet and carries me all the way back to my bedroom.

I don't fight to get out of his hold.

I let him carry me, and I'm not sure if that makes me weak or makes me strong.

12

Arden - present day

Two months after Cyn's arrival I'm sitting in the outhouse sketching in my notebook. It's become a habit of mine to draw all the ingredients and equipment she uses, and to make notes whilst she attempts to create diamonds. Her methodical approach is impressive, and there's a lot more science to the process than I'd previously given her credit for, and all of it self taught.

It used to piss me off when she'd disappear for hours in the science lab at Silver Oaks even after we got Mr Rancliffe fired. She'd experiment for hours with her herbs, flowers and plants, distracting herself by making tonics and tinctures, honing her craft, all the while becoming as impenetrable as a prison. We quickly learned that whatever we tried to do to provoke her into speaking proved ineffective.

I can tell you, it fucked with my head. I wasn't used to not getting what I want, and Cyn was adept at torturing us with her silence. Not even that night when we took things too far and bound her to a tree, stripping her of her dignity, did she speak.

Fuck, how I'd wanted her to scream, to rage, to throw hate at us.

But she hadn't.

She remained silent, her tears washing over her cheeks with a flood of emotion that made me feel sick inside. Sick because I was the cause of her pain. Sick because in my righteousness I believed she deserved it, and yet deep down I *knew* she didn't. Sick because before we had bound her tight with rope we had all touched her in a way that wasn't hateful.

She was so deep asleep that she hadn't heard us break into her room. She hadn't felt her cover being pulled off her body or seen how the three of us had silently stood and watched her sleeping, enthralled. She didn't see how one by one we touched her like she was a treasure, like she was something worth keeping, something precious.

But then something shifted, and I remembered who she was, who her father was friends with. Hatred had slid back into my veins like a silent assassin, distorting everything. But in all that time she never made a sound.

Even her tears were silent, accusing.

The only time we ever got close to hearing her voice was the day Carrick drank something he shouldn't and she brought him back to life. The way he'd struggled for breath, foaming at the mouth, the sheer panic of almost losing him, had been a moment in our shared history that none of us have ever forgotten.

I know it haunts him still. Maybe it always will.

Opposite me, Cyn pulls off her face mask and swipes the tendrils of mousy brown hair that have escaped from her pony-tail behind her ear. Her cheeks are flush and her grey eyes are, for once, bright with excitement. It's not often I see her eyes filled with anything more than a controlled calm, so that one look makes me sit up straighter in my seat and take notice.

"What is it?" I ask, knowing that she's finally made a break-through.

Frustratingly, so far every attempt at trying to create the drug has been fruitless, and I've begun to wonder whether she's making the process fail by design. Then I'm reminded that she doesn't want to be here, and that would serve her no purpose other than to prolong her stay.

"Well?" I insist.

In answer, Cyn scribbles a message on her pad and slides it across the table towards me.

I've done it.

I look up from her neat cursive, meeting the confidence of her gaze. "What makes you certain that you've got it right this time?" I ask her, closing my notebook and resting my hands on the smooth wood of the table.

The clarity, she explains.

Placing her pencil on the notepad, she pinches the crystal between her thumb and forefinger, holding it up to the light. If I didn't know any better I'd assume it was a real diamond, one destined to end up set in twenty-four carat gold, gleaming and glistening on someone's finger, or dangling from a necklace.

"It's no longer opaque," I note, taking it from her proffered hand, and studying the multi-faceted surface with interest.

She nods, picking up her pencil once more, the pink tip of her tongue poking out between her lips as she writes. *I needed to adjust my process slightly.*

"Why?" I ask.

To allow for environmental differences.

I frown, cocking my head as I try to understand. "Is this not a good environment?"

She shakes her head. *It's not that exactly. Although I have had to make slight adjustments to the process due to the dampness in here. It would be better if this outhouse was insulated.*

"If we were to insulate, would the process be quicker?"

Yes, she nods.

"Then why didn't you say something before now?"

She raises her brows a fraction of an inch at the tone of my voice, then flicks her gaze back to her notepad and writes, *I didn't think you'd be happy to take the time to make this outhouse weather proof in order to assist me, so I figured out how to adjust to the environment instead.*

"So you waste almost two months experimenting when we could've had this place weather-proofed in a quarter of that time?"

She pinches her mouth together, and I know I've pissed her off. I can't really blame her for it, but that doesn't mean I'm going to acknowledge the fact or try to ease our fraught relationship with words of encouragement. It's enough that I've taken her drops to dampen my desires, I draw the line at stroking her ego too.

"Is there anything else that you require in order to fulfil your debt? I don't need any more delays. As you know our deal with Soren hinges on expediency. If you can't fulfil the quota in time, we will lose the deal and gain an enemy."

And that bothers you? she asks, pissing me off even more.

"Losing the deal? Of course it does."

She shakes her head. *No, I meant gaining an enemy. I thought the infamous Deana-dhe weren't afraid of anyone.*

I snort, her tone undeniable despite her even features. "We're not. We do however prefer to keep our enemies to a minimum."

She begins to roll her eyes, then stops mid roll, censoring herself as she so often does. Instead, her fingers tap against the lined notepad as she focuses her attention on the perfectly formed drug, thoughtful now. I want to demand what she's thinking but force myself to be civil instead knowing that she will double-down if she feels threatened or disrespected.

"You can speak freely," I offer instead, opening up my book and making a quick sketch of the drug. My tone is light, almost disinterested, as I try to use reverse psychology to engage her in a conversation. And it works, just not in the way I expected.

Out of the corner of my eye I watch Cyn as she moves around the table, coming to a standstill at my side with her pad and pencil in hand. Ordinarily Cyn keeps herself as physically closed off from us as she does verbally and emotionally, so it's a surprise to me that she's now willing to stand so close that I can actually feel the heat of her body penetrating mine. Then again she's confident in her abilities, and given I don't immediately want to pull her into my arms and ravage her, I'd say that she's right to be.

"Yes?"

Pulling up the stool she takes a seat, staring at my notepad with the neatly written notes and pencil drawings.

Your drawings are very detailed, she writes.

"Is that a compliment?"

An observation.

I guess I deserved that. Compliments aren't something enemies normally give each other, and it's not something I've ever indulged in, except maybe that one time when I took her virginity and came so hard that I'd forgotten my hatred for a moment and told her how much I loved the feel of her pussy fisting my cock.

"Any other observations you care to share with me?" I ask.

You're troubled.

"Troubled? No." I brush off her remark with a sharp laugh. "Why would *I* be troubled?"

Biting on her lip, Cyn narrows her eyes at me. *You think you're immune to the consequences of stress.*

"Why would I be stressed?"

Because you live a lie, she retorts. *You're not untouchable, or invincible, or a god dressed up in mortal men's clothing like you want everyone to think. You're just a man. A gifted one, yes, but still just a man.*

"What people choose to believe about the Deana-dhe is up to them. If that elevates me and my brothers to a god-like status, that is just as well. Isn't God all-seeing, all-knowing? There is very little the Deana-dhe do not know. So please, don't tell me I'm stressed when I'm not."

You have a patch of eczema on the crook of your arm, she points out. *Your tongue is cracked and skin is sallow. At best you're not getting enough sleep, at worst your immune system is struggling because you are.*

I curse myself internally for rolling up my sleeves earlier. "It's nothing."

Her gaze drifts back to my arm, and it takes everything in me not to roll down my sleeves and hide my inflamed skin from her.

When was the last time you saw things that are yet to pass? she asks, her question snapping my spine straight.

"What are you talking about?"

Do you still draw images that you see of the future?

"You said you didn't remember," I grind out, recalling the night when she'd witnessed what very few people have.

After saving Cyn from falling to her death after she slipped and fell from her window ledge back at Silver Oaks, we shared a joint during which I'd fallen under the influence of a vision, and my need to draw what I'd seen took over. I barely even registered her still sitting in the room. By the time I'd realised what I'd done, she'd already left. The next day when I confronted her about it she denied seeing anything. I'd believed her.

She gives me a pointed look. *I remembered back then. I remember now.*

Setting the pencil down and closing my notepad, I reply, "You lied to me."

I did, she writes, shifting her body slightly so that her knees graze my thighs. She doesn't balk at the contact and this time neither do I, but for some reason that makes me more tense, not less. Her tincture certainly works, but in truth, I'm not sure I like it.

If you try to ignore what your heart and soul yearn to tell you," she writes quickly, *"it will eventually make you sick. Your eczema is an outward sign that your soul is suffering.*

"And yet you never used that information against me?" I state, ignoring her statement. Information like that is valuable. The Deana-dhe's whole business model is based on uncovering people's secrets and lies. It's why we're so feared and respected. She shakes her head, her brow creasing.

Not everyone wants to hurt someone just because they can.

I read her words three times over and each time they make no more sense than the last. That kind of information would've gotten me a long stint in confinement with electrical probes stuck to my head had Dr Lynch found out what she'd witnessed. It would've been the perfect opportunity for her to seek revenge for the way we treated her.

Yet she didn't take it.

"You could've destroyed me. Why didn't you?" I ask.

Because who you are, the heart of you, that's not something I would ever wish to take advantage of. This gift you have was given to you for a reason, much like mine has been given to me. Why would I wish to destroy you and risk your potential to do good?

"Because you hated me. You hated us. Is that not a good enough reason?"

Cyn shakes her head. *Two wrongs don't make a right.*

"Yet in the forest at Silver Oaks a few weeks after you arrived, you threatened us. You said that you would destroy us long before we could ever destroy you," I remind her, clinging onto anything to make myself feel better about the fucked-up way we treated her.

She chews on her lip, a tell she sees fit not to hide, before she writes, *I was angry, scared, and at that time I meant what I said. But the difference between me and you is that I will never capitalise on someone's gift or their secrets to use against them, no matter how tempting. I couldn't do it. I won't do it.*

When I've finished reading her response, I slowly raise my gaze to look at her, to see in her eyes whether she's telling the truth. People lie all the time to get what they want. Lying to someone's face is a hell of a lot harder than in written form, so I need to see whether she's playing me or if she's sincere. There's no doubt that when I look in her eyes, she's telling the truth. Yet, still I question her.

"What's your angle?" I ask, snatching up the drug and fisting it, her honesty, her kindness, angering me. How dare she be a martyr. How dare she make me feel guilty.

Apart from avoiding getting hurt by you? she asks bluntly.

I grit my teeth. "I said no one would hurt you. I meant it."

I'm trying to understand, she writes.

"Understand what?"

Why, when someone is born with such an incredible gift that has the power to do so much good, they deny its existence, even to themselves.

"Because this isn't a gift. It's a curse."

Shifting her penetrating gaze back to her notepad, she writes, *I find that all depends on how you view yourself. Are you cursed, Arden, or do you tell yourself that so you don't have to feel guilty about turning your back on a part of you that's so fundamental to your very existence?*

My fist tightens around the diamond so hard I fear I might crush it with my bare hands. She's perceptive, and I don't like feeling as though someone knows me better than I know myself. Because of that, I tell her something I wouldn't have otherwise.

I tell her the truth, or at least *a* truth.

"In answer to your earlier question, the last time I drew a vision of the future was when three people in love smoked diamonds and performed for us."

Who were they?

"It was Pen and two of her four boyfriends, York and Xeno," I reply, knowing that she'll recognise the names given Malik Brov, the father of her childhood friends, was so obsessed with the woman. "As you know, Malik was killed to protect Pen. He'd wanted her to perform in The Menagerie alongside the other talented artists he'd stolen. But she had powerful friends and four boyfriends who'd sooner die than let him take her."

She nods. *So what did you draw?*

"The tattoo of one of the men Pen loved."

Why?

"Because I had told Pen that someone she cares about was going to make a huge sacrifice."

And the man with the tattoo you drew was that person?

I rake a hand through my hair, nodding. "Yes."

So you helped them. You gave them a warning?

I read her response and see the hope in it, as though she's trying to find a part of me that's selfless, good. But she should know by now that everything is an exchange of information. Nothing I do is given without getting something in return.

"No. I coerced them into performing under the influence of diamonds in exchange for that information. I used my gift for my *own* gain. I am not and never will be like you," I say.

She swallows, her eyes blinking at me as she registers my truth.

And what did you gain? she writes.

If she were able to talk I know that question would've been asked in a whisper, as though she's afraid to know the answer.

"Knowledge, understanding."

Explain... she persists, the softness of her cursive, somehow demanding now.

"I wanted to know what it means to truly be in love, to have found your soulmate, or in Pen's case her soulmates."

She doesn't move to pick up her pencil to ask the question I see swimming in her eyes, instead she flicks her gaze away, drawing her bottom lip into her mouth as she stands. Without thinking about it, I reach for her, grasping her fingers in mine.

"Look at me."

When she refuses, when she tries to snatch her hand away, I

stand and grip her jaw forcing her to look at me, refusing to save her from the ugly truth.

"I did it so that the next time we were faced with you I'd know that this connection between us is nothing more than a foolish mistake, a *curse*, one we'll all have to endure for the rest of our lives."

She's shocked by my words, hurt even, and that triggers me even more.

"I didn't just take the tincture to protect you from me, I did it to save myself from this desire that burns inside of me because it's a *lie*," I say, then I release her from my hold and storm out of the outhouse, angry for losing my cool around her, angry for a deeper reason that I can't quite fathom.

13

Cyn - Sixteen years old

Ms Weatherby looks at me from behind her wire-rimmed glasses, and waits for me to respond. "Well?" she persists. "Are you willing to put this unfortunate incident behind you and move on?"

Unfortunate incident? I write, unable to hide my disgust. *They tied me to a tree, tore the clothes from my body and marked my skin with names. Tell me how that's unfortunate?!*

"I'm trying my best to find a resolution here. The instigators have been suitably punished."

Ten days in solitary is a suitable punishment, is it? I argue.

"What would you propose I do?" she asks, resting her palms on her desk.

How about expelling them?

She arches her brow. "That's not possible. Your father wishes you to stay here until you're eighteen. Arden, Lorcan and Carrick will do the same. There is nothing that I can do to change that, Cynthia," she says, throwing her hands up in the air as though I'm the problem, not everyone else around me.

I shake my head, this conversation is futile. She isn't on my side, she never will be.

Is that all? I ask, more than ready to get out of her oppressive office and back to the science lab. I'm over this conversation, and I'm done waiting for someone to step in and help me. It's time I figure this out for myself.

"There is one last thing, Cynthia," she begins, pulling out a letter from her desk drawer. "This came in the post today from your grandmother. She made it clear that I was to give it to you the moment I received it."

Eyeing her with suspicion, I take the letter from her pinched fingers. Ms Weatherby doesn't strike me as a woman who keeps her promises, let alone has enough restraint not to steam open a letter to read the contents. Despite that, the letter looks untampered with.

My suspicion must be clear on my face because next she says, "Your grandmother also made it clear that if I failed to give this letter to you, or opened it, she would have no issue hiring someone to *take me out*. Her words, not mine."

I widen my eyes in shock, which is quickly replaced with

amusement. My grandmother wouldn't hurt a soul, not even some stuck-up principal who has less spine than a worm. Ms Weatherby doesn't know that though, her only experience with my family is me and my father, and he's got enough badness inside of him that it rubs off on everyone around him, tarnishing them.

I stand, snatching up my notebook and pencil and tucking them, alongside my grandmother's letter, into my rucksack. I walk out of her office and head outside towards the graveyard situated at the back of the chapel, seeking peace amongst the dead because all the living have ever done is hurt me.

The air is crisp, the ground lightly dusted with frost as I enter the graveyard and take a seat at the wooden bench situated right in the centre. Winter is here and with it a reminder of the hardest day of my life. Tomorrow is the anniversary of my mother's death. It's been twelve years since she passed. Twelve long years since I lost her and my ability to speak. I miss her so much that sometimes I think that I must've died too and this deep, bottomless loneliness I feel is me living in purgatory as punishment for not saving her. I should've ignored her pleas to stay quiet and screamed for help instead, perhaps if I had she could've been saved. With a heavy sigh that sends clouds of warm air up into the atmosphere, I shrug off my rucksack, pull my grandmother's letter from it and begin to read.

To my dearest Cynthia,
I send you this letter with so much love, and with a heavy heart burdened with the knowledge that you are so far away from me and I cannot do a damn thing about it.

Cynthia, I am sorry. I am sorry my son saw fit to send you away from us.

I am sorry I am not well enough to give him a good hiding and force him to bring you home, or that I am not strong enough of mind to challenge his decisions.

I make no excuses for my son's behaviour. I abhor it, and if the truth is known, despite loving him as any mother would their child, I do not like him.

Please forgive me for my weaknesses. If I could force my legs to work again, I would drive to you myself and get you out of that place. As it is, I am as much a prisoner of this life as you are.

But I am not writing to you for sympathy, I am in part responsible for my son's behaviour and I will live with that for the rest of my days. If I had been a better mother, a stronger woman, perhaps things would be different.

My only saving grace is you, dear child. You are a gift, and so very like your mother that I know only goodness resides in your heart. Tomorrow is the anniversary of your mother's death and I know you will feel her loss even more keenly than even I do. It has been many years since her passing and it never gets any easier. She was and will be missed. She tried so hard to love your father enough to make him a better man, and it was working, Cynthia. It was working. But then she was taken from us and any light she shone onto his soul was put out.

There is no saving him now.

I drag in a stuttering breath, tears glistening on my lashes as the words blur beneath me. Swiping at them, I force myself to read on.

Cynthia, I have never told you this before, but there is something very important you need to know. Your mother wasn't just a gifted healer, she also had magic running in her veins. Magic that she used for good. I know it may be hard to believe that magic exists outside of stories and fairytales, but it's true.

For what is magic truly?

Is it not magic that a woman can grow a life inside her womb? Or a mother's intuition saving her child's life? Your mother healed with her herbs and flowers as much as she healed with the goodness inside her heart. She helped people. That was her calling.

She didn't need to cast a spell, or make a sacrifice to imbue her magic into her craft. Everything she made was blessed by her goodness. It was a combination of her skill as a herbalist, and the kindness she wore like a talisman that made them so powerful.

And I believe with every fibre of my being that her gift has been passed on to you. Not just because my heart knows this to be true but because when your uncle Jack found you covered in your mother's blood, barely conscious, it was me he brought you to. You probably don't remember in the aftermath of her death and all the trauma that followed, but your mother had used her blood to draw on the palm of your hand the witch's knot. A symbol of protection, yes, but also a sign from mother to daughter that you too have the power to do good.

Use it wisely.

Gach mo ghrá,

Máthair chríona.

. . .

*A*ll my love, mother of thy heart, I read.

Silent tears fall at her words and the Irish Gaelic she taught me to understand. My father hated that we used to converse in a language he chose not to learn, even if it was on paper, but it was something that brought us closer together, and I'm grateful for that gift she bestowed upon me. Reading my grandmother's letter through once more, I fold it up and slide it back inside the envelope, placing it in my bag.

I love my grandmother, and miss her terribly, but her words are no more comforting than the chill air wrapping around me now. In fact they only make me long for my mother more. There is no comfort knowing that she did everything in her power to save my life, only a sense of guilt.

It should have been me.

If my mother could make a cold, hard man like my father soften in his love for her, then her gift of healing people is far greater than my ability to throw a few herbs together to make a relaxing high or a sleep tonic. It's with that thought that I sit staring off into space as the first drops of snow begin to fall, scattering over my shoulders and head. I should go inside, get warm, but I don't. I sit in the cold, snow falling heavier as I stare at the gravestones, lost to my own thoughts.

"What are you doing out here?"

I flinch. It's Carrick.

"I asked you a question," he adds, but I continue to stare ahead.

He doesn't deserve my attention, let alone my words. When he sits beside me, I don't leave. I remain where I am, allowing the cold to penetrate my bones, wondering if this is how my mother felt as the blood drained from her body taking all the life-sustaining warmth from her.

"You'll freeze out here. You're already covered in snow," he says, sitting down beside me.

Still I refuse to acknowledge him.

"I get it. You're mad."

Mad? I'm beyond that now.

I'm *tired*.

He hesitates, and out of the corner of my eye I see him cup his hands over his mouth and blow warm air into his palms. Eventually he blows out a shaky breath, then turns his body slightly towards mine.

"I don't know why I want to hurt you one minute and then kiss you the next," he admits so quietly that I have to question whether I actually heard him right. "All I know is that I don't know how to stop."

I remain like a statue, unmoving, the snow falling thicker and wrapping us both up in a stillness that somehow encourages truthfulness. He leans forward, his elbows pressing against his knees, his head dropping between his shoulders, flakes of snow covering up the black leather of his jacket inch by inch.

Refusing to allow him to offload his sins so he can feel better about himself, I get to my feet and shake off some of the snow. Then walk away.

"Cynthia, I'm trying to explain," he calls after me, a touch of sadness in his voice that makes my steps falter. "I'm not a good person. I'm broken inside and I lash out at everyone who isn't Arden or Lorcan. It's wrong. I know it is…"

His voice cracks, and I shouldn't feel empathy towards him because he deserves none of my sympathy, but the pain in his voice is like a siren's call to that part of me who wants to heal whoever's hurting, regardless of the cost to myself. So, rightly or wrongly, I turn on my heel to face him, and wait.

He walks slowly towards me, the snow falling thicker now, and making it almost impossible to see beyond a few metres, but I don't feel the cold, I feel numb.

"I can't promise you that I won't hurt you again," he admits, lifting his ice-cold fingers to my equally cold cheek. "But I promise that if I do, I'll pay for it here."

Then he presses his palm against his chest, and bows his head briefly. When he lifts his gaze to meet mine, a single tear slides from his coal black eye. I'm not sure if it's from the cold, or some deeply hidden emotions but either way I don't reach up to swipe it away, or try to comfort him. I simply dip my head in acknowledgement, then turn on my heel and walk away, knowing that in his truth I did find some comfort.

14

C yn - present day

Thunder claps overhead and I bolt upright, the sound ripping me from my restless sleep. A flash of lightning flashing across the midnight sky as fingers of terror grip my throat. I force myself to relax, to remind myself that I don't need to give into my fears, that I'm stronger than that. Thunder and lightning can't hurt me. If I can survive a prolonged stay in this house with these men, then I'm strong enough to weather this passing storm.

Pulling off my cover, I press my bare feet against the hard-wood floor and grab my dressing gown thrown over the armchair by the fire, and slide it on. Knowing from experience that I won't fall back to sleep now, I head downstairs towards the kitchen. The only thing that will keep my fear at bay is my craft, and I will make a start on Arden's skin cream for his eczema to distract me.

As I head downstairs, I pass several doors, my feet silently slipping over the threadbare rug that runs the length of the corridor. The kitchen is the last room on the right and as I near it, I hear the sound of voices coming from a door opposite that I believe leads into the cellar. I've never been down there, but I know that they use it to store the majority of their supplies.

Stopping by the door, I recognise the harsher timber of Carrick's voice and the more lyrical tone of Arden's. I strain to hear what they're saying but the conversation is muffled as though at the end of a long, dark corridor. Pushing open the door, I look down onto a staircase, lit only by the soft light in the hallway behind me. I know better than to step into the darkness, but curiosity gets the better of me and I press my hand against the wall, slowly descending the steps.

When I reach the bottom of the staircase, lit by a stream of light sneaking through the crack of a door standing ajar at the end of another long corridor, I pause to listen.

"I've got you, Brother," Arden says, his voice is gentle, soothing, but with a hint of something else that makes my pulse beat faster. "Let me take care of this for you."

The groan that follows is familiar, and it speaks to a part of me that I pushed deep inside a long, long time ago. Despite everything I promised myself before arriving here about not allowing myself to be drawn to the alluring darkness that is the Deana-dhe, I follow the sound of Carrick's groans, and Arden's gentle encouragement. Finding myself standing outside the door, I peer through the gap. What I see makes me smother the gasp that releases from my throat, and my heart squeezes painfully.

God, if they'd heard me.

Pretending that I'm still unable to speak has been a lot harder than I thought it would be after years of not being able to. Arden, Lorcan and Carrick spent so long trying to get me to talk, to make a sound, and if they find out I found my voice during my year long stay with The Masks, their bitter enemies, I'm not sure what they'd do. All I know is that in order for my plan to work, I have to remain silent.

They can't know why I'm truly here. They can't know that I'm protecting the people I love.

Breathing out slowly to steady the erratic thump of my heart, I watch as Arden presses his mouth against the bare skin of Carrick's shoulder and bites down. Carrick's body shudders and he reaches up with one hand to cup the back of Arden's head encouraging him to continue.

"Harder," he utters, the guttural sound reminding me of all the times Carrick had begged me to bite him, to draw blood in our youth.

For years after I left Silver Oaks, I convinced myself that I bit Carrick to appease my need for revenge for all the ways he hurt me growing up, but with time and clarity I know that's only partly true. I bit him because I liked the way it made me feel. I liked the power it gave me. I liked the way he succumbed to me.

It turned me on.

It still turns me on.

I can admit that now.

With age comes wisdom, and with time comes forgiveness. It's been a long, hard road, but seeing what my friends, The Masks, went through for the woman they love, and the sacrifices she made for them has made me see things clearer. Nothing is straightforward.

There is no black and white, only varying shades of grey.

Growing up with the Deana-dhe I was a victim of their evolution, an eye-witness to their transformation. I know them perhaps better than they know themselves. I know that their relationship extends beyond best friends, that it's more than a brotherhood. As young adults, I witnessed their friendship pushing boundaries, rewriting them. It had shocked me back then. It doesn't shock me now.

Arden withdraws his mouth, unlatching his teeth from Carrick's muscular flesh. He licks at the drops of blood, like tiny rubies sparkling on his skin. My hand drops from my mouth as I grip the doorframe, entranced by the way Carrick leans back into his arms and Arden hugs him to his chest.

"You want more?" he asks, brushing his lips along Carrick's shoulder, one hand reaching up to cup his throat, the other sliding down his bare chest over the rivulets and grooves of his cut muscles, sliding through the dark smattering of hair covering his lower abdomen.

"I *need* more. I can't do this without it," Carrick replies, eyes pressed shut as though in pain.

Do this? Is he referring to me being here? He's made it no secret that I'm a bane to his existence. That I'm a temptation he's finding hard to ignore. Is he asking Arden to bite him so that he can survive in this house with me? Given his refusal to take the tincture I made or to wear the necklace I'd offered, it makes sense.

"You will do this, and I promise I'll help you through it," Arden replies, arching Carrick's neck as he runs his lips up and down it.

It's sensual, erotic, and I feel my body react to Carrick's obvious arousal. To know that in part I've caused this to happen makes me feel powerful in a way that I can't explain. My skin becomes hot, my pulse thready, and my clit throbs as I watch this intimate act of one powerful man relieving another with his lips and teeth. Carrick groans as Arden bites down again, sucking his skin into his mouth, marking his flesh with purple bruises as he repeats the act over and over again all so that he can temper his feelings towards me.

It's been years since we were last together, the four of us, and the three of them fought against themselves around me constantly. Regardless of their shaky self-control, their attention was like the fierce heat of the sun. It had the power to do great harm, yet without it nothing would grow.

That's what this moment feels like now, what being here feels like.

It's hard to understand, to even comprehend, but my feelings towards the Deana-dhe are as complicated as theirs are towards me. I've spent years both hating them and wanting them. Fluctuating between needing atonement for all the ways they hurt me, to wanting to heal them of all the pain they carry.

My grandmother believed that I'm a healer, a woman gifted

with magic capable of doing good, and she was right, I am. This past year I spent with The Masks caring for the Numbers taught me that. But I'm also my father's daughter. I have a darkness in me that if left to fester and putrefy would undo all the good I've done in my past and turn me into the *cailleach* Carrick accuses me of being.

He's right to fear me, I do have the power to kill, to harm, to maim, but I don't do that for all the same reasons I am here now, and that isn't just because I owe the Deana-dhe a debt, it's because I am protecting the people I care about most in this world.

I'm protecting The Masks.

I'm protecting their love for a woman who changed them irrevocably.

You see, despite what the Deana-dhe think, they're not dead.

They're alive and well and that's all down to my ability to stop a beating heart with poison, and revive it with an antidote.

That is my secret, that is the real reason why I'm here, and that is why I must, at all costs, keep them distracted from the truth in any way possible until I can figure out how to persuade them not to kill The Masks the second they find out that they're still alive.

I promised my friends time, and that's what I'm giving them.

Taking my time to make diamonds was the only way I thought I could do that, but now, as I watch Arden slide his hand beneath the waistband of Carrick's joggers and fist his cock, I'm beginning to understand that perhaps there is something more that I can do.

They've always called me Cyn, that I was their original sin.

Perhaps it's time I show them the true meaning of that word.

As Arden strokes Carrick's cock, bringing him to orgasm, a plan begins to form. A plan that looks very much like the vision he drew all those years ago. The one I stole from him the night he saved my life.

15

C yn - sixteen years old

"Very good, Cynthia. I feel we've made some progress," Dr Lynch says, pushing his glasses up his nose and smiling at me. "Don't you?"

I nod, giving him a fake smile. I've been at Silver Oaks for over a year and all he's managed to coax out of me are a couple of mouthed words. Hasn't he read my file? Doesn't he realise I've been doing that for years already? God, it's frustrating. No, it's futile.

"Excellent, excellent," he says, jotting something down on his notepad before resting the pen on top of it, studying me. "Now that the rather unfortunate incident in the chapel with Carrick and the resulting repercussions of such behaviour is behind us, I think it's time we get back to our usual scheduled group sessions, shall we?"

I shake my head. *No.*

Despite the fact that they've backed off, and left me in peace, I'm still raw from the whole experience. I'm not sure that I'll ever get over it.

"It is imperative that we heal the wounds and forgive," he continues as I scowl at him.

But I refuse to give him an inch, I'm not budging on this and I tell him as much with my body language. Crossing my arms over my chest, I narrow my eyes at him and shake my head.

No!

"Need I remind you that had you not bit Carrick then none of this would've happened."

What?! So this is *my* fault? Of course it must be. It can't be the three boys who've done nothing but torment me. It can only be the girl who bit a boy in retaliation.

And liked it... that annoying voice reminds me.

I ignore it.

He takes my silence as agreement, and smiles. "Very well, I shall see you tomorrow at the group session. In the meantime, keep practising what we've discussed. Mouthing the words you wish to speak may eventually encourage the sound to follow, agreed?"

I grit my jaw, wishing I had the voice to tell him what I really think of him.

"Mouth your response, please," he says.

Yes, I mouth.

A pleased look slides across his face. "Perhaps we can reward you all with a movie in the common room, it might help to build some bridges?" he says, smiling again as he drops his gaze back to his pad and jots down something else.

Standing abruptly, I have the sudden urge to reach over the desk, grab Dr Lynch's tie and slam his face against the surface for even suggesting something so ridiculous.

I don't, of course.

Instead, I gather my bag and head towards the Olympic-sized swimming pool that's tucked away in a brick building just beyond the main campus, thinking of all the ways I could poison Dr Lynch for being such a blinkered old fool, and whether I'd do it slowly over time or in one go.

Maybe a few dozen lengths will help to ease this pressure building in my chest? I can't name what it is, but it's a mixture of anxiety, rage, and the need for retribution, because it isn't just Dr Lynch I have the desire to hurt but Arden, Lorcan and Carrick too.

I've never been the kind of person to harbour hate. I've always tried to find the good in people, however small, but these boys, this place, it's changing me.

Heading into the pool house, I push open the door to the changing room and find that it's empty. Getting undressed quickly, I put on my swimsuit and head towards the pool. I'm hopeful that the pool itself will be just as empty this morning as it so often is when I've used the facilities during the day, but as I pass the showers on the far side of the changing room, I hear the sound of something wet and slippery that makes me pause.

The low moan that follows, and the prickle that covers my skin, has my throat tightening in recognition.

I should keep walking.

Actually, I should turn around, get dressed, and get the hell out of here.

But I do neither of those things.

Instead, I peer around the tiled wall into the shared showers, and come face to face with Lorcan butt naked, his swim trunks bunched around his ankles, getting sucked off by a blonde girl wearing a tiny string bikini. He's gripping the back of her head, smiling down at her as she bobs up and down on his dick.

Fuck!

Shit!

With my heart lodged in my throat and my pulse rushing in my ears, I wince, moving as slowly as possible, hoping to hell he doesn't notice me.

I should be so lucky.

The second I feel his eyes on me, I stiffen. My neck and cheeks flame pink, my heart pounds out of my chest, but instead of running, what do I do next?

I close my eyes.

I close my eyes as though that alone will make me invisible because if I can't see him, he can't see me, right?

Wrong.

So so wrong.

"Look at me," he demands.

And I know, I *know* he isn't talking to the girl on her knees with his dick rammed down her throat. He's talking to me. I squeeze my eyes shut tighter, trying to edge away. I can't be here. I can't be a witness to this.

"If you don't do as I ask, there'll be consequences," he says.

I believe him.

I'm an idiot.

A fool.

A moron.

I should've gone back to my room and smoked some herbs. Why did I even think I could get a moment's respite from these boys? They're everywhere I go, in every room I enter, stalking the hallways, the science lab, the forest, the graveyard and now the swimming pool. They're even in my dreams.

Will I never get any peace from them?

When they're dead, that voice growing louder inside of me says.

"Open. Your. Eyes."

The girl gags, mumbling around his dick because she has no idea there's another person witnessing this moment, and she thinks he's talking to her.

"Do as I say."

I don't even know if he's talking to me or to the blonde on her knees, but she continues to suck him off, the slippery, wet sound making my skin burn with heat as I open my eyes and meet his gaze head on.

Everything in me is screaming to run. To rip my gaze away from the intense heat of his. The ice-grey of his eyes is a knife blade at my throat as he warns me not to move.

But he needn't worry, I'm stuck in place, unable to take my eyes off the scene before me.

It's torture.

It's...

It's disturbing.

It's *erotic*.

My mouth parts, heat flooding every inch of me as I look and look and look, forgetting that not so long ago Lorcan, alongside Arden and Carrick, had tied me to a tree and encouraged half the school to mark my skin with obscenities just for the hell of it.

I'm angry at myself for being too cowardly to leave. I'm frustrated that I somehow find this attractive. I feel like one of those people who drives slowly past a crash on the motorway because they're drawn to the macabre. I can't not look. So despite my hatred towards him, I give in to the moment, knowing that one way or the other I don't really have a choice.

I drink in the sight as his cheeks flush pink, his pale skin illuminated in lust as droplets of water slide over his pecs. I watch fascinated as his stomach muscles flex and retract with every slip and slide of her mouth against him, and I find myself wondering what it would feel like to be in her position, so vulnerable and yet so powerful at the same time.

Shoving that disturbing thought away, I allow my eyes to wander as I take in the smattering of ice-blonde hair across his chest and the pale pink of his nipples. He has the figure of a swimmer, with broad shoulders, defined pecs, strong arms and a slim waist. Clearly, the girl who's deepthroating him appreciates his physique, given the way she slides her free hand up and over his stomach and chest like she can't get enough of him.

He smiles, a groan parting his lips as the girl sucking him

off takes him deeper, gagging as the veins in his forearms bulge whilst he guides her head up and down, up and down.

"That's it, eyes on me," he croaks out, never once taking his heated gaze off *me*.

I keep my eyes on him. I drink in his pleasure, half sick with shame and self-hatred, half filled with a growing desire and lust. Internally, I battle with myself. This is wrong, not just because of what they're doing but because he's someone I hate, loath, detest, and yet...

"Don't. Stop."

Each word is a demand, a desperate plea and I don't know if it's me or her he's talking to, or a combination of both. Either way, every slide of her lips down his cock and every groan of satisfaction he emits is like a burst of pleasure right between *my* thighs. Even if I wanted to leave, I couldn't. I have to see how this ends. For him. For her. For *me*.

I feel so much shame, so much self-loathing because I'm turned on by what she's doing to Lorcan, who's only ever hurt me.

"That's so good, so fucking hot. I feel your eyes all over me," he says, his voice low, husky as he penetrates me with his gaze. "You see *me*."

The girl's responding groan hides the sharp intake of breath I make as the air snaps and crackles with electricity and I'm suddenly hot all over. I'm a burning inferno, a stupid foolish moth drawn to the dangerous flames of his attention. As his gaze sears into mine, I feel something shift between us, something fundamental, and instead of running away, I take a step closer.

Chest heaving, heart pounding, clit throbbing, God help me, I step closer.

And the look he gives me as I step towards them, it could burn us both to ash.

"You want this?" he questions, eyes lit with something so far removed to what I'm used to, that I nod almost involuntarily.

A dark smile rolls up his lips as he grabs the girl roughly with both hands and jerks into her mouth, a keening sound rumbling up his chest as he comes, his eyes still on me.

It's an intimate moment.

So intimate that I see his vulnerability right there on his face when he falls apart. For long seconds he's lost to the sensation that I'm not a part of, but so wholly and deeply involved in by witnessing this act.

And I'm affected deeply, irreversibly.

My fingers flutter to my lips as heat pools between my legs, and I feel an unfamiliar throbbing there that I desperately want to relieve, and I might've, had the girl not pulled her lips from his cock, wiped her mouth across the back of her hand and stood, breaking the eye contact between Lorcan and I.

Breaking the connection.

Like a flood, reality and a whole dose of shame washes over me, making me stumble backwards. The girl senses me, and she twists on her heels, her eyes widening, her face contorting angrily.

I don't wait to hear what she says. I run.

I run straight into the swimming pool area and dive into the water in a vain attempt to wash away the shame and cool my heated skin.

It only occurs to me after I've come up for breath after swimming half a lap beneath the water that I've made another foolish mistake, one I instantly regret when I hear a splashing sound behind me. I know, without needing to look, that it's Lorcan, and I'm in deep, deep water both figuratively and literally.

Swimming as hard as I can towards the edge of the pool I try not to let the panic slide into my veins. A brief glance over my shoulder, and that panic escalates tenfold.

I see Lorcan's strong arms cutting through the water and the swell of his shoulders as he moves like an Olympic medalist towards me.

That swell of panic becomes a brick lodged in my chest and my fear weighs me down. Suddenly my legs feel leaden and my arms weak, and it's a battle to even gasp for breath as my throat closes over.

What's he going to do with me?

A second later, I find out.

Long fingers wrap around my ankle and I'm yanked beneath the surface of the water so suddenly that I don't even have a moment to drag in much of a breath.

His other hand reaches for my waist, a strong arm locking around me as he holds me back against his chest and drags me further beneath the water. Above me the surface ripples, taunting me with freedom and the oxygen I so desperately need.

He's going to drown me.

This is where I die.

No.

NO!

A surge of energy rushes through my body as I go into fight mode. Elbowing Lorcan as hard as I can in the ribs, I kick my feet and wriggle as much as I can. I am *not* dying today.

Bubbles shoot up in the air around us both as I struggle to get free. I can't see clearly from a combination of panic, stinging chlorine and the bubbles blurring my vision. I don't know how long he's held me underwater, but I do know that my lungs are screaming for me to get oxygen.

With one final burst of energy, I flick my head back hard and feel it meet something equally hard. I'm hoping it's his nose as his arms finally release me and I'm kicking frantically, swimming upwards.

The second I break through the surface I drag in huge lungfuls of air, coughing and spluttering. Tears pool in my eyes but the second I catch my breath, I force myself to swim towards the steps a few feet from me, my knees and hands hitting the tiles as I half sob, half choke, half wheeze.

My legs feel like jelly and won't carry me, so all I can do is twist around and scramble backwards, shifting my bum up each step, trying my best to ignore the severe shaking of my body and the tears falling freely now.

"Hey, calm down. I was just playing. I wouldn't have drowned you," he has the gall to say.

I blink back my tears, swiping at my face and glare at him with as much hate as I can possibly muster. Which, believe me, isn't hard.

He was just *playing*? *Calm down*?

Bastard.

Bastard.

BASTARD!

"You know you could've broken my nose with that move you just did," he says, treading water a few feet away from me, a brilliant smile on his face.

Why is he smiling? Why is this even remotely amusing?

FUCK YOU! I scream inside my head, forcing myself to suck in deep lungfuls of air so that my body still doesn't feel like it's drowning and give me back the use of my legs so that I can get the hell out of here. As it is, I'm shivering from a combination of fear, relief and anger.

"Can't have this beautiful face fucked-up if I want to keep getting blowjobs like the one Luscious Lorna just gave me," he continues, swimming towards me. A smirk creeps across his face as he hits the bottom step and stands. "Unless, of course, you *wanted* to ugly me up for everyone else so you can have me all to yourself?"

What?! I'm so shocked by what he's just said that my mouth parts and this rush of something unfamiliar rises up my chest. It's only milliseconds before I realise what it is, and I slam my mouth shut, swallowing the voice he had somehow almost lured from my chest.

No.

No to sucking his cock.

No to him forcing me to speak.

No to him.

No to anything to do with him.

No. No. NO!

He smirks, oblivious to what he almost did. If he had any

idea how close he was to provoking me into speaking I'm sure that smirk would erupt into the biggest, smuggest smile he's ever worn. As it is, he's too self-centred to notice and I'm too angry to care.

"Don't tell me you don't want to. I saw the look on your face, *Cynthia*, or should I call you *Cyn*? Seems far more appropriate, don't you think?"

Before I even know what I'm doing, I'm launching myself at him, fingers curled into talons as I grip his shoulders and shove him back into the water with all my might. He didn't expect me to attack him so he goes down easily.

Ha!

In the split second it takes for me to submerge him, he's back up out of the water, his hands beneath my armpits, like Poseidon emerging from the ocean, staff in hand.

"What the FUCK do you think you're doing?" he shouts, gripping me tightly, his body crushing mine against the pool wall as I pant angrily in his face. My nails dig into his shoulders, drawing blood. "Well?!"

My chest heaves with self-righteousness as I allow my features to morph into a look not dissimilar to one he gave me a moment ago. He tried to drown me, so I returned the favour.

"It was a joke!" he eventually says, his gaze loosening, not softening exactly, because he's Lorcan Sheehan and nothing about him is *soft*. Not his attitude, not his body, and certainly not his cock that is stiffening between us as we speak.

Something slides inside my belly like a snake through long grass. This closeness, this anger, this hate and violent lust between us is wrong, it's dangerous. My instinct is to scream, but I can't do that. Whatever he'd manage to pull from me earlier is gone, lost now to some unreachable place locked inside of me.

"You're scared," he states, as though that's a surprise to him, and just like the night they tied me to a tree, something in him softens.

Does he honestly think that just because he was the only one not to write some horrid word on my body that I should somehow trust him? That because he was the one to untie me and carry me back to my room, his coat covering my nakedness that I forgave him for his part in the whole ordeal?

Of course, I'm scared of him. Whatever just happened in the shower room doesn't negate that.

I suck in a breath and pin my backside tighter to the wall, trying to put even the tiniest amount of space between us, but he must feel the water slide between our bodies because he presses himself harder against me to close the gap.

"But earlier you weren't scared. Earlier you wanted me. You wanted *me*," he whispers, as though he can't quite believe that I would.

Even if I did, which I don't, why would someone being attracted to him be so hard to believe? It's not as if he isn't good looking, he had a girl on her knees sucking him off, for Christ's sake.

"You think she wanted me?" he asks, reading me far more easily than I thought possible.

I frown, caught by the bitterness of the laugh that follows his question.

"Don't misunderstand what you saw," he says. "She was

blowing me thinking of Arden and Carrick. I'm not the one she really wants. I never am."

His confession confuses me so much that I almost forget the predicament I'm in. When he shifts his hold on me, his hands sliding up my arms towards my wrists, his gentle touch sends shockwaves over my body, fear and pleasure intertwining.

"You don't believe me?" he asks, his voice softer, searching, and that snake in my belly morphs into something else that I refuse to acknowledge.

In truth, I'm not sure what's more frightening, the callous, insensitive arsehole who thought it was funny to almost drown me or the boy who looks at me now with confusion on his face and pain in his eyes.

Grasping my wrists, his thumbs slide over the tiny slashes I put there. The scars that litter my wrists and forearms are a constant reminder that not even pain can drive my voice out of my body. Wincing, he takes a step back.

"You're not the only one with scars, Cyn," he says, then turns his back to me.

What I see shocks me deeply, and all I can do is stare at the horrific patchwork of skin that covers the expanse of flesh from just below his shoulder blades to the centre of his spine. It's not a burn scar, nor is it some kind of chemical injury. This is something else altogether, as though several layers of the upper epidermis have been removed and replaced with skin that's a slightly different shade, as though it's come from another part of his body. I lift my hand, wanting to touch it, to check for myself that it's actually real and not some elaborate prosthetic he's wearing to mess with my head, but he looks over his shoulder at me right at that moment, and turns around, capturing my wrist once more.

"Don't."

I want to ask him how it happened, and maybe he already sees the question in my eyes because he sighs, lowering his hand, still holding mine within its grasp.

"Skin cancer. I have a rare genetic disorder which means I'm more susceptible to getting it. My mum didn't give much of a shit about me and let me run around our backyard as a kid half naked most summers. I ended up having multiple melanomas on my back, and a few more scattered over my chest. The ones on my chest weren't as bad," he says, lifting my hand and trailing my fingers over his left pec, then right rib cage and finally just above his navel where three smaller scars sit. "I had skin removed from my thigh to cover the expanse on my back. Most people are turned off by what they see..."

His voice trails off as he studies my face, and I'm not sure what he sees, but whatever it is he must decide he's done with torturing me for one day. Stepping back, he allows me the space to move.

As I leave the pool, my pulse rushing in my ears, and my heart racing for an altogether different reason, I hear him whisper something under his breath.

"I'm sorry if I scared you. I'm sorry for it all."

I don't acknowledge him.

I keep walking and don't look back.

16

Lorcan - present day

"You're up early. What are you making?" I ask, leaning against the doorframe as Cyn stirs something in a glass bowl over a saucepan filled with bubbling water.

The heat from the Aga is warming the room and through the window dawn is breaking in deep pinks and opalescent oranges and yellows. For once the sky is free from clouds and the sea is calm.

A good omen perhaps?

Cyn beckons me over. When I reach her side, she points to her leather-bound recipe book, the one she carries with her wherever she goes. Each recipe is illustrated with intricate drawings of the ingredients and equipment she uses on thick cream paper. Accompanying the drawings are detailed instructions written in her neatest cursive. Her artwork is stunning, the attention to detail impressive.

"Skin cream, useful for eczema and on dry, itchy skin," I read.

She nods, concentrating on the melting honey-coloured liquid. Given the list of ingredients, I surmise that it's beeswax which, according to her notes, when added with glycerin is a much gentler base for creams used to moisturise the skin.

"You have dry skin?" I ask, watching as Cyn uses a wooden spatula to stir the beeswax until it's completely melted. She then adds a cup of glycerin and water to the mix.

Shaking her head, she hands me the wooden spoon, urging me to stir so she can pick up her notepad and pencil to communicate.

This is for Arden, she explains.

"Arden? Why would he need cream for eczema?"

Because he has a patch in the crook of his arm.

I stop stirring the liquid, frowning. "He does?"

She nods, pressing her fingers to my wrist gently encouraging me to keep stirring. I glance at where her skin meets mine, enjoying the warmth from her touch. Despite the necklace I wear around my neck, enchanted with some spell that's supposed to keep my desires under control, I still feel acutely attracted to her. Maybe I don't have the desperate need to make her mine right at this moment, but I *still* want her. That hasn't changed.

Removing her hand, she replies, *He isn't taking care of himself. The stress he's under is showing in his skin.*

"What do you mean by that?" I ask, watching as she drops dried chamomile and witch hazel into the mixture as I stir.

He's a seer, but he's denying that part of himself, she writes, frowning. *It's making him sick.*

"You know about that?"

She nods. *I've known for some time.*

"And you think that a bit of dry skin has something to do with his gift?"

The body will outwardly show what the heart is denied, what the soul craves. He needs to embrace who he is.

"Like you do?"

Taking the spoon from me she nods, then covers the glass bowl with the saucepan lid, lowering the temperature. Then she flicks on the kettle, takes two mugs from the cupboard and lifts up a jar of tea.

"Yes, sure," I say, taking up her offer as I sit at the table.

She places two heaped tablespoons of tea into a teapot, fills it with hot water from the kettle then brings it over to the table, alongside two mugs, a tea strainer, some milk in a jar, and her notepad and pencil.

"You're concerned about him?"

There's no denying the surprise in my voice. Why would she even care enough to want to help?

She shrugs, pouring the tea over the strainer, before handing me a mug. I help myself to milk and take a sip, waiting for her response.

It's who I am. It's what I do. I heal people.

"Even those who don't deserve it..."

Does a doctor turn a sick patient away just because he doesn't like them? I'm no different.

"You didn't sign a Hippocratic Oath, you're not bound by the same ethics," I argue.

I have my own ethics, and oaths that I will not break.

"Which are?"

Heal the sick.

"That's it?"

That's not enough?

"That's more than enough," I reply, contrite.

Do as I will, but harm no one, she continues. *And finally, respect my gift and use it for good.*

"For good? Doesn't being here making diamonds that we're going to sell to the Skull Brotherhood break that?"

I'm not the one selling it to them. You are, she argues.

"But you're here because you sought information from us in order for you to get vengeance."

I didn't know at the time my debt would be to make diamonds.

"Maybe so, but it is, and here you are doing exactly that."

You make it sound like I have a choice. Everyone knows that if you make a deal with the Deana-dhe there's no backing out of it.

"Okay, there's that. But that doesn't negate the fact that diamonds are drugs that alter the conscious state."

You're making an assumption that diamonds are bad, they're not. In fact, I'd argue that diamonds are the antithesis of bad.

"They're a drug that manipulates emotions and enhances sensation. They're hallucinogenic. How can anything like that be good?"

You're wrong. There is no manipulation, though you're correct that they do enhance sensation and open the mind's eye, which I would argue isn't a hallucination but a realisation of truth.

"I remember," I say, my gaze slipping to the collar of her t-shirt and the triangle of skin there. Fuck, how I remember. Though I think Carrick and Arden would beg to differ about the manipulation part.

"And the side effects?"

Tell me what they are then, she urges.

I frown, trying to remember how I felt when the four of us took diamonds. There was no downer after the high. We weren't unwell in any way. It was as though we'd woken up from a really vivid, sensual dream, our bodies rested, our minds revitalised. I didn't even feel the urge to take them again, despite their potency.

The only thing I wanted was her. Not the drug. But Cyn.

Carrick and Arden put that down to the blood pact we made whilst under the influence, and for a long time I agreed with them, but now? Now I'm not certain of anything.

Sitting back in my seat, I let out a long breath, trying to understand my scattered thoughts.

Diamonds only enhance. They don't manipulate. That's the beauty of them.

"Carrick and Arden would disagree."

Carrick and Arden are afraid.

"And you're not?"

I'm here, aren't I?

"Are you saying what I think you're saying?"

I'm saying I was an eighteen year old girl attracted to three boys who hurt me. That's my truth I have to live with.

"You wanted us? I never thought–"

Time has passed. I'm not that girl anymore.

"That's fair," I reply, thoughtful as I study her.

There's something unconventionally attractive about Cyn that goes beyond her strong roman nose, sharp cheekbones and long unruly hair, something within her that I've always been fascinated by. Yes, her silence makes her compelling, and the three of us are all egotistical enough to believe that we'll be the ones to get her to talk despite failing in the past. But there's so much more to her than her looks and her silence. She's smart as a whip, for starters. She carries herself with grace and dignity. She's intriguing, mysterious, alluring in a way that's difficult to pinpoint. I've been with many women, as have my brothers, but no one has occupied my thoughts the same way Cyn has, and I would bet my life that Arden and Carrick feel the same even if they can't admit that right now.

"Is that what you tried to do for The Masks, heal them?" I ask after a while, needing to divert the conversation in another direction if only to distract myself from a truth I'd always known deep down. Placing her mug of tea on the table she licks her lips, then after a moment picks up her pencil and writes.

I didn't heal them. No.

I nod. Her honesty is unsettling somehow. I expected her to come to their defence. To try and persuade me that they were good men underneath it all. She hasn't. I respect that.

"Yet they were your friends? How does someone like you become friends with men like that?"

Someone like me?

"Someone with a kind heart, a good soul."

She smiles then, and it's such a shock that for a moment all I can do is blink at her, totally entranced by the way her smile illuminates her face, like the sun catching a crystal hanging in a window, the kaleidoscopic light bringing colour to everything it touches. After a second, that smile stretches wider and her shoulders begin to shake. It takes me a moment to realise that she's laughing, given no sound is coming from her mouth.

Cynthia O'Farrell is laughing... *At me.*

"What's so funny?" I ask, unable to do anything other than laugh with her. I don't care if she thinks I'm amusing, all I care about is the joy on her face, even if it is at my expense.

I might heal people, but my heart harbours the same things yours does. It seeks revenge. It wants retribution. It has needs.

"So Carrick's right about you then?"

Her laughter dies at the mention of his name.

Carrick sees in me his own reflection.

"What's that supposed to mean?"

It means Carrick can't see beyond the darkness in his own heart.

"He's not all bad, Cyn," I say, realising how feeble that sounds given Cyn's experiences with him. Carrick is a complicated man.

No one is all bad.

"Not even The Masks?" I ask, waiting to see whether she engages in a conversation about her childhood friends or changes the subject like she tends to do whenever any of us mentions them.

Forcing myself not to fill the silence, I sit back in my chair and wait as Cyn chews on the inside of her cheek, doodling on her notepad. It's the equivalent of someone stumbling over their words.

I was going to say that no one is all bad, but everyone has a choice not to let their darkness take them over. People who are truly evil give in to their urges, let it consume them.

"Yes, I'd agree with that statement," I concur.

The Masks were bad men with deviant needs, she continues.

"They were."

Pausing, she places the pencil between her teeth, and I find myself fascinated with the way her lips wrap around the end, remembering how those same bee-stung lips felt sucking my cock. It's been years since that night, and what should be a faded memory is still as real in my mind as it was the moment it happened.

But they were also human, complicated, and not impervious to love despite what everyone thought of them.

Ah, so this is where she tries to convince me that beneath it all they were good.

"Come on, Cyn, you can't be that naive. There are some people who're incapable of love, of empathy and kindness. The Masks were devils wearing human skin."

You think you know them?

I arch an eyebrow. "You think we don't? We collect secrets like other people collect antiques, or jewellery, or expensive bottles of wine. Over the years we've gathered a lot of information about The Masks and the people who attended their infamous balls."

I don't doubt that you've heard many stories, and I'm sure most were true, but no, you couldn't possibly know the real men behind the masks they wore.

"Do you want to enlighten me then? I'm assuming you know of some redeeming qualities, given you were such good friends with them?"

Cyn nods, then writes. *They never hurt me.*

"Because they saw in you something they recognised? Is Carrick right to fear you, Cyn?"

Have I not proven myself enough over the years that I'm not a threat, not in that way?

There's a weariness in her response, as though she's tired of trying to defend herself to us. If the truth be known, I wouldn't judge her for wanting to seek revenge on us. We fucking deserve it.

"Why haven't you tried to hurt us like we hurt you?"

It's a straightforward question but given her hesitation, I'm guessing her answer isn't.

Let's just say a wise man once said: "I destroy my enemies when I make them my friends."

"Abraham Lincoln, right?"

She nods, a hint of surprise lighting her eyes.

"Is that what you meant when you once said that you'd destroy us before we ever destroyed you."

Revenge can come in many forms, Lorcan. I guess this is one of them.

"By making us your friends? How is that revenge?"

Would you rather I poison you?

I can hear the sarcasm in her words as though she's spoken them out loud.

"No, I wouldn't, but I still don't understand why. You want to kill the man who was responsible for your mother's death and yet you don't want to seek revenge on the men who hurt you repeatedly growing up. It doesn't make any sense to me."

Does it have to? she asks, her ash-grey eyes probing.

"Yes, it does," I say, rubbing at my face in frustration. "I feel like there's something I'm missing. Something you're not telling us, Cyn. Carrick thinks you're manipulating me. Are you?"

No. I'm not.

"I want to believe you."

I'm not here to convince you that I have good intentions, or bad for that matter. I'm simply here to fulfil my debt. I made a deal and I intend on sticking to it. All I ask is that I'm given time to do that. There's no ulterior motive, Lorcan.

The truth is, I would've believed her if she hadn't at that moment broken eye contact with me and glanced at her recipe book. Over the years, we've all become adept at reading people, and I think in part that's due to the woman sitting before me now. There were so many times at Silver Oaks when she refused to converse with us that we learnt how to read her, to interpret what she wasn't saying consciously, but subconsciously through her body language. So in that split second when she casts her gaze away, I know she's hiding something important, and that something can be found in the pages of her recipe book.

Tucking that piece of information away, I push back my chair and stand. "Well, it's been good talking with you. Carrick will be down soon to watch over you."

He's already up, she writes. *Arden too.*

"They are?"

She bites her lip, heat warming her cheeks.

"What is it?"

It takes her a moment to respond but when she does she writes; *I saw them together, in the basement.*

"Ah," I say, understanding now why her cheeks are so flush. Carrick is struggling and I know Arden is the best person to relieve him of that suffering. They've always been close that way, and whilst we've shared each other, and women, in the past, their connection has always been more sexual. "Does it bother you to know they're intimate that way with each other?"

Cyn meets my gaze, then shakes her head. *No. It's reassuring.*

"How so?"

It shows me that even if they dislike me, they're still capable of empathy, affection, and love.

I nod, tucking that information away to digest another time. "I've got some work to do in the den."

She dips her head in acknowledgement.

"I trust you not to make a run for it," I add as an afterthought.

Why would I do that? You'd only catch me, right?

"Oh, we both know that it was always Carrick who caught you first," I reply, smiling at the shocked expression on her face as I get up and leave the room.

The Deana-dhe might be the ones who collect secrets, but we each have a few of our own, including Carrick.

17

C yn - Seventeen years old

"Come out, come out, wherever you are," Carrick sings, his voice echoing around the graveyard as mist rolls across the ground like ghostly fingers, sliding over my feet and legs, making me shiver.

Crouching behind a gravestone, I ignore the sharp stab to my arm from the thistle digging into it and make myself as small as possible. He can't possibly check behind each gravestone, it would take him too long. But somehow, like always, he seems to know exactly where I'm hiding.

"You know you can't hide from me. I'll always find you," he continues, his heavy footsteps creeping closer.

I can hear the excitement in his voice as clearly as I feel the trepidation tremble in my heart. I know what'll happen when he finds me. He'll bruise me with his kisses and he'll mark me with his fingers. Then he'll beg me to bite him, to taste his blood before disappearing into the night.

He'll do all of that, and then when Lorcan and Arden find me, he'll turn up a few minutes after them pretending that the flush in my cheeks, the tears trembling on my lashes and the heat between my legs had nothing to do with him and everything to do with them.

My fingers shake, and my pulse quickens in a combination of fear and this strange, abhorrent arousal. I hate him, I hate this, but I *want* it.

The first time they chased me, my fear almost got the better of me. It was three months after my interaction with Lorcan in the pool and had started after Dr Lynch finally persuaded us to watch a movie together to build bridges. I knew it was a bad idea. Had felt their intent the whole way through the movie. Every passing second had built up the tension between us. Dr Lynch had stayed the entirety of the movie, preventing them from whatever malicious thoughts they might've had, but as I was heading back to my bedroom, Arden had cut me off with a devious smile on his face.

"*Run, Little Mouse,*" he'd said.

I ran.

And later when each of them had caught me, they'd end the chase with stolen kisses.

Then as the weeks passed less kisses were stolen and more were given up as I began to understand that there was power in my touch. That for some reason I was their weakness as much as their enemy.

It became addictive, and we've been playing this cat and mouse game for months now. Maybe it was Lorcan who convinced them that this kind of game was far more entertaining than tying me to a tree. All I know is I run and they chase me until I'm caught.

When Carrick's so close that I can practically hear the thumping beat of his heart, I push up from my feet and make a run for it, half stumbling, half running through the graveyard. The only sources of light are the moon and a blanket of stars hanging from the pitch black sky above our heads.

Reaching a large tomb, I hide behind it, gasping for breath. My vision blurs as I suck in lungfuls of oxygen, trying and failing to regain some control over my heart that's intent on punching its way out of my chest.

"Cynthia, I'm disappointed in you..." Carrick says.

His voice is a deathly whisper that scatters across my skin, both heating and cooling it simultaneously. Pressing my palms against the stone, I wait for my punishment, anticipating the complicated emotions that will follow.

"Why give up so easily?" he asks, stepping in front of me, his dark eyes a void I can't help but be sucked into. "Anyone would think you wanted me to catch you."

I draw a slow breath into my lungs, blowing it out through my nose as he lifts his hand to my face and cups my cheek. His hands are surprisingly warm despite the chilly spring air.

"Did you want me to catch you, Cyn?"

Cyn.

It's as though I'm *their* sin and not the other way around. As though I'm the person they have to guard their hearts against, that I'm the temptation, the devilish woman who wants to coerce them into doing things they wouldn't ordinarily do, as if *I'm* the problem.

Me.

"Do you know what I think?" he says, drawing his thumb across my lips as he presses his body against mine. "I think you're screaming inside. I think you're screaming for me to touch you, to kiss you. I think you want me, despite hating everything about me. I think you want to bite me. That's what I think."

I don't argue. Not with my words, obviously, but not with my body either. I don't shake my head. I don't push him away. I don't cry or knee him in the balls even though I could easily. I don't protest or use my eyes to tell him that he's wrong. That it's all in his imagination.

I don't do anything like that because he's right.

I do want him to kiss me, to touch me.

I do want to bite him, and feel him succumb beneath my lips and teeth, my tongue and hands.

I hate him, but I want *this*.

I want to *feel* his reaction to me, I want to swim in his submission.

He hurt me by tying me to a tree with rope, by calling me names, by seeking out ways to humiliate me, and in turn I will hurt him by making him want me, to need me.

That's my revenge.

For I am Cyn.

I am their sin.

And that gives me power.

Sliding the tip of his nose against the bridge of mine, he cups my face in his hands and kisses me. The boy who sang like an angel kisses me. But this time he doesn't force himself upon me. He doesn't consume me with rough kisses and hateful lips. He kisses me with a gentleness that surprises me.

He kisses me like I'm something precious. Something delicate. Something breakable. Something worshipped, adored. Something *loved*.

In this moment, in this graveyard, with mist trailing around us both and the moonlit night shining stars upon our skin, Carrick kisses me like we're no longer two people who despise each other.

We're not enemies. We're not afraid of each other. We don't want to hurt or maim.

He kisses me as though his heart is mine, and when his fingers stroke my cheeks, my neck, my chest, he does it with reverence. In worship. When he moans against my mouth, tipping his head to the side and presses himself so close against me, it's in adoration, not hate.

When he groans, and whispers my name. It's not in disgust or in anger.

And then, when he breaks the kiss and pulls the collar of his t-shirt over his shoulder and asks me to bite him, it's with a dark need that shreds my own reservations to tiny, tattered pieces.

"Cyn, bite me... *Please*," he begs.

Inside I smile as I scrape my teeth against his warm, salty

skin, my tongue licking over the pulse in his neck and across the leather-steeped scent of him. He groans as I bite down on his shoulder, gently at first, then harder as he reaches for the back of my head and holds me in place.

Revenge doesn't taste sweet, it tastes metallic, warm and viscous. It tastes like blood.

"Fuck," he mutters, his throat bobbing, his pulse throbbing. "Just do it. Draw blood, Cyn."

So I do.

I bite down harder, my teeth breaking his skin, the familiar taste of him coating my tongue.

"Oh fuck," he cries, cupping my head, curving his body around mine as though the pain is cathartic, a release.

I think it is.

In fact, when he grinds against me, his cock stiff in his jeans, I know it is.

The pain and the pleasure I bring him cuts through the gross, hateful feelings he has towards me and turns it into something else, something meaningful.

I don't know if he understands it other than a feeling of need.

His need for me to hurt him.

My need to hurt him.

And the mutual pleasure it brings us both.

But there's also something giving in the act. Something that goes beyond the surface level feelings we hold for one another. My revenge, his pleasure. His submission, my power.

It is a connection that is undeniable, but secret, perhaps even to ourselves.

When I pull back, licking and kissing the place I hurt, he shivers. His whole body trembles against mine, and instead of pushing him away in disgust and self-loathing like I have done on previous occasions, I wrap my arms around his back and hold him.

I hold my enemy and press butterfly kisses against his bare skin.

Eventually he pulls back, slowly, regretfully, a pained expression on his face.

My heart leaps into my throat and I swallow hard, my lips parting.

There's so much I want to say, but can't. There's so much I don't understand.

"Cyn," he begins, his eyes filled with pain, with hope, with something that battles against my need to hurt him, that weakens it.

And then he stiffens, his head cocked, his attention pulled away from me.

A twig snaps, someone clears their throat, another familiar voice says, "I know you're here, Cyn. I feel you in the shadows, my nightmare come to life. My fucking wet dream taunting me."

Arden.

Go. I mouth, keeping Carrick's secret, holding it close.

For in his eyes I don't see hate. I don't see fear. I see the first stirrings of love.

Carrick is falling in love with me but he doesn't know it, and it's at the point I know I have him under my spell.

Go. I repeat.

And just like a thief in the night, he turns on his heels and slips into the darkness, taking that love with him and tucking it deep, deep down inside of him, burying it beneath half-truths and lies, burying it beneath a mountain of past hurts and disappointment that has nothing to do with me and everything to do with the trauma he can't bear to speak of.

As Arden steps into my periphery, another feeling descends over me. Different to how I feel in Carrick's presence. It's familiar in a way that ought not to be true. It's like the passing of a rainbow through a bottomless ocean, the colours distorted beneath the waves, making the depths infinitely more beautiful. It's like magic.

"There you are," he says, stepping closer, his feet pressing into the footprints Carrick had made only moments before, one boy replaced with another.

Two best friends, two people who've hurt me.

"I've been looking everywhere for you, and here you are hidden amongst the dead. Seems fitting."

Pressing the palm of his hand against the tomb, he ducks his head, his black hair falling into his amber eyes as he grips my jaw in his fingers. I don't know if he can tell that Carrick has been here before him, or if he has no idea. Either way, he licks his lips and tips my head back.

"Finders keepers," he says, then replaces Carrick's kisses with one that takes the breath from my lungs and rearranges my cells.

And just like with Carrick, I don't push him away. I accept what is, and succumb to it. I'm oblivious to anything going on around us.

I'm oblivious to Carrick watching us on the far side of the graveyard, his fingers curling into fists, his jealousy cutting him deep.

I'm oblivious to Lorcan stepping out of the shadows he's been standing in for the past half an hour, witness not only to my kisses with Arden, but with Carrick too.

I'm oblivious to the hands of fate binding the four of us together under a moonlit night as the ghosts of people long since dead dance and weave around us.

I'm oblivious to the real magic that tethers us to each other, that seals the bond between us when Arden slips away into the night and Lorcan takes his place, staking his claim on me just like his best friends had done not moments before. And when Lorcan leaves, his kisses lingering on my lips, I'm oblivious to my own soul tethering itself to theirs, refusing to let go.

18

Carrick - present day

"Where the hell are you going now?" I mutter to myself as I follow Cyn towards the small pebbled beach on the west coast of our island.

Keeping my distance, I pull my coat tightly around my body, flipping up my collar as I try to fend off the high winds that are turning strands of my hair into sharp little whips. Today is my turn to chaperone our little *cailleach*. She's been with us for three months now, and every day is a battle. If it weren't for Arden and his promise to keep me sane, I would've cracked.

To add salt to the wound, I'm sick as a dog and could do with hibernating in my room until I get rid of this fucking virus that has suddenly plagued my body. Instead, I'm traipsing after Cyn in this god-awful weather.

Narrowing my eyes on her back as she scrambles down the semi-treacherous coastal path, I think about all the ways I'd like to punish her, starting with my cock buried down her throat and ending with me smothering her screams of pleasure with my lips, because if anyone deserves to consume her voice, it's me. She's had her fair share of gorging on my voice over the years. I don't see why I should be deprived of hers.

All's fair in love and war, minus the love, *of course.*

Losing Cyn momentarily as she descends the coastal path, I pick up speed, jogging to catch up with her. By the time I reach the bluff, she's part way down, and I watch her as she traverses the rocky pathway, hiking up her ankle-length skirt as she does so.

My cock stirs at the sight of her bare legs, her shapely calves and a hint of thigh as she takes sturdy steps in her walking boots. My attraction to her pisses me off. I loathe it, actually, but it remains inside of me like a sick, twisted little demon wanting to feast off of her unhappiness and gorge on the sins of her flesh.

"Fuck!" I hiss, a wave of dizziness hitting me at the thought.

I'm not sure if it's from my sudden need to fuck her or the fact I've broken out in a sweat from my high temperature. Either way, I blame the witch.

Pressing my eyes shut, I rock on my feet, fighting the dizziness until it passes. When I open my eyes again, blinking away the double-vision, Cyn is no longer on the path but waist deep in the ocean, reaching for something under the surface.

"What are you doing, *cailleach*?" I ask, my words ripped from my mouth as another gust of wind forces a wave to pick up speed. Cyn is completely oblivious.

"Cyn!" I shout, but my warning is lost beneath the howling wind and the crashing, violent waves. "CYN!"

This time she hears, but it's too late, the wave is upon her and within seconds she's pulled under.

I run.

I run like the fucking wind.

My feet find flight on the back of another angry gust, and I ignore the cold creeping into my bones, my pounding headache and aching muscles. None of that matters as I stumble down the rocky path, tripping and sliding as earth and stone give way to heavy, pounding feet.

Nothing matters but saving Cyn.

"Hold on!" I yell, watching as her head breaks free of the surface and she gasps for breath before being wrenched back under once more.

As my feet hit the pebbled shore and I pump my arms, ignoring the way my body screams at me to rest, it occurs to me as I rip off my boots and coat that I could let her drown.

That's what she thinks I want, but it isn't true. At least not entirely.

What I want isn't something she can give me. Since the moment she crept inside my head and taunted me with her subtle beauty and soundless voice, I've been cursed.

My soul yearns for hers. But we're *not* soul mates. We've been tied together by a blood pact and her witchcraft, and because of that I will never know what it feels to love wholly, truly, deeply.

She fucked us.

And I hate her for it.

Right here and now, I could end the hold she has had over the three of us. Cyn could drown, and I could let her. It's the only way to end this bullshit. But as another huge wave tumbles over her, that thought is ripped right out of my head, the blood pact we made forcing my feet to move, to save her.

Running into the ocean, I dive over the next crashing wave and into the ice-cold water. My body registers the cold, but I fight the urge to lock up. Forcing my limbs to move, I focus on the billowing material of her skirt, and swim as hard and fast as I can towards her.

Every metre forward, I'm forced back, and I can feel the weight of my own clothes dragging me down, like a lead anchor on the hull of a ship. It's hard to tell if she's still fighting the currents because she makes no sound. Despite this life or death situation, her voice remains stubbornly quiet.

Yet, I *know* she's still fighting, Cyn is too stubborn, too pig-headed to give up. Her threat in the kitchen that first morning after we brought her home had been as empty as Arden's promise. She will no more kill herself than Arden will stay away from her. He can lie to himself all he likes, but I know him. The second she's finished making the agreed amount of diamonds, he will take what he wants from her. Perhaps it's that thought, and not the fact she truly could die right now, that has me using every last ounce of energy to battle the current and reach her, because if Arden's going to take his pound of flesh, then so am I. One way or another I'm going to sever this connection between us all, but it will be on my terms and not from the ocean's greedy grasp.

Another few strokes and several hard kicks of my legs later, I see the billowing material of her skirt like a boat's sail floating on top of the water, and there right before me is Cyn. My relief is short-lived as another wave comes crashing down. We're both turned over, and as I'm tumbling, fighting against the current, I open my eyes and catch a glimpse of Cyn. Her mouth is open, her hair floating around her head, a beautiful siren floating in the water as bubbles are forced out of her mouth. Is she screaming?

That impossible thought is yanked from my head as I'm tumbling once again. Panic seizes my lungs as they beg for oxygen and then, miraculously, I feel the material of her skirt.

Grasping it, I yank hard, feeling the weight of her body as another wave passes over our heads. The ocean wants me to let her go, but I refuse to release my grip. I tug, hauling her towards me, until she's in my arms, then I kick my legs towards the surface, gasping for air.

Cyn coughs, struggling in my hold, fighting me as though I'm the ocean trying to drown her.

She might be blue-lipped, but she's alive.

She's alive.

"Keep calm, don't fight me. I'll get us to the shore," I say, hauling her back against my chest as another wave threatens to take us both under.

She coughs, spluttering salty liquid from her lungs, wheezing and choking. Something unfamiliar tugs inside my chest as she struggles in my hold. Her natural instinct is to escape the person who's hurt her the most over the years, and I don't blame her for it. She has every reason to fear me, to hate me, but despite everything that has passed between us I need her to trust me, just this once.

"Cyn, calm down. Let me help you... *Please*," I add.

Somehow those words are like magic. She lets out a breath, her body relaxing against mine despite her shivering, and in that moment, as the ocean still tries its best to drown us both, Cyn puts her trust in me.

It takes me what feels like hours to reach the shallows, but when my feet hit the shore, relief and a deep sense of foreboding overrides the exhaustion I feel. Pushing upwards, taking our combined weight on my unsteady legs, I haul Cyn into my arms, carrying her bridal style up the shore. One brief look at her blue lips and vacant eyes tells me she's hypothermic and that if I don't get these wet clothes off her soon and her body temperature back to normal levels, she's going to be in serious trouble.

"Hold on," I say, meaning it, wanting to see the fight back in her glassy eyes, and the heat of anger in her cheeks once more.

Ignoring the way my own teeth clack and my body cries out for me to stop and rest, I climb the path back up the cliff. As I hit the bluff, a familiar voice calls my name.

"Carrick! What the fuck happened?" Lorcan shouts, running towards us, close behind him is Arden.

One look at Cyn and the blood drains from his face. My knees buckle just as they reach me, and on instinct Arden catches Cyn, hauling her into his strong arms.

"She got c-caught in a current, I p-pulled her out," I manage to stutter out, my whole body shaking with cold as Lorcan wraps his arm around my waist and hauls me upright.

"You're freezing. We need to get you inside," he says, taking off his jacket and wrapping it around my shoulders.

"Don't w-worry about me. She's h-hypothermic," I reply, ignoring the concern in his voice. "I'll l-live. I always do, r-right?"

"Lean on me. I've got you," Lorcan says.

Arden presses his lips against Cyn's cheek. "I need to remove her clothes, and get her body temperature up. I'll take her to my room."

"G-go ahead. We'll f-follow," I bite out, feeling my legs buckle again.

Lorcan takes more of my weight, but urges Arden to move. "Go. I've got him."

"When you get inside, you'll need to do the same," Arden says, looking from me to Lorcan. "Bring up something warm to drink. We need to get her internal temperature up."

"Understood. Go," Lorcan replies.

We enter the house a minute or two behind Arden, and he calls for us the second we step into the hall.

"She needs something warm inside of her now!" he shouts, looking over the balustrade down at us both.

"You good?" Lorcan asks, worry pulling his brows together in a frown.

"Get the drink. I'll go up."

"You can manage?"

"I'm not dead yet," I reply sardonically.

"LORCAN!" Arden yells, and it's enough to urge him into action.

"On it!"

Arden looks down at me. "Get up here. Now," he orders, before twisting on his feet and rushing back to his room.

By the time I enter his bedroom, the fire in the grate has caught light and is giving off life-saving warmth. Arden is pulling off Cyn's wet jumper and skirt, leaving her in just her underwear, her shoes and walking boots are already discarded. She's conscious, but somehow not in the room with us. There's a blankness behind her eyes that makes me want to shake her back to life. Instead, I drag my gaze lower, curling my fingers into fists as my eyes take in the puckered buds of her nipples, a deep pink beneath the drenched cotton of her white bra.

I'm well aware I should be getting out of my own wet clothes, but I can't seem to drag my gaze away. Her skin is almost as pale as Lorcan's, the raised scars on her inner thighs a reminder of the harm she's done to herself over the years. I also notice the way the white cotton of her knickers moulds to her pussy lips, and how dark the dash of hair is beneath the wet material.

Fuck.

"Get undressed now," Arden barks as he pulls off her knickers and bra.

If he's as affected by her nakedness as I am, he doesn't show it. Perhaps the tonic she made worked just like she said it would. It certainly hasn't killed him... Yet.

"Go sit by the fire, wrap yourself up in that blanket."

His voice is clipped, filled with concern and as he begins to strip, relieving himself of his own clothes, I understand what he's about to do without the need for him to tell me, but he does anyway. "My body heat will help to warm her up," he says.

I nod, gritting my teeth around my chattering words. "I know t-that."

Stripping my clothes with shaking hands, I watch Arden climb onto the mattress beside Cyn and roll her onto her side, sliding in behind her. His body is muscular, virile, and his sculpted chest and strong legs are covered in dark hair that is as thick as Lorcan's is sparse. Against her slight figure, he looks like a giant of a man.

There's something about the way he could so easily crush her, that any one of us could, that turns me on. Physically, she's so fucking fragile. Breakable. But mentally? This woman has the strength of a mountain lion.

Dragging my eyes up from his hardening cock I meet his gaze, understanding passing between us. He wants her. I want her. But neither of us will fuck her.

Not like this.

Pulling up the thick duck-down duvet and top quilt, they disappear beneath the covers, just the tops of their heads visible. "Get warm, Brother," he instructs, his voice strained.

In her weakened state, Cyn's as vulnerable as she's ever been, and now she's naked with nothing between them but the beckoning call of death. If I had enough warmth in my body, my cock would harden at the thought. As it is, I'm too damn cold.

Pulling off the rest of my clothes I'm reminded of all the ways that death is a constant lingering presence in my life. It's had its clutches in me ever since Cyn killed me then snatched me from his claws just over six years ago.

I can't shake it.

Just like I can't shake her.

Naked and with the blanket wrapped around me, I sit next to the fire in Arden's worn leather armchair and allow the heat to penetrate the cold. By the time Lorcan arrives with the drinks, my teeth have stopped chattering and I'm warmer, despite still having a cloudy head and aching muscles.

"Drink this," he says, handing me a cup of hot chocolate.

I take it from him with a raised brow. "Hot chocolate?"

"You need the sugar, and the hit of thirty-year old bourbon I've added to your cup. That'll warm you up, Brother..." His voice trails off as he looks over at the bed and the two bodies hidden beneath the covers. "How is she?" he asks.

"Conscious, but still fucking cold," comes Arden's murmured reply.

Lorcan swears under his breath. "What can I do to help?"

Sometimes even I have to question whether Lorcan's sincerity is an act. No matter how many times I question his motives, there's always a hint of truth to his actions and his words, a kindness that Arden and I lack. Maybe underneath it all he's a good guy... or a really good fucking actor.

"You can make soup. Chicken if we have it, vegetable if not."

"That I can do," Lorcan agrees.

"Carrick, drink up and get into bed," Arden orders. His need to remain in control is the only thing getting him through this moment of sheer, blind panic.

Conflicted, I hesitate.

A large part of me doesn't want to get under the covers and press my body against hers in a way that is comforting or life-giving because I still harbour this deep hatred that I can't seem to rid myself of. The other part of me, that part that always wants to be near her, wants nothing more than to feel her naked against my skin and abuse the situation, taking what I want and damn the consequences.

Neither are good, at least, not for Cyn.

"I'm not sure that's a good idea," I admit.

"Get under the fucking covers."

"Lorcan can do it," I snap back, chugging back the last of the drink, silently thanking Lorcan for topping it up with bourbon. The burn is fucking delicious.

"Lorcan needs to keep the fire stoked and make soup because you both need warm fluids and lots of them. Don't fucking argue, and do as I say, or so help me, Carrick...!"

"When you put it like that," I mutter sarcastically, gritting my teeth and hauling myself upright, glad that Lorcan is busy helping Cyn to take a sip of hot chocolate and doesn't notice how I have to grip the armchair to stop myself from collapsing. I don't need anyone fussing over me. I've survived far worse than the common cold and a dip in the Atlantic Ocean.

Death might be a constant, silent companion in my life, but today is not the day I die.

Gritting my teeth to stop them from chattering, I head over to the bed. Lorcan eyes me warily as he places the mug on the side table and steps out of my way. By the look he gives me, I know he thinks I'm going to take advantage.

"Now isn't the time," he says, and whilst his voice is neutral, the look in his eyes is not.

He's giving me a warning, as he should.

"I'm not in any position to fuck," I say, and it's the nearest to the truth as I can give him.

Lorcan nods. "I'll make that soup. You get her warm. That's it. That's all," he bites out before leaving, and just like that Cyn's only form of protection is gone.

"Are you getting in, or are you just going to stand there?"

I grind my teeth.

"Carrick?!"

"Fuck. Alright."

Shrugging off the blanket, I pull back the covers and slide in, trying my damndest not to look at Cyn's naked body. She's staring right at me as I pull the covers back over us all, and I find myself unable to look at the stuttering grey of her eyes.

"You need to get closer. It's your body heat she needs," Arden reminds me as I meet his gaze.

He's as close to a woman as a man can get without actually being inside of her. There's no denying the need in his eyes as he tips his nose to the spot just below her ear and breathes in deeply. She smells of the ocean, of course she does, but beneath that is the scent of her. To me she smells like Christmas spices, cinnamon and frosted pine. She smells like a warm toffee pudding, and melted chocolate. She smells like happiness and comfort. Warmth and love.

She smells like all of the things I was deprived of as a child.

It's why I *can't* be near her, and why I'm drawn to her over and over again.

Arden locks eyes with me, and I know that look.

"Arden..." It's supposed to be a warning, but it comes out as broken as my need for her is.

"I'm just keeping her warm," he replies, then opens his mouth over the bare skin of her neck, and puffs out his cheeks, blowing warm air across her skin.

Cyn shudders violently, her teeth clacking and that movement makes Arden groan like an animal caught in a snare. It's a painful sound. One I can identify with.

Inching closer, I feel the hair on Arden's arm whispering against my skin. He has one arm wrapped around her waist and the other positioned diagonally between her breasts as he clutches her to him, and I'm not sure whether he's doing it for her benefit or his.

"Press against her. Chest-to-chest," he says, adjusting his position so that one arm slides beneath her neck and around my back, and the other over our waists.

I do as he demands, sucking in a ragged breath at how cold she still feels. She's like a marble statue, soundless, perfectly sculptured, smooth as stone. A huge part of me wants to chip away at her, carving through the layers she's encased herself in until I reach inside and yank her voice free.

I want to hear her scream.

Whether that's in pleasure or in pain, I'm not entirely sure.

All I know is that I want to do it over and over again, then I want her to beg me for more.

Of course, she doesn't make a sound as I press my chest against hers. There's not a gasp or a whisper, not a whimper or a curse.

Nothing.

Yet the look in her eyes speaks volumes, and for the first time in my life I'm humbled by the unspoken words she conveys to me now. Relief, gratitude, and maybe beneath all of that, *hope.*

For long moments, I allow myself to really look at her. To really *see* her. I brave it out as my legs entwine with hers and Arden's, our bodies pressed together. Confused by the lack of distrust, and openness, I stare and stare. I'm unable now to remove my gaze from hers, when only moments before, I couldn't even stand to look.

"That was so fucking stupid," I mutter, my head resting on the pillow beside her as she shifts minutely in our arms. "You could've died."

Behind her, Arden runs his lips over her shoulder, finding a new spot to blow heat over. Her eyelids flicker shut and I'm uncertain if it's because she likes what he's doing, hates it, or is so fatigued she can barely keep them open.

"When you said you'd kill yourself, I didn't think you actually meant it," I say, swallowing hard, not because it hurts me to say those words but because she shifts again, her nipples grazing the hard plains of my pecs.

When she opens her eyes there's a different emotion held within them. One that doesn't make sense given the very dangerous situation she's in right now.

"I don't understand," I say roughly, and I'm not just talking about why she walked into the ocean, it's also because I don't understand what she's trying to convey with her eyes.

Her mouth parts, the tiniest breath releasing from her lips, and my fucking throat clogs as her lips move silently. Is she going to speak?

Milliseconds pass, a moment in time so minute that barely a breath leaves my body, and yet it feels like we've been here for a millenia, pressed together like this. Chest to chest, stomach to stomach, hip to hip, thigh to thigh. It feels more right than it does wrong, and my muddled brain can't understand or even comprehend why I feel this way when my heart hates this woman.

Doesn't it?

"Perhaps I should've let the ocean take you."

The moment is shattered. Her shoulders drop as disappointment flickers across her face.

"Carrick," Arden scolds, oblivious to the silent communication from Cyn.

Cyn drops her gaze, and I expect her to withdraw to that silent world that none of us can reach, but then she does something that surprises me. She lifts her hand and slips it between us, pressing her palm against my chest, and with the gentleness and caution of someone approaching a feral animal caught in a snare, she leans forward and presses a soft kiss against my lips.

Behind her, Arden gasps, but I'm too stunned to do anything other than revel in the softness of her lips and the gentleness of her touch as she strokes my chest with her fingers, as though trying to tame the wild thrashing of my heart.

And this feeling her kiss evokes... It's familiar.

We've kissed before, many times. Yet somehow this kiss unearths something I've buried deep beneath the boggy soil of a manipulated history. Underneath all the mud and detritus of our fucked-up past is a memory that is sweet, tender, *heartfelt*. This kiss unveils a memory of me kissing her gently, reverently, just like she's kissing me now.

When she pulls back and locks gazes with me, I understand what this is. This is a thank you for saving her life, one I don't deserve, considering a part of me still wonders if it would have been better for all of us if I'd let her drown. As I drag my gaze back up to meet Arden's, I can't help but wish he'd been the one to let her die that night back at Silver Oaks when she'd slipped from her window ledge onto the rooftop beneath her window. Perhaps if he had, then I'd be free of this guilt and these confusing feelings churned up by ocean waves, our warm bodies and gentle kisses.

That thought tortures me as Cyn's eyes drift shut, sleep claiming her.

19

C*yn - seventeen years old*

I stare up at the night sky, the cold tiles of the sloped roof beneath my window hard beneath my spine. If it weren't for the six inch railing designed to keep pigeons from nesting in the gutter, I would've fallen to my death the instant my arse slid off the window ledge.

Luckily for me, someone here hates pigeons.

If I could laugh, I would.

Instead I smile.

I stare up at the moon and grin so hard my cheeks ache.

Because if I don't, I'd surely cry and I'm sick of crying.

I'm also sick to death of receiving curt messages from my

emotionally stunted father.

I'm sick of feeling like an outcast.

I'm sick of reliving that moment in the chapel where I lost all sense of myself and drank Carrick's blood.

I'm sick of yearning for more kisses from each of the boys who chase me through the grounds of the school, hunting me down.

I'm sick of the constant ache in my chest.

I'm sick of being silent.

"What's so funny?" a familiar voice asks.

And I'm sick of Arden Dálaigh popping up at my most vulnerable moments.

My smile drops as I turn my head to the side and look up to find Arden leaning out of his window with an amused expression on his face.

"I thought we'd have a little longer before you decided to throw yourself off the roof. I'm pretty disappointed actually. Torturing someone isn't much fun when they're dead."

I press my eyes shut and drag in a calming breath. There's no way to explain that this was an accident and I'm not trying to kill myself, that I was sitting on my window ledge having a cigarette and leant out a bit too far, losing my footing. So I let him make his stupid assumptions and wait for whatever it is he wants to say next.

"I mean it could be fun," he muses. "I could message Carrick and Lorcan and make this a party. We could even place a bet on how long we think that railing is going to keep you from falling..."

He lets his voice trail off as he thinks about it, then he slaps his hand against the window ledge.

"Stay where you are. I just need to grab something," he says, disappearing from view, a sudden burst of laughter floating out of his bedroom window.

Stay where you are...? It's not as if I can go anywhere, arsehole.

Expecting him to come back with his phone to capture my humiliation on camera, I'm surprised to find him chucking me a length of rope. It lands across my stomach, thick and coarse.

I grab hold of it, simultaneously relieved and disgusted. It's the same rope that they used to tie me to a tree all those months ago.

"Tie it around your chest, under your shoulders. I'll pull you in," he instructs, securing the rope around his own waist before showing me his handiwork. "See, nice and secure."

I hesitate, knowing I shouldn't trust him but not having any other choice. The railing was only put in place to prevent pigeons nesting in the gutter and not designed to hold the weight of a seventeen year old girl. Besides, as much as I hate to admit it, I really don't have any other option.

"I mean you could stay where you are and wait for that railing to give way, or you can trust that I'm having way too much fun playing cat and mouse with you, and allow me to pull you up."

Fine, I agree with a sharp nod of my head, then with shaking hands, I tie the rope around my chest and hold on for dear life.

"Good, now slide yourself along the roof until you're directly beneath my window," he says.

I follow his instructions, edging slowly across the roof, my legs shaking now that I'm no longer rigid. Keeping still was the only thing stopping me from realising that I could actually die. Moving makes this whole thing even more dangerous.

What if the railing suddenly gives way?

What if I slip?

"That's it. Now I need you to turn around so that you're facing the roof."

I shake my head, tears pricking my eyes. Edging sideways was bad enough. I don't want to shift my body off the tiles in case I lose my footing and fall.

"It will be easier for you to grab the ledge if you're facing me," he points out.

He's right of course, but that doesn't stop the fear from eating me alive. I want to throw up.

"Cynthia. You can do this," he says, and the amusement in his voice is gone now. What's left behind is concern that is as alien to me as lying on this roof and trying not to die is. "I won't let you fall."

Cursing myself and ignoring the fact that fat droplets of rain begin to fall, I twist my body to the side, the rail biting into the soles of my feet as I move. A tile comes loose beneath my toes, causing my foot to slip and my heart to stop beating. I slam my eyes shut, my mouth opening to let out a scream that never comes as my chest presses against the roof.

"You're okay, I've got you!" Arden calls, and I feel the rope pull taut as he holds me in place.

It takes me half a minute to blink back the panic and allow my heart to calm a little before I have the courage to look up at him.

"Easy now. Don't be afraid."

If my face wasn't frozen into a permanent state of fear, I would've laughed. He's joking, right?

Above me, a thunderclap sounds, followed almost instantly by a bolt of lightning that rips through the sky and makes me jump almost out of my skin. Thunderstorms have never bothered me before but if I don't die tonight, I know I'll be placing them in the ever growing box of triggers I've been collecting since I was a child.

"Good. Now grab the rope above your head and hold on tight!" he calls, just as the heavens open. Within seconds I'm saturated. My thin t-shirt and leggings soaked through.

Following his orders, I pray to Mother Nature not to strike me down with a bolt of lightning as my feet lift off the rail. Then inch by terrifying inch, Arden pulls me to safety.

By the time my fingers hit the ledge, I'm shaking from mind-numbing terror and ice-cold rain.

"I've got you," Arden says, and with one final tug, he manages to drag my top half over the window ledge, grab the rope tied around me, and pull me all the way in.

I fall directly on top of him, my chest pressed against his chest, my legs tangled with his. Beneath me Arden is panting from exertion whilst I shiver and shake, crying silent tears into his neck. On instinct my arms wrap around his chest and I hold on tight, not able to let go. Needing to feel the steady thrum of his heart and something solid and warm beneath me.

"It's okay," he murmurs, wrapping his arms around my back and sliding his legs out from beneath mine to wrap around my hips.

In any other situation warning bells would ring in my head, but here and now it doesn't feel like he's trying to scare me, it feels like he's trying to comfort me by wrapping my whole body up in his.

"It's over," he says.

I curl into him tighter, unable to let go.

"Cyn, it's over."

Maybe it's my near death experience or maybe I've smoked too much weed, but it sounds like he isn't just talking about the fact I nearly fell from the roof, but his shitty behaviour towards me. I nod into his shoulder, pulling back a little. His arms loosen and I find myself looking down into his amber eyes, my face just inches from his. For the first time since I met him there's no spite or hatred aimed at me, just... I don't know, curiosity, I guess.

"You good?" he asks, his gaze flicking from my eyes to my mouth and back again.

A strand of wet hair falls forward onto his face as I nod, and he reaches up, pushing it behind my ear, his warm fingers lingering on the sensitive spot where my jaw and neck meet. Even though my teeth are chattering and I'm soaked through, I feel a familiar warmth spread out from my middle at his touch, and without thinking I shift in his hold, trying to disperse the feeling only to *feel* something else altogether.

He's hard.

Jerking upwards, I push off the floor.

Arden releases me, but he doesn't bother to hide his hard on beneath his grey joggers, nor does he apologise for it. He simply sits up and leans against his bed whilst I press my back against the wall beneath his window opposite. Outside thunder claps and I jump, feeling on edge once more.

"It's just thunder," he says, his gaze dropping from my face to my chest as I untie the rope and let it drop to the floor.

It's at that point I realise that I'm not wearing a bra, and the warmth I felt in my chest moments before now burns a fierce path up my neck as I cross my arms, trying to regain some dignity. I wish I had the confidence to not care that he can see my breasts through my sodden white t-shirt, but I don't. Nor do I have the energy to fight him off should he decide to act on his obvious arousal.

I need to get out of here, but when I try to stand, my legs don't seem to want to cooperate and they sag beneath me. It's like they've detached themselves from the rest of my body and are still out on the ledge, waiting to plunge sixty feet to the ground below.

"You're in shock," he says, unravelling the rope from around his waist and dropping it to the floor as he heads into the bathroom. "Don't try and move, I'll get you a towel so you can dry off."

My gaze drifts to the rope, and as silence descends I try my best not to remember the humiliation of that night he used it to tie me up, and the harm it caused. We've shared many kisses since. Kisses that have made me question myself and these boys and their intentions.

One minute they're hurting me, the next kissing me.

Then they're tying me up and humiliating me, the next saving my life.

What are we? Enemies. Lovers. Neither?

Arden clears his throat as he steps out of the bathroom topless, with a towel thrown over his shoulder and another one gripped in his hand. Noticing how I remain focused on the rope, he says, "You've had enough excitement for one day. We won't be tying you to a tree any time soon."

I flinch, wrapping my arms around myself at the dispassion in his voice. What has made him so cruel? It's the first time that I've really asked myself that question. Do I really want to know?

"You should dry yourself off, otherwise you might catch a cold," he adds, standing above me.

I feel his penetrating stare, like he's trying to work out if I'm a worthy opponent, or still just some amusing toy he can play with to pass his time. Perhaps I really am just a mouse to him, something to snag his claws into until he gets bored and either kills me or casts me aside.

Taking the towel from him, I pat dry my face and neck, and rough dry my hair. I do this all one handed, trying to hide my breasts whilst he rubs the towel over his own chest, still a little damp from me being pressed against him.

"You want a jumper or something?" he asks, grasping his sweater off his bed and handing it to me before I can even nod my head. "I have sweatpants too if you want them?"

I frown, not able to keep up with the way he's being kind and saving my life one minute, and threatening my safety the next.

"Maybe just stick with the jumper for now. I'm guessing you don't want my help to remove your leggings?"

I shake my head vigorously, glad that I still have use of that part of my body.

"Fair enough, but you should remove your wet t-shirt. There's no point in giving you my jumper to wear if you're just going to keep it on. Getting pneumonia isn't fun. Believe me, I know."

Dropping the towel, I grasp the jumper to my chest and wait, willing my legs to come back to life so I can get the hell out of his room. There's no way I'm stripping off in front of him.

"Don't mind me, once you've seen one pair of tits, you've seen them all," he says with a smirk, the Arden I know coming back full force. Is he really being a prick right now? Then I look at the rope and remind myself that doing one good deed doesn't magically change someone's personality. Like he said earlier, if I die, who's he going to torment? Correction. Who are *they* going to torment?

"I'll put this away whilst you change," he says when he realises I'm not going to budge.

I watch him sceptically, expecting him to go back on his word and tie me up whilst I'm unable to fight him off, but he surprises me yet again by turning his back to me, and gathering up the rope. I can't tell if he's taken pity on me and is finally being a gentleman, or if he's lulling me into a false sense of security so that I drop my rapidly rising guard. Either way, he gives me privacy to strip off my t-shirt and pull on his jumper.

It takes me less than half the time to change than it does for him to gather the rope, and instead of trying to get my legs to work, I find myself staring at his naked back, riveted by the way his muscles tighten and loosen beneath his skin as he winds the rope around his right hand and elbow. He may only be a little more than a year older than me, but he's built like a man, with broad shoulders and a defined waist. The muscles on his back and arms flex as he carries the rope to the ottoman at the end of the bed, lifting the lid to drop it inside.

With one hand gripping the lid, his gaze skims over me, and I find myself shrinking into his jumper, my nose disappearing inside the collar as he stares, trying not to breathe in the scent of him, but failing. There's something about the way he looks at me in this moment that has me quaking for a different reason, and I physically have to pinch myself to stop those dangerous thoughts in their tracks. Just because he has a beautiful face doesn't mean he has a soul to match. In fact, I already know he doesn't.

Reaching inside the ottoman he pulls out a paper bag and then drops the lid shut before settling down next to me.

"You know, this has been sitting in my ottoman for quite some time," Arden says, opening up the paper bag and pulling out a bag of weed that looks all too familiar. "You should really put better locks on your door."

I fold my arms across my chest, refusing to show him that his complete disregard for my privacy affects me. I may as well leave my door open for all the good the locks do.

"*But*," he continues, "It wasn't until recently that I found out *you* supplied Mr Rancliffe with this very same weed too."

There's no point in denying it, so I just nod, though I do wonder how he found out that information, given that it was a secret between me and Mr Rancliffe.

"So it's just as well that we got him fired for inappropriate behaviour with a minor when we did–"

I snap my head around, scowling. He was never inappropriate with me. Never.

Arden lifts his finger and presses it against the crease between my brows. "Just because he hadn't touched you, doesn't mean he hadn't touched others, or that he wasn't going to try and feel you up eventually. The man was a creep."

I shake my head, refusing to believe him.

"I don't expect you to believe me, but it's the truth," he says, then pulls out a pack of Rizla papers and starts rolling a joint with the lavender, mugwort and raspberry leaf mixture.

"You really are full of hidden talents, aren't you Cyn? Does your dad know you make this?" he asks, as I watch him lick the seam of the Rizla paper and roll a perfect joint. A moment later he lights it, inhaling a deep breath before passing it to me.

I shake my head in answer, drawing in a lungful and holding my breath for a few seconds before blowing the scented blue-grey smoke out of my mouth. The hit is as pleasant as smoking marijuana, but without the food cravings and hysterical laughter that goes with it, and I instantly feel my muscles relax and the tension, fear and stress I've been holding onto begin to ease.

"What would you say to making more of this?" he asks as I pass the joint back and he takes another hit.

When I remain thoughtful, partly due to the way this mixture relaxes me, and partly because I can't actually have a proper conversation without a pad and pencil, Arden fills the silence.

"We can come to an agreement. If you supply me regularly with enough of this to sell to the other students, I will leave you in peace... *We* will leave you in peace," he adds, when I raise a brow at him.

I think for a moment, taking another hit and holding the smoke in my lungs, revelling in the way it laces my veins with a relaxing high that temporarily eradicates all the anxiety I've been bottling up since my arrival here. I know from experience that it won't rid me of all these anxious, fearful, angry feelings forever, but it will allow me a couple of hours respite, and right now I'll take it.

"Well, what do you think?" Arden asks, his gaze a little glassy as he studies me. "Will you do it?"

What do I think?

I think he's out of his damn mind.

I think agreeing to anything Arden wants is foolish.

I think I should turn him down.

But instead of doing that, I find myself holding out my hand to shake on the deal. He takes it, gripping it firmly.

"No more cat and mouse, Cyn," he says, taking the joint from me and placing it between his lips. A moment later he blows out a stream of lavender scented smoke. "No more kisses..."

His voice trails off as he turns his head to the side and stares at me.

I nod my head, feeling this weight lift off my shoulders, but instead of leaving me, it settles into my heart instead, sinking it to the bottom of my rib cage. Why is that thought so painful?

"I'll miss them," he admits, the joint making his lips loose and his thoughts unfiltered. "Perhaps we should share just one more to seal the deal?"

He doesn't wait for my agreement. He slowly leans in and then, just when I think he's about to kiss me, the blackness of his pupils widen, eating up his amber irises in milliseconds.

Shock holds me rigid as the expression on his face changes from relaxed and open to troubled and pained. I reach for him, worried that he might be having a reaction to the joint, but he just shrugs me off and pushes to his feet, stumbling towards the desk in the corner of his room where he blindly grabs a sketchbook and pencil and starts to draw.

For over an hour he scribbles fiercely on several pieces of paper, ripping the sheets away as he finishes one sketch then moves onto another. I find my feet after fifteen minutes, and approach him with caution, uncertain what's happening but instinctively knowing that I shouldn't disturb him. All I can do is watch as he draws sketch after sketch after sketch. He's frantic, manic, but despite his state of mind every drawing is incredibly intricate, so lifelike that they look like photographs.

One sketch that he's discarded is of a man with a skull tattooed across his face. He has mean eyes and a wicked smile. There's something so very *wrong* about him. I shudder, dropping the sketch and picking up another.

This one makes my stomach flip and my heart squeeze. It's of Arden, Lorcan and Carrick, not as they are now, but older. They have broader shoulders, thicker arms and butterfly tattoos inked onto their throats. They're beautiful, but deadly, like a black panther or a Siberian wolf.

The next is a room of glass cabinets filled to the brim with all manner of strange yet beautiful objects. There's jewellery dripping over human skulls, china dolls with cracked and broken faces, a foetus in a glass jar, a stuffed cat with an extra leg. But the focus of the drawing appears to be a knife, the handle of which has the same tattoo wrapped around it. Something about that knife makes my skin crawl.

Casting that sketch aside, he presses the nub of his pencil into a fresh sheet of paper. His agitation seems to worsen as he tries and fails to draw whatever it is that consumes him. I watch helplessly as time after time he begins to draw, then screws up the sheet of paper, only to start all over again.

"No. No. No," he mutters, angry, harsh lines scratching across a brand new page again and again and again.

With a trembling hand, I press my fingers onto his forearm, hoping that somehow I can draw him out of whatever trance he's under.

It doesn't work.

So all I can do is stay by his side, bearing witness to a side of Arden Dálaigh that he's kept hidden. A chill passes over my skin, nothing more than the breeze from the open window, and yet as thunder rumbles and lightning dashes across the sky it feels like a portent.

Something's coming, something big, and I know it will change all of our lives forever.

Hunching over his desk, Arden wraps his arm around the piece of paper and draws, finally able to get down on paper whatever it is that he sees in his head. Another twenty minutes pass, and eventually he sits up, resting the pencil on the table, staring at his art, his shoulders softening, whilst my spine snaps straight.

Right there in perfect detail is a full length sketch of an

older version of me standing naked in the middle of a bedroom I don't recognise. Behind me stands the broad shouldered, tattooed version of Arden. His mouth is pressed against my shoulder, his arm around my waist. Kneeling at my feet is Lorcan, his head buried between my spread legs, one hand grabbing my tit whilst the other grips my hip, and standing to his right is Carrick, his hand grasping my chin as he kisses me whilst fisting his cock.

I'm fucking them. They're fucking me.

Snatching up the sketch I stare at it, cheeks flaming, pulse thumping, the spot between my legs heating.

What's this?

My thoughts are so loud I could've sworn I heard them, but when I look back down at Arden, he's still staring off into the distance. He's in this room physically, but his mind is somewhere far, far away. Folding up the sketch, I slide it up the cuff of Arden's jumper just as he seems to return to the room. For some reason I don't want him to see it.

"Cyn?" he questions, his brows pulled together in a frown before his gaze drops to the sketches discarded on the floor. He leans over to pick them up, hands trembling. When he finally looks back up at me, I'm already opening his bedroom door making my escape.

He doesn't come after me, and when he finds me the following day, questioning me about what I might've seen, I claim ignorance, pretending I was too high to remember.

Neither of us bring it up again.

20

Arden - present day

"Where are you going, Carrick?" I ask, watching him pull back the covers and slide out of my bed a few hours after I made him get into it. Cyn is fast asleep, her body warm and relaxed against mine.

"To my room," he replies curtly as he helps himself to some of my clothes, pulling on a pair of tracksuit bottoms, a t-shirt and a sweater.

"You're running."

He sits down on the leather ottoman situated beneath the window, pulling on a pair of thick, woollen socks, answering me only when he's finished. Flicking his gaze to Cyn, he swallows hard, his Adam's apple bobbing up and down beneath the butterfly tattoo we all wear on our necks, its black wings given life with the movement.

"I'm not running."

"I know you," I insist.

"You ordered me not to fuck her. I'm following your orders."

"I ordered you to take her elixir so it would subdue your need to fuck her. You ignored me."

He laughs. "It didn't work on you. I bet your cock is still as hard as it was the moment you slipped into bed behind her."

"It worked. I haven't taken advantage."

"You don't want to?"

"I do..." My voice trails off as I try to articulate how I feel. "My urge to fuck her is still there and evidently so is my physical reaction to the idea of it, but regardless I won't act on it. The elixir has taken the edge off, it's given me the ability to think with a clear head despite my feeling of wanting. Do you understand?"

"Believe me, I understand wanting to fuck her, you know I do. That's why I need to get out of here, because if I allow myself to let go, I *will* destroy her."

"You want her that badly?"

He laughs then, and it's a bitter sound. Hollow. "Are you kidding? I want to fuck her so hard that she'll scream my name. I want to make her scream so bad. I *always* have, haven't you?"

I nod, feeling my cock stir at his words and the fire they stoke in my own black soul, but moments later I feel a soothing kind of calm that is like a balm to the darkness. "But you won't because I asked you not to."

"I won't because, like you said, she has a job to do and she won't do it if we hurt her."

"Yet she kissed you," I say.

"Yes," he replies tightly. Again he looks at Cyn, again he forces himself to look away.

Carrick has needed me to help relieve him of some of the pressure, and I've done so willingly because I love him, but it isn't enough. There's a war going on inside of him right now, and I need to know which side is going to win.

So I push harder, forcing him to face up to what he's hiding from us, from himself.

"*She* kissed *you*," I repeat.

"She was delirious. I could've been anyone."

"We both know that isn't true. She kissed you and you didn't act on it. Why?"

"You asked me not to fuck her. I didn't fuck her," he repeats.

"She was naked. She initiated intimacy," I press, wanting him to admit the truth. He didn't take advantage of that moment for the same reason he's running now. Something is shifting within him. I can sense it.

"She was fucking hypothermic, Arden."

"And?"

"And what? I was barely warm myself. She felt like a fucking corpse. I might be a twisted fucker, but I'm not into necrophilia."

"She's warm now."

"This conversation is over," he grinds out, standing.

"You don't *want* to hurt her," I say, forcing him to face the truth.

"The sooner she's completed her debt, the sooner this is over," he replies, avoiding the truth altogether.

"Is that really why you didn't let her drown, because of the debt?" I ask, choosing a different tactic.

Beside me, Cyn moves in her sleep, distracting me momentarily as her arm brushes against my bare chest. My first instinct is to grasp her to me, pin her down, slide into her half-sleeping form and fuck her until she comes, but that soothing feeling returns, like the gentle hand of something tender, kind, reminding me of the promise I made to her.

"I saved her from drowning for the same reason you kept her from dying from hypothermia. She's here to make diamonds. That's *all* we should focus on."

"And what if I want to keep her beyond the fulfilment of her debt? What then?" I ask before I can stop myself.

"You're confusing lust with affection, respect with tenderness," he grinds out angrily. "Cyn is not our friend. She's not our lover. She's not one of us, Arden. We only want her as badly as we do because of the pact we made, and right now we *only* need her because of the gift she has."

He's right, of course. Our relationship with Cyn, if you can call it that, has always been confusing, complicated. I took an immediate dislike to Cyn on that first day when she arrived at Silver Oaks. I hated her because of who her father was and who she was friends with. It didn't matter that she was a victim of a war she had no part in. All that mattered was that she was Niall O'Farrell's daughter, and he was best friends and business acquaintances with Malik Brov, the man who murdered my father.

"I'm not the one who's confused. You assumed I meant something that I didn't. This is a *business* decision. There's no one else who can do what she can. No one, Carrick. She's valuable. That's why I suggested keeping her."

Cyn is our cash cow, and to be totally honest, the hate I once had for her as a teenager has grown into a begrudging respect, given her inexplicable gift to produce a drug that has the ability to make a person come multiple times and give them a high like no other but without any dangerous side-effects. The attraction we all feel is just an inconvenience that we stupidly brought to life in a night of drugged out bliss.

I should've seen that coming.

I didn't.

And now we're all victims of a bond we cannot shake.

Cyn stirs, shifting in her sleep and I catch the soft swell of her breasts as she turns her body towards mine, strands of ocean-scented hair falling across her cheek. I brush them aside, my fingers trailing over the warmth of her skin. She's so fucking tempting, there's no denying that, but I have no emotional attachment. We've already established that I want to fuck her but I also want to keep her so she can bring in money.

"Are we done?" Carrick snaps, dragging my attention back to him.

"Not until you've eaten," Lorcan says, as he steps into the room, carrying a tray with four bowls of steaming soup. If he notices the disharmony between us, he doesn't say a word. He simply places the tray on the table in front of the fire then hands Carrick a bowl.

"I'm not hungry," Carrick says.

"Eat the damn soup," Lorcan retorts, picking up another bowl and bringing it to me, his gaze falling to Cyn as he waits for me to take it from him. "You should wake her."

Shifting slightly, I place my hand on Cyn's shoulder and give her a gentle shake. "Wake up." She stirs, but not enough to awaken, so I shake her a little harder. "Cyn, wake up."

This time her eyes flutter open, and for a moment she looks up at me without any kind of hate or distrust in her eyes as her sleepy brain tries to figure out what's going on. It takes a few seconds, but the reality of her situation soon comes rushing back, and within moments she shifts away from me in bed, cautious, untrusting. It takes a great deal of effort not to grab her and pull her flush against me, so that I can feel her arse pressed up against my aching cock once more.

Fuck, I want to sink inside of her.

Blood pact or not, I've wanted to feel her pussy pulse around my dick just like it did when we were younger. The elixir she gave me to take is the only thing stopping me from doing that again right now.

"Goddamn it," I mutter under my breath, as pissed off with her reaction as I am for mine.

Cyn grasps the duvet cover, and pulls it up against her chest, her gaze tracking over my bare chest as I sit unashamedly naked before her. There's no denying that I've changed a lot physically since we fucked. My shoulders have broadened, my chest is covered in more hair, and my abs and pecs are defined from years of street fighting, something we all do for fun when the mood takes us.

"Like what you see?" I ask, papering over my feelings with smugness, being an arsehole.

She swallows hard, her gaze tracking over my chest and lowering to the dark trail of hair leading to my dick, which hardens further under her perusal. There's something about the way she looks at me that is different. It reminds me of the way she used to kiss me when we were kids. There's heat behind it. Need.

"Perhaps you want to rub your arse against my dick again, just like you've been doing these past few hours in your sleep, huh?" I taunt, unable to help myself, because if she doesn't stop looking at me like that, no fucking tincture is going to stop me from taking what I want.

She presses her eyes shut briefly, and heaves a sigh then cuts a look at Lorcan, her brows rising a fraction as he offers her the bowl of soup.

"You need to eat. It'll help. Then you can go back to sleep if you want," he says.

"Don't worry, *cailleach*, Lorcan isn't the type to slip poison into your food. He's more interested in buttering you up so he can fuck you without feeling bad about it," Carrick says, lifting the spoon to his mouth and taking a mouthful.

To his credit, Lorcan doesn't rise to the bait, he simply sits on the bed, grips the spoon in his fingers and eats some of the soup. "See, all good."

Cyn nods, her fingers loosening on the covers as she tucks

the edge of the duvet beneath her armpits, taking the bowl of soup from him, and eats.

With a satisfied smile, Lorcan rises to his feet and passes me a bowl, taking the last one left on the tray for himself. He sits down in the armchair next to the fire and we eat in silence, the only sounds coming from the chink of the spoons against the china bowls and the crackle of the fire still lit in the hearth. By the time Cyn has finished eating there's a deep pink tint to her cheeks and lips. It pleases me.

"Better?" Lorcan asks, taking the bowl from her, his gaze softening.

Cyn dips her head, a thank you we've all come to understand given it's so rare, but it's the hint of a smile that follows which is even rarer. Cyn's smiles are few and far between, and the fact that Lorcan's kindness coaxed it into being is even more telling.

Lorcan grins. "You're welcome. It's good to see some colour in your cheeks."

Carrick snorts, discarding his empty bowl on the ottoman as he strides across the room "You're so fucking transparent. I'm out of here."

That fleeting smile dies on Cyn's lip as she scowls at Carrick's retreating back, and despite him having his back to us all he seems to sense her change in mood. Slamming his hand against the doorframe, he rounds on her.

"What, Cyn?" he demands, striding over to her bedside and getting in her face. "Just say what's on your damn mind!"

She glares at him, her mouth sealed shut, her eyes blazing.

"Well?" he insists, his knuckles white from his tight grip on the headboard either side of her head. "You've got a lot to say, I see it in your eyes."

"Carrick," I say, offering a half-hearted warning because I'm curious to see where this is going, despite my promise to keep Cyn safe. Carrick has always been a hothead around Cyn, quick to blow up in her presence. She gets under his skin, and we all know it.

"Just. Say. It!" he demands, hissing at her.

Cyn shifts backwards, trying to press herself into the headboard and away from the aggression leaching from him. How many times have these two been in this very same position over the years? Too many to count. Except this time there isn't a therapist or a teacher who can step in and put a stop to it. There's only us, and right now I'm not inclined to help her.

"You know him, you know us," Carrick says, filling in the silence. "We don't do nice. Everything comes at a fucking price, even that soup Lorcan made. You *know* this."

Cyn flinches, her fingers gripping hold of the duvet cover as though she expects him to rip it off her any moment now. Part of me wants him to, but then I remember Cyn's warning and I heave out a breath.

"Let it go, Carrick," I say, pulling back the covers and striding out of the bed, not caring I'm still sporting a semi.

"Why? You know I'm speaking the truth."

He doesn't even acknowledge my nakedness. It's not as if he or Lorcan haven't seen me naked before. We've grown up together, shared women together, shared each other. My body is as familiar to them as theirs are to mine.

"I do know that."

"Then what's the fucking problem?" he counters.

"You are, Brother."

"Because she kissed me? Is that it?"

"You kissed *him*?" Lorcan exclaims, casting a look at Cyn who just lifts her chin and looks away from his probing gaze and the jealousy slashing across his features. "Carrick?"

"Yes, Cyn kissed me and Arden is pissed about it."

I swipe a hand through my hair, willing myself not to react. Instead, I grab a pair of jeans from my wardrobe, and pull them on. "No, I'm not pissed off because Cyn kissed you."

"What then?"

"The problem we have here really isn't about the kiss, the problem as I see it, is you."

"Me?!" Carrick exclaims.

"Yes, you. Lorcan's behaviour has never bothered you before. In fact, you used to encourage it because, like me, you wanted to see how hard she would break when she realised his kindness and empathy was as hollow as our hearts. Now you're protecting her from that pain. *Why*?"

Carrick grits his jaw. "I'm not. I pulled her out of the fucking ocean because she owes us a debt. I got into bed with her because you ordered me to."

"And you didn't take advantage of her kiss because you've grown a conscience where she's concerned," I press.

"No."

"Yes," I insist.

Carrick's nostrils flare. "Think what you like, Arden, I know how I feel."

Lorcan cocks a brow. "Seems to me Cyn's kisses are as powerful as they ever were. Isn't that right, Carrick?"

"And you'd know all about that, wouldn't you, Lorcan, given it's you who's coerced the most out of her," Carrick retorts, giving Cyn one last lingering look before striding from the room.

21

Cyn - Seventeen years old

Where are the others? I write on my notepad as we sit at our table in the furthest corner of the library where huge floor to ceiling bookshelves are filled with all manner of books from fairytales to textbooks, encyclopaedias to romances.

Twice a week for the past month I've been meeting Arden, Lorcan and Carrick in the library to study. Our tentative truce is held together by the thinnest of threads ever since Arden saved me from falling from the roof and I agreed to supply them with weed to sell to the other students.

I'm under no illusion that this truce will last forever, but I'm willing to try and keep it going for as long as possible, or at least until I get out of Silver Oaks and I never have to see them again.

Lorcan cups his chin in his hand, his elbow pressing against the hardwood of the table, and grins. "Pretty sure they're supplying half the school with your weed. It's really good stuff."

I nod. *Of course it is. I made it.*

"Arden said that you're working on another batch, something with a bit more oomph? A different recipe or something?"

I am. Though last night I tested it and it made me feel weird.

"Weird how?"

Not myself. I pause, my pencil hovering over the paper as I try to articulate what I mean. A few tokes and I'd been taken out of myself. It wasn't a relaxing high, it made me feel on edge as though the barrier between right and wrong was removed. But I don't say this, instead I write; *I need to adjust the ingredients slightly. The balance is off.*

"You really know your shit, don't you? I mean, how did you even know those herbs were safe to smoke? Where did you learn all this stuff?"

You're full of questions today, I reply.

"I'm just curious," he shrugs. "I don't have a hidden agenda if that's what you're worried about?"

If you want to know then you're going to have to share some things with me first.

I push the notepad across the table towards him, jerking my chin.

"Fair enough. What do you want to know?"

Standing I push back my chair then round the table, sitting next to him. His smile broadens.

"You can't keep away, can you?"

I roll my eyes. *It's easier for you to read what I write if I'm sitting next to you.*

"Why don't you just use your phone to communicate? Wouldn't it be quicker to send a text?"

I pull a face that makes Lorcan grin, then write, *Texting is so impersonal. Besides, people can ignore a text, they can't ignore a notepad shoved under their nose.*

"Fair point. Good for sending dick pics though," he remarks with a smirk.

That's disgusting.

"Lucious Lorna would beg to differ."

Lorna's a sex pest, I write before I can stop myself.

Laughter bursts out of Lorcan's mouth. "You're not wrong there."

I huff out a breath. *Do you want the answers to your questions or not?*

"Fine. Fine," he agrees, forcing himself to be serious. "Okay, so ask me a question and I'll answer you. Then you can tell me how you know so much about making drugs."

Chewing on the end of the pencil, I take a moment to think about what I want to know. I don't want to end this conversation before it has even begun by asking him something that's too personal, so I start off with a question that shouldn't be too hard to answer.

How did you become friends with Carrick and Arden?

"We grew up together in Ballydavid. Friends since we were barely out of nappies. They looked out for me."

So how did the three of you end up here?

He tuts, wagging his finger. "My turn now," he reminds me.

I shrug. *Go ahead.*

"Who taught you what you know? How does someone like you learn how to make drugs?"

Someone like me?

"You know what I mean. You don't seem the type."

Firstly, I'm not a drug dealer. These are natural herbs.

"Marijuana is natural, it's also illegal," he points out.

What I use isn't illegal.

"Okay..." he replies, waiting.

My mother was a herbalist, someone who spent her life working with medicinal plants to heal. Instead of reading me bedtime stories, she would show me her notebooks filled with everything you need to know about plants, flowers and herbs. When she passed away my grandmother took over the role of teaching me.

"But how did you know which plants would have that effect? I'm pretty sure there are a lot of poisonous plants out there."

Of course there are, but like with anything, knowledge is power. I've learnt a great deal about species of plants, what can be used to aid digestion, to ease headaches, to calm nerves. Which plants are poisonous, and those that are safe to use. Wolfsbane, for example, belongs to the Aconitum plant genus. It can be found throughout the UK, and the toxins in the plant can slow the heart if ingested.

"Damn," he replies, whistling.

Foxglove, that pretty plant with long tubular purple flowers and very popular in gardens, has the same effect if consumed, I explain, grabbing the encyclopaedia of plants I had open on the desk and finding the page detailing all there is to know about Foxglove.

"I recognise that plant," he says, studying the page. "I had no idea."

Not many people do. Interestingly, drugs derived from the Foxglove have actually saved more lives than killed. So whilst a plant or flower can be poisonous, they can also be lifesavers too so long as you know the correct quantities to use and how to extract the part that's useful.

"No shit," he mutters, eyeing me with a little bit of caution. "So what you're saying is that you could kill us if you wanted?"

I chew on the inside of my cheek. *I could. Yes.*

"Fuuuccck," he exclaims quietly, blowing out a slow breath as he leans back in his chair. "I'm starting to think we fucked with the wrong girl," he says, almost as an afterthought.

I side-eye him. *I'm not a murderer, so I guess you're all in luck.*

"What are you then?"

I'm a healer. Like my mother.

"A healer?"

Yes.

Silence descends between us and he looks thoughtful for a moment. Then without warning he reaches over and grasps my hand in his, his fingers curling around my palm. He doesn't try to kiss me or ask me any more questions. This seems more intimate than all the kisses we've shared, more meaningful somehow. Eventually, I slide my hand from his.

I have a question.

"Sure, go ahead," he replies.

Why me?

"I thought you wanted to know how we ended up at Silver Oaks?"

I guess I want to know why you chose to be cruel to me more than I want to know why the three of you ended up here, I write, setting my pencil on the pad and twisting my body to face him.

That question above all others has plagued me since I arrived here and I need to know the answer. I need to understand.

Lorcan swipes a hand through his white-blonde hair, his leg jumping beneath the table with nerves, setting my own on edge. My stomach turns over at the way he seems to battle with himself. I'd expected him to say something along the lines that a girl who can't speak, who's mute, quiet, *different*, is an easy target. He doesn't. What he does say shocks me.

"Your father is friends with Malik Brov. Malik Brov had Arden's dad murdered."

My mouth drops open in shock as sickness rolls in my stomach.

No. You're lying, I write. It can't be true.

I've only ever seen Malik in passing on the occasions when my father took me to Ardelby Castle. I was always ushered into another room by their butler, Renard, to spend time with Konrad, Jakub and Leon, his sons, but he never struck me as the type of man to commit murder. He's intense, a little odd, and has only ever said a handful of words to me, but a murderer?

Then I remember the bruises on Jakub's arm the first time we visited, the swelling on Konrad's cheek the next, and the way Leon sat so stiffly the last time I saw them, as though in pain. In fact, each time my dad has taken me with him to visit Malik, the three boys have become more and more distant, cold. My hands begin to shake, and I clasp them together to try to force myself to calm down.

"I swear on my life, it's true. Malik murdered Arden's father. Your dad was a part of that, Cyn. He might not have been the one to actually do it, but he knew. He was involved."

But why?

"That's not my story to tell. You'll have to ask Arden that. I've said too much already."

I sit in shock, trying to come to terms with what Lorcan has told me. It makes sense now. Arden knew who I was when I arrived, and because of who my father is and the friendship he has with Malik, that hate Arden has for them both extended to me. But I'm not responsible for my father's actions, let alone Malik Brov's. What they did wasn't my fault.

Lorcan sighs, pressing his fingertips gently under my chin and urging me to look at him. "I know what you're thinking. Why take it out on you, right?"

I nod.

"Because he couldn't reach Malik or your father, so why not get his revenge by hurting the person most precious to the infamous Niall O'Farrell?"

I shake my head, reaching up to push his hand away, and pick up my pencil instead.

That was his first mistake. The only person who was precious to my father was my mother and she's already dead. He only had enough room in his heart for her, and when she died any kind of love he had died with her. He doesn't care what happens to me. The only thing he cares about is getting me to speak so he doesn't have a daughter to be ashamed of.

"Cyn, I'm–"

Sorry? For what? For what Arden did, or the role you played?

Lorcan drops his head in shame. "For it all."

I understand Arden's reasons for doing what he did, even if I don't agree with them. But what about you, Lorcan? What about Carrick? What's your excuse for hurting me?

Maybe he can't sense the bitterness I feel from the words I write down on paper, but he sure as hell can sense it from my body language.

Folding my arms across my chest, I wait, disappointment and a huge well of sadness opening up inside of me. How can anyone hurt another person just because of who their parents are? I've had to live with the cold absence of love from my father for years, alone except for my grandmother. I've had to live without my mother, with the memory of her dying, my tiny hands unable to stem the flow of blood from her wound. I've had to live with that trauma my whole life, my voice stolen because of it. Haven't I been through enough at the hands of my father and the war he started by taking my mother from her family and forcing her to marry him?

"I can't speak for Carrick, his reasons are his own, but me?" Lorcan sighs, chewing on his lip as he takes my hands in his, refusing to let me pull away from his grasp. "At first it was because I sympathised with Arden. His father was a good man, he practically brought me up as his own son when my own mother was incapable of doing the same. He made sure I had the best care after my operation and skin graft. He took me in as his when my mother couldn't, *didn't* want the responsibility of looking after me. His murder affected me deeply. I carry the same hatred for Malik and your father as he does, and yet..."

I cock my head to the side, frowning. *Yet?*

He reads the question on my face, answering me. "I realised what Arden and Carrick failed to understand. You're no more responsible for your father's or Malik's actions as I am for my own mother's treatment of me. You're innocent in all of this, and for my part in it, I'm sorry. I'm truly sorry, Cyn."

I sigh. For me, words mean everything, and none that I use are wasted, yet I can't trust his words. We might've formed a tentative truce of late, but how many times has Lorcan been kind one minute and cruel the next? How do I know that this isn't just him playing his games again?

I don't. I can't trust him, no matter how sincere he seems.

"You don't believe me. I see that," he says softly as I get to my feet and pack up my rucksack.

I don't need to acknowledge what he's said, he already knows he's right. Despite that, when I've finished packing up, he grasps my elbow, turning me to face him.

"Cyn, I'm sorry."

Then he kisses me, apologising with his lips and his tongue, his hands gently cupping my face until I feel his apology all the way down to my toes, even though I still don't believe it.

Because here's the thing... Lorcan might apologise to me in private, he might be kind when we're alone together, but whenever he's around Arden and Carrick, he's different and I don't know which side of him is the true Lorcan.

Perhaps I never will.

22

L orcan - present day

"Are you certain she's well enough?" I ask Arden as Cyn busies herself making more diamonds. Her hair is pulled back off her face and tied up into a high bun, loose strands fall from behind her ears as she adjusts her goggles.

"It's been almost a week since Carrick pulled her from the ocean," Arden replies, leaning against the wall as we both watch her at work. "She's been taking a tonic, something with echinacea. She said that it's good for warding off colds."

"Is it?"

"She's not coughing, unlike Carrick, and looks a darn sight

healthier than he does right now. That tells me all I need to know," Arden replies, swiping his palm over his face.

"I heard him last night. Didn't sound too good," I admit, sensing his concern, feeling my own.

"He's refusing Cyn's help. She offered him cough syrup to loosen the phlegm, and made him a tea to help with his blocked sinuses, as well as a tonic to help lower his temperature, but he's stubborn. He thinks he's immune to death given he survived it once..."

"Because of Cyn. Because *she* saved him," I point out.

"And now they're even..."

Arden's voice trails off and I drag my gaze away from Cyn. Since her near-death experience, we've all been on edge. None of us want to admit it, but knowing she could've drowned has forced us all to confront some deep-seated, complicated feelings towards her. For me, it's only confirmed what I've always known to be true, that I like Cyn, that I care for her, more than perhaps I thought possible.

Carrick has doubled-down, refusing to acknowledge the fact that his feelings are beginning to change, or perhaps the ones he's buried deep down are finally surfacing, and Arden?

Arden is focusing on getting this shipment for Soren fulfilled. He's burying his head in work. He's strung out, wired, and despite the cream Cyn made to heal the patch of eczema on his arm, another patch has popped up on his leg. She's right to be concerned about him, I am too. I've never seen him like this, so *human*.

"Should we be worrying?"

"Put it this way, if he doesn't accept Cyn's help soon then I'm going to have to leave the island with him and get him medical help that he will accept."

"And you're okay with that?"

"Taking Carrick to the mainland? Of course, I am."

"No, I meant leaving Cyn here, alone with me."

Arden stares at Cyn, a muscle in his jaw jumping as he grits his teeth. "I don't have any reason to be concerned. You're wearing the necklace, you've kept to your word. I trust you," he says eventually.

"Arden, don't tell me the thought of leaving her doesn't kill you. I know you, Brother."

"You're projecting," he counters, pushing off from the wall.

I grip his arm and his bicep tenses beneath my touch. "No, I'm not. Need I remind you of what you said the other day?"

"I was pushing Carrick to admit *his* feelings. I know where I stand when it comes to Cyn. This is just a business transaction to me. Nothing more."

"You're lying to yourself," I say, lowering my voice. "This is more than a business transaction, it's more than wanting to fuck her. Don't you see, it *always* was."

Arden rounds on me, grasping my throat and shoving me back up against the wall with force. Behind us Cyn gasps, her hand flying to her mouth. Arden points at her.

"Get the fuck out."

She takes a step towards us both, holding her hands up as though trying to placate him. I see the concern in her eyes. She *cares*. Despite the terrible way we treated her, she always did.

"Go and check on Carrick," I urge her. She doesn't need to witness this.

"GO!" Arden roars when she doesn't immediately leave.

Cyn flicks her gaze to me, and I nod. "It's okay. Go."

The second she's left the outhouse, Arden rounds on me. "Don't you dare insinuate that this is anything more than me making a good business decision. I made a statement to push Carrick into admitting how *he* feels," Arden hisses, getting in my face, his body pressed against mine, his heart thumping against my chest.

"So why are you so angry, huh?"

"Because she's getting between us again. Just like before."

"We're *allowing* that to happen, just like before. You can't deny that we each have an instinct to protect her, even from each other. Carrick was protecting Cyn from me because he thinks I'm manipulating her. You tried to protect Cyn from us both by forcing us to take the tincture, and I'm trying to protect her from you both by getting you to see how you really feel."

"Need I remind you that neither of you fucking took it, so there was no forcing of any kind," he grinds out.

"Yet you've been spending time in the basement with Carrick, helping him to relieve himself of his needs. Don't tell me that's just for his benefit, or yours for that matter. I *know* you're protecting her."

Arden blanches. "You know about that?"

"You don't need to keep that from me. I'm not jealous. If you didn't do it for him, then I would've. We have each other's backs. Haven't we always understood each other? You're my *bráthair sól*, and as my soul brother I am going to always tell you the truth, no matter what. You care for Cyn too."

Arden shakes his head. "No. We're acting this way because

of the blood pact which *she* coerced us to make when we were under the influence of diamonds. She did it to protect herself, and at the time we would've done anything for her because that drug is potent, it manipulates emotions. *You* know this. *You* experienced it for yourself," he says, forcing his point home.

"Maybe you're right and maybe I'm the one who's wrong," I respond. "But what if the way we feel towards Cyn has nothing to do with diamonds or the blood pact and everything to do with what we've kept hidden deep in here?" I say, placing my hand over his heart.

Arden's fingers tighten around my throat, his heart pounding beneath my hand. I don't try to break free from his hold, I just let him absorb what I've said.

"Impossible," he grinds out. "I don't feel anything for her. *Nothing*."

Releasing me, he twists on his feet, strides across the room and picks up a diamond. He holds it up to the light. "This is all I'm concerned with."

"Do you remember the night we took her virginity?" I ask, watching him as he inspects the diamonds. There are thirty, and each one is worth five thousand euros. She has another ten to make. That's a lot of money sitting there on the table.

"Of course, I fucking remember," he replies with a sharp look.

"Do you remember what you said?"

He places the Diamond carefully back on the table, folding over the velvet cloth they're resting on, then turns to face me. "What about it?"

"You said then she was our soulmate. You believed it. I

believed it. I know Carrick did too."

"It was the drug," he counters.

"But what if diamonds forced us to see the truth we'd all been denying? What then?"

"It manipulated us into saying that shit."

"What if that isn't true? What if that's what we've convinced ourselves of, instead of seeing the truth?"

Arden folds his arms across his chest. "Where are you going with this?"

"You were convinced that the diamonds had fucked with our heads. You convinced us all she wasn't our soulmate, the person we'd been yearning for our whole lives. You were wrong. That drug forced us to see the truth. Don't you see, she was already ours before we made the blood pact."

"You're twisting shit. Diamonds are powerful, they manipulate our thoughts and feelings. She's not ours."

"You turned your back on the truth because you couldn't face it," I insist. "You convinced us all that it was a mistake. What we did, what we felt. Need I remind you that the only reason Carrick is alive today is because Cyn saved his life. She saved him. She could've let him die. She could've given up your secret. She could've made me feel like shit because of the scars on my back. She never hurt us, not once. Not after everything we did to her."

"So what are you saying? That we owe her?"

"Fuck yes, of course we do. But I'm also saying that buried beneath all the shit we've convinced ourselves of is the truth," I say, resting my palms on his shoulders, and squeezing.

"You really do care for her, don't you? This isn't an act."

"Yes. I did as a kid, and I do as a man. I'm not afraid to admit that now, Arden, but I was back then. I should've stood up for her more. I should've trusted my gut. But I wasn't the one gifted in magic, so I trusted you instead," I accuse. "Blood pact or not, that won't fucking change. It's about time you and Carrick face the truth. These feelings we have, this need for Cyn, was there way before that fucking night, and you know it."

"Even if you're right, even if what you say is true, Cyn doesn't feel the same way," he argues stubbornly.

"Doesn't she?" I reply, reaching over the table to grab her leather-bound recipe book.

I flip through the pages, hoping my hunch is right, that she's hiding something important in there. When a piece of folded-up paper falls out, I know instinctively that I've found what I've been looking for. The paper is discoloured with age, the edges frayed, but the image isn't.

Fuck, the sketch before me is as finely detailed, as beautifully drawn and powerfully moving as all of Arden's artwork is.

"What's this?" Arden asks, snatching it from me.

A gasp releases from his lips as we both stare at the drawing of the three of us worshipping Cyn with our lips, fingers and tongues. My fucking heart skips a beat at the look of sheer joy on Cyn's face, and the easy way she is with us, and us with her. This isn't a drawing of what happened between us when we were younger, this is of us sometime in the future. She isn't fighting against us whilst we take pleasure from her body and give her pleasure in return, she's a part of the exchange, wholly and fully. We're not stealing kisses or taking what doesn't belong to us. This is mutual affection, and maybe, maybe even love. And if you look close enough, right there on her ring finger is a tattoo of three tiny butterflies. Butterflies that do not sit on her hand now.

"Do you see that tattoo on her ring finger?" I ask.

"Fuck!" Arden exclaims, looking up at me. Shocked. He sees what I see. It's undeniable. "The mark of the Deana-dhe."

"Sometime in the future we will make her ours officially, Arden. There's no denying it."

He frowns, tracing a finger over the drawing. "Look at us," he murmurs.

"You don't remember drawing this?" I ask.

"It's my drawing, there's no doubt about that..." His voice trails off as he tries to think. "But I go into a trance-like state when I have a vision, and sometimes the only reminder of what I've seen is the drawing I produce. I don't remember drawing this, but I know I must've had a vision of the four of us together."

"Do you know when it happened? When did you draw this?"

"There can only be one possible time. Remember I told you about the night I saved Cyn from falling to her death from the roof at Silver Oaks?"

"Yeah, I remember. You saved her life. That's when shit changed between us and Cyn."

Arden nods. "I told you both to back off because I wanted her to make more weed to sell and I knew she wouldn't do it if we continued to mess with her, but that's only partly true. When I'd looked her in the eye the next morning and she denied seeing me do anything out of the ordinary, I knew she was lying, and I had every intention of fucking her over and going back on my word. Yet she never said anything to anyone, and over time I convinced myself she hadn't seen anything, because fuck if she had surely she would've used it against me, right? It was only recently that she admitted that she remembered everything, and I admitted to myself that I'd known that all along."

"She kept your secret," I say.

Arden nods. "And that drawing, all this time."

"Why do you think that is, Arden?" I ask, urging him to uncover what I already understand to be true.

He blows out a long, hard breath. "But it can't be true. She can't be ours."

"Why? Because we convinced ourselves she wasn't?

He nods. "All this time, Brother. She's been *ours* all this time. We were just too fucking blind. I was too fucking wrapped up in my need for revenge to see it."

Folding up the sketch, I tuck it back inside her notebook and place it back on the table just as Cyn pushes open the outhouse door, a blast of cold hair rushing in behind her and blowing her hair wildly about her head. That wildness is reflected in her eyes and I know instantly that something is very, very wrong.

"What is it?" Arden asks, picking up on her fear.

Cyn swallows hard, urging us to follow her, then spins on her heel and runs from the outhouse back to the monastery. Without saying a word, we run after her, knowing that it's Carrick facing death once more, just like he did when we were kids, and that Cyn is the only one capable of saving him.

23

Cyn - aged seventeen

As I sit in the peaceful midnight silence of the science lab, the building empty of students as they slumber, I stare at the tiny green bottle filled with poison and consider my options.

After my conversation with Lorcan in the library, I've been going back and forth over what to do. Surely if my father had known the true identity of my bullies he'd have handled them, right? If he had been in on the murder of Arden's father, then why wouldn't he want to deal with Arden too, especially after what he's done to me? Then again, my father had demanded that I have therapy with the nastiest, cruellest boys in the

school, so why would he order the murder of the boy who he believes has the power to make me talk?

The truth is, he wouldn't.

Nothing is more important to him than getting me to talk, and I would bet my life that my father already knew he was here, and that Arden would take an immediate dislike to me because of my relationship to him. It makes so much sense now.

It doesn't hurt any less to know that though.

The reality is, my father had underestimated me before with Jakub, Konrad and Leon and I want to prove him wrong again. I'm nothing if not stubborn, and I want to prove that I can handle these boys myself, and I will do so *silently*.

Not speaking is a part of my identity, of who I am as a person. If my father can't accept that part of me, he can't accept any of me.

I think deep down that's why I never told my father what was happening at Silver Oaks, though after the incident in the church, and later in the forest, there's no doubt my father knew I was a victim of their cruelty. Then as things began getting more complicated between us, I still didn't say anything because I liked their kisses, despite still hating them.

But now that I know the truth about Malik Brov, about my father, about why the three boys hate me so much, I have a difficult choice to make.

Despite all the kisses, the recent truce, Lorcan's kindness, Carrick's confession, and the fact Arden saved my life, they're a threat to me, to my family, and I have the power to do something about that. Sighing, I look at the bottle of poison, wondering what the right course of action is.

Am I really capable of murder?

Is my father really worth protecting? I know he isn't a good man. I know since my mother's death he has become the worst possible version of himself. I know that the world would be better off without him, and yet my mother had loved him, and I had loved her.

Part of me wants to end this now. I could poison them all and it would be over.

My father would protect me from any repercussions, I know he would. In fact, doing this would gain his respect, and that is better than the absence of love. But my mother would turn in her grave, and my grandmother would be devastated. She had sent me that letter for a reason, she had told me I had the power to do good just like my mother had. So what do I do? What path do I take?

For the next hour I go back and forth, until eventually the decision is made for me.

"You know you really need to stop sneaking about the school at night, Cyn, someone could take advantage of a girl all on her own," Carrick says as he steps into the science lab, a devious glint in his obsidian eyes.

I wonder, if he knew what I was thinking, whether he'd take as much pleasure in trying to scare me. The truth is, right now I'm more scared of myself than I am of him. Meeting his gaze, I force myself to breathe, to stay and not run.

"Here's the problem, Cyn, I can't stop thinking about you. I stay awake every fucking night wanting nothing more than to chase you down, to capture you like I always do. These past few weeks have been fucking torture not being able to do that. I want you and I never wanted anything in my life. Why am I so drawn to you? Why are any of us drawn to you? You're our enemy, I don't understand."

Well, that makes two of us. At least we have common ground there.

Carrick strides towards me, his intent clear. He wants me to run, but this time I won't. Instead I pick up the tiny bottle and place it in the pocket of my cardigan, then wait.

"You sit there, torturing me with your silence, goading me with your serenity. I want to hear your voice, *cailleach*. I want to hear you moan in pleasure, in pain. I want..." His voice trails off as he fists his fingers at his side.

There's something about the agony of his voice, the need in it that makes me turn to face him. Twisting around on the stool, he looks down at me edging between my legs as he reaches up and cups my face. My eyes flutter shut at the contact, at his gentleness.

It's as though the minute we touch something comes over him and he's no longer the threatening boy who wants to hurt me, but someone who has such great capacity to be tender, soft, *loving*.

In his touch I feel the same kind of overwhelming feeling as I did when I heard him sing. In his touch, the fissure that his voice opened in the chapel widens and more of the real Carrick, the true heart of him, appears.

"I want to kiss you. Fuck, I want you," he murmurs, lowering his mouth to meet mine.

His kiss begins like nothing more than a whisper. It's a butterfly's wing against my lips, a soft sweep before the pressure increases ever so slightly. His fingers curl into my hair, his body trembles as I lift my palms and press them against his chest, feeling the steady thrum of his heart beneath my hands. He's so alive, so warm, so welcoming and so so far removed from the boy who takes pleasure in hurting me.

Pressed together like this, I don't feel like the tragic, mute girl everyone passes me off as. I feel worshipped. I feel adored. In the arms of my enemy, I feel seen.

Groaning, Carrick slides his mouth over mine and I part my lips, wanting the tender touch of his tongue, needing more, wanting more. My fingers grip his jumper and I shift closer to him, widening my legs as he slides one hand down my back, squeezing my hip, and kisses me with more heat, more passion, more *everything* than he has before now.

"Fuck, Cyn. Fuck," he moans, his fingers pulling my hair, breaking the kiss. He stares down at me, his eyes liquid pools of midnight. "Tell me what's happening? Tell me, Cyn."

My chest heaves and my lips part as I look up at him, wanting nothing more to tell him what he wants to know, but even if I had the capability I couldn't explain what this is between us because I don't understand it myself.

It's the same connection I feel with Arden and Lorcan. It's overwhelming, confusing, and addictive. It's calming, soothing, a feeling of belonging.

So all I can do is reach for him. All I can do is drag his face back down to mine and kiss him with the same passion he kisses me with, until he's scooped me up in his arms and deposited me on the table. Our mouths remain fused together as we kiss, but this time our hands move as if of their own accord. I grab his arse, hauling him against me as he cups my breast over my cardigan, squeezing gently. His mouth slides across my cheek and down my neck as I arch it for him, kissing and licking a fiery path across my skin, lighting me up from the inside out.

God, how he makes me burn.

Then he breaks away, asking me permission with his gaze to go further.

I should tell him no. I should tell him to stop. I should explain that only minutes before I was considering poisoning him, poisoning Arden and Lorcan. I should confess my sins, beg for forgiveness. Give him mine.

But I don't do any of those things. I simply nod.

Carrick drops his gaze to my chest as his fingers reach for the top button of my cardigan. The backs of his knuckles drag over my breasts through my vest top beneath as he undoes every one. Then slowly, as I press my palms into the wooden desk below me, he trails his fingers upwards, over the swell of my breast and tugs on the neck of my vest top, pulling it down with my bra.

Cold air scatters across my skin, making my nipples pucker. Heat blooms in my belly as he passes the pad of his thumb over one of my nipples, his dark brown hair falling into his eyes as he lifts his gaze to mine, staring at me.

He doesn't say a word, he doesn't need to.

I can see the need in his eyes, feel it in the air zinging with electricity between us.

Then he lowers his mouth to my breast and takes me in his mouth, sucking gently.

I arch my back, my mouth opening in silent release.

"Cyn. Oh fuck, Cyn," he mutters, sucking and licking.

I'm so distracted by his lament, by his lips worshipping me, that I don't notice Arden and Lorcan walk into the lab until it's too late.

"I told you to stay away from her," Arden bites out.

My eyes snap open, my cheeks flush with heat and on instinct I push Carrick away roughly. I push him away and pull up my top, shame creeping over my skin as all the softness he'd shown me is replaced with hardness. Right before my eyes, the Carrick who kissed and touched me with adoration disappears.

Carrick smirks. "She offered herself up on a platter, what was I supposed to do Arden, walk away?"

"Yes!" he snaps, rage twisting his features into an ugly mask as he strides across the room and swings for him. Arden's clenched fist meets Carrick's jaw and his head snaps sideways.

"STOP!" Lorcan shouts, racing over to them both. He wraps his arms around Arden, yanking him backwards. "Fucking stop!"

Carrick doesn't listen, he stalks towards them both as Lorcan drags Arden back, murder in his eyes. Without thinking I get between them, my hands pressing against Carrick's chest as I shake my head furiously.

I should let them fight it out. I should let them hurt each other.

It would be no more than either of them deserve, but

Carrick's kisses are still warm on my skin and I can't let them do that. I can't.

"Get out of the way," Carrick snarls.

I shake my head. *No.*

Behind me, I can hear Arden roar in frustration and Lorcan telling him to calm down, to stop, to think.

"Let him go, Lorcan. Let's end this," Carrick spits, trying to sidestep me, but I just get in his way again, pushing against his chest harder this time.

"No. Calm the fuck down, both of you!" Lorcan replies.

"Don't tell me to calm down," Carrick shouts before his attention snaps back to me. "This is your fault," he accuses.

My fault?

How is any of this my fault? My hands drop, and I back away from him but he grips my arm, turning his rage on me. I shake my head. I'm not to blame. It's not my fault. None of it.

Something in his eyes makes my instincts kick in, and I reach into the pocket of my cardigan, my fingers wrapping around the poison, holding onto it like it's some kind of talisman. It gives me strength to know it's there.

"What have you got in your pocket, Cyn?" Carrick asks, his gaze zeroing in on my fingers wrapped around the tiny glass bottle.

I back away, shaking my head. My heart pounds with fear. Fear of Carrick. Fear of these volatile emotions the four of us draw out of each other. My head hurts from the whiplash. My emotions are all over the place.

A dark voice inside of me tells me to show him what I'm hiding. I don't. I just back away, edging towards the door.

Carrick lunges for me, gripping my arm as he yanks me against his chest. I fight him, twisting in his hold, kicking and slapping at his hands as I try to get away.

"Leave her alone! I'm going to fucking kill you!" Arden roars.

"Stop!" Lorcan shouts, exasperated, angry, afraid.

Carrick doesn't listen. He pins me against the wall of the classroom with his body and grabs my hands, pressing them against the wall above my head and says, "Show me what you're hiding. Now."

A tear trickles down my cheek and I swallow back a sob. I'm not crying because of the way he's acting so brutally after being so gentle, I'm crying because I nod in my defeat, my fingers uncurling from around the bottle as he lowers my hands and takes it from me.

"What's this?" he asks, holding the bottle between his finger and thumb. He unscrews the lid, and sniffs.

Unlike some poisons the smell is pleasant, like almonds and honey. It doesn't give any indication from its scent that it's dangerous. I made it that way on purpose. Deadly nightshade has a bitter taste, but I've covered it up by making it smell and taste sweet.

"What kind of potion is this, Cyn?"

My eyes widen as he lifts it to his lips.

Let him swallow it, that dark voice inside my head whispers. *He deserves it.*

"What have you got there, Carrick?" Lorcan asks, still trying to calm a heaving, angry, rage-infested Arden.

Carrick ignores him, gaze laser-focused on me as he whispers, "Will this take all the pain away?"

"Carrick, what the fuck are you doing?" Lorcan insists.

Time slows as Carrick crowds me in, blocking my view of Arden and Lorcan. There's a deep sadness in his eyes, a pain that's bigger than the four of us, and I realise in that moment that I'm not my mother. I can't fix this. I can't fix him. So when he asks me again if it will take the pain away, I nod minutely.

God help me, I nod.

The second he lifts the bottle to his lips, regret rushes through my veins and my mouth opens, one word rising up my throat.

STOP!

But it comes out as nothing more than a broken croak as I slap at his hand knocking the bottle away.

It flies across the room and relief floods my veins as it smashes into tiny pieces against the wall.

But when I turn back around, Carrick's eyes are wide, his hands are at his throat, a tiny bead of poison sliding from the corner of his mouth.

No! No! No! No!

As he drops to his knees, choking on death, Lorcan lets go of Arden and they both rush forward.

"What's happening to him?" Lorcan shouts, frantic as he catches him in his arms and Carrick writhes within them, saliva frothing from his mouth as his eyes roll to the back of his head and he starts to convulse.

"What did he just drink?" Arden shouts as I run across the science lab to the store cupboard grabbing liquid charcoal, bottled water, metric tubing and a syringe, all items I use separately for my experiments.

Rushing back to Carrick, I shove Arden out of the way and urge Lorcan to lay Carrick flat, showing him how to hold his shoulders down. I turn towards Arden and place his hands on Carrick's knees urging him to do the same.

"What are you doing?!" Arden asks, fear making his jaw clack.

I give him a look with my eyes that I hope conveys that I'm trying to save his damn life. Then I tip Carrick's head back, pick up the metric tubing, pry his mouth open and hold his tongue down with my fingers then slide the tube down his throat.

I don't think, I just do.

Through some sheer miracle I manage to slide the tube down his oesophagus and not the trachea on the first go. Once it's in place, I grab the water, fill the syringe up, then pump it down the tube. I do this over and over until I think there is enough in his stomach, then I pull out the tube, push at Lorcan and Arden, then turn Carrick on his side and shove my fingers down his throat to engage his gag reflex.

It works.

All the water, and with it the poison, is evacuated from his stomach alongside whatever he ate earlier. Rubbing his back, Carrick coughs and splutters, chokes and spits as he throws up over and over again until his stomach is empty.

"Fuck, fuck!" Arden swears as I glance over at him, shock, fear, relief and gratitude passing over his features as his brain catches up with what's happened.

"You're okay Carrick, you're okay," Lorcan says, replacing my hand on Carrick's back, rubbing up and down as I reach for the charcoal.

It's the only thing that will neutralise any of the poison that might've been absorbed before I could pump Carrick's stomach. It's unlikely, given how quickly I acted, but it's better to be safe than sorry.

Carrick stops retching and allows Lorcan to haul him back into his arms, tears pouring from his eyes, puke surrounding his mouth as he sobs. The sound he makes is heartbreaking, soul-destroying. There's so much pain in it, so much fear, and it tears at my skin, reaches inside of my chest and shreds my heart.

I cry with him, for him. I cry for me and what *I've* done.

He could've died. I almost killed him.

My god, who am I?

What kind of person would do that?

Guilt grips my throat and threatens to take my consciousness, but I fight off the feeling. I can't afford to be selfish and pass out now. He still needs me. I owe him.

Lorcan holds him, wrapping his arms and legs around him until the tears finally stop and all we're left with is the raw aftermath of such a traumatic experience.

Without saying a word, I remove my cardigan, using it to clean his face. He stares up at me, not moving, not speaking, just breathing.

At least he's breathing.

Reaching for the charcoal, I unscrew the cap, lifting it to his lips.

"What's that?" Arden asks.

I point to the label, unable to explain given I don't have a notepad or pencil to communicate with.

"Charcoal?" Arden reads aloud.

"It's a neutraliser, right?" Lorcan asks.

I nod, pressing it back against Carrick's lips, urging him with my eyes to drink.

"Drink it, Carrick," Lorcan says.

Carrick opens his mouth and swallows the liquid charcoal, not once taking his eyes off mine. I can't read him. I don't know if he blames me, if he's grateful that I saved his life, if he wants to hurt me or thank me.

But none of that matters.

What matters is that he's alive.

Once he's drunk a quarter of the bottle, I screw the lid back on and take his hands in mine. For a long time we just look at one another, unable to express what we're feeling in the moment. I can feel the heat of Lorcan and Arden's stare, feel their shock as though it's my own. My heart aches for us all, for the mess we've made in the name of others. They're victims of Malik and my father's darkness. I'm a victim of their hatred.

"You saved his life," Lorcan says, eyes wide in wonder.

Nausea rolls through my stomach. I might've saved his life but it wouldn't have needed saving if I hadn't made the poison in the first place.

I don't deserve his gratitude or his appreciation.

Not knowing what else to do, I lean in and press a kiss against Carrick's cheek, my eyes shutting on the tears that slide down my face, mingling with his.

Silently, I apologise.

Then I get up and leave, hating myself for what I did, wondering how I can fix the wrongs between us, wondering how I can make it right.

For three months we avoid each other. For three months I work on my apology in the science lab, experimenting with all manner of herbs and flowers until eventually I make something that I hope will give peace between us. Then during the last week of our attendance at Silver Oaks Institute, I offer them my apology in the form of a new drug I've named diamonds, and with my body.

24

C arrick - present day

I sense her next to me, the woman who plagues my waking thoughts and my every dream. Her fingers slide over my forehead as she presses something cold against it. If I had the energy, I'd flinch away from her touch. But I can't seem to move, let alone open my eyes to see what she's doing.

Everything is an effort. Breathing hurts. My throat is lined with razor blades. My head swells with grey storm clouds filled with lightning and thunder. My limbs are weak, my bones ache.

And somewhere along a long dark tunnel is death, just waiting to sink its bony claws into me again. If I had the words

I'd tell death to back the fuck off. But I have neither the words nor the energy.

"You think he has pneumonia?" Arden asks, the fear in his voice unmistakable as it permeates my consciousness, trickling like grains of sand through an hourglass timer.

I try to move, to reach for him and tell him not to be scared because I won't fucking let death take me from my brothers. I refuse. But I can't open my mouth. I feel like I'm at the bottom of a well, stuck in sludge and mud, my voice taken, my nails split and broken as I try to climb the walls and reach the light high above me.

Cyn must nod her head, or write her response down because Arden swears.

"Fuck. Can you heal him?"

Why is he asking her that? I don't want her to heal me. I don't want her near me. I don't want her help. I don't want her. Fuck, I don't need her.

"Good. Do whatever you need to do. *Whatever* you need to do. Understand?"

No!

Death laughs.

He grins beneath the wide brim of his hood.

"Can I help? What do you need, Cyn?" Lorcan, my brother, my best friend asks.

I hear the faith in his voice. He trusts in her to heal me. But doesn't he see, she's not ours.

It's a lie. All of it.

It's all a lie.

They talk above me, so close yet so very far away. I strain to hear them, to understand the conversation going on around me, but as time passes it becomes more and more difficult. The words scatter like snowflakes across my too hot skin, dissolving, lost to the fever overtaking my body. I try to fight the exhaustion and the fatigue that drags me into the sinking well of darkness.

Fuck, I fight.

I fight so hard.

But with every breath I feel weaker, I feel myself slipping away, and in the distance Death takes another step closer. I reach out for something, anything to keep me anchored to the mortal world.

The scent of Christmas spices fill my senses, cinnamon and frosted pine, warm toffee pudding, and melted chocolate. I smell happiness, comfort, hope.

I smell her.

I smell sin.

I smell Cyn.

And for just a moment my chest isn't so tight, my breathing isn't as laboured, my heart isn't so heavy and my soul not as fractured.

I bask in the feeling. I succumb to the comfort it brings me. My body relaxes. The rapid beat of my heart slows. Memories of her kisses settle the panic swelling inside my mind, and I'm lost to the gentle press of her lips, the tender slide of her tongue against mine.

Cyn. Sin. Cyn. Sin.

The girl, the woman, the healer, the witch.

She's comfort and warmth.

She's fear and pain.

She's magic and mysticism.

She's all of those things.

Then the comfort fades away and I feel the dark tendrils of the blood pact swirling around me, it caresses my skin, seeps into my pores, wraps around my throat and Death takes another step closer, grinning mercilessly.

My thoughts scatter, confused and bewildered. I don't understand why she's both a comfort and endless misery, the feeling of home and desperate heartbreak.

All I know is that I'm under her spell. I'm at the mercy of her magic.

My heart aches, my voice cracks as I call her name. Unsure if I'm warning her to leave me alone or beckoning her closer. My feelings towards her make no sense. I don't understand them.

I don't understand any of it.

Silence descends and I sense Cyn move away. I should be relieved. I should be grateful she's gone, but somewhere deep inside yearns for her nearness, yearns for her.

"Don't go..." I whisper.

Don't go. Don't go. Don't go.

My voice is muffled, as though the strong current of the ocean is dragging me beneath the waves. I reach for her, my fingers grasping the material of her skirt, reality merging with memory as I thrash about trying to swim to the surface, to breathe. I need to save her.

I'm drowning.

I need to get to her.

I need her.

I can't breathe.

I.

Can't.

Breathe.

Then I feel the strong hands of my brothers on me, pinning me down, urging me to take a breath, to remain calm, to stop fighting, to trust them, to trust her.

"Do it. Give it to him now," Arden says, and I feel my mouth pried open and moments later a bitter taste coats my tongue.

Then I feel the power of her magic seeping into my taste-buds, hurtling along my bloodstream, slowing the panic in my veins, calming the frantic beat of my heart until exhaustion takes over, and I'm no longer drowning but drifting into a bottomless sleep filled with the scent of Cyn, her gentle touch, and her *voice...*

Cyn sits in a chair at the side of my bed, her hair pulled back in a low ponytail as she reaches over me and swipes a damp cloth over my heated cheeks, her grey eyes filled with concern. I try to speak, but it's only when the words won't come that I realise I'm not watching this unfold from within my body, but somehow outside of it.

Right now, she sees a sleeping man, eyes shut, lips parted, breathing ragged.

Yet I feel her touch. Sense her closeness. Smell her comforting scent. See her concern.

It's as though I'm both inside of my body, and out of it.

But that doesn't make any sense, so I must be dreaming, right?

Then she speaks, and I know I am.

It doesn't matter though, because in that moment her voice is everything I need, everything I crave. It's like a soft caress, the gentle flow of a babbling brook, the chirp of a bird singing in summer, the soft buzz of a bee collecting pollen, the velvety petals of a flower drifting to the ground. It has a rhythmic cadence, a lyricism that is as pure as it is sultry.

"Your hatred always felt like the rumbling presence of a storm on the horizon. I could sense the danger in it, and I began to realise that to survive you I'd either have to embrace the danger or fight back with everything I had," she says, her words washing over me, prickling my skin as the untethered part of me floats around her, one minute watching from above, like a bird hovering on the slipstreams in the air, and the next standing beside her, a shadow just out of sight.

"I didn't understand you back then, but every now and then I saw glimpses of the person you hid from the world. That night you sang in the chapel, I saw between the cracks, Carrick. I felt you in that moment. I felt the person that you hid from the world. That night I'd found a kind of kinship in your voice. I felt your pain as if it were my own, and I knew you'd been hurt badly. Like always recognises like," she whispers, her voice trailing off as another sound distracts her.

It's a moan.

It's me moaning, and the untethered part of me angers at the sound. I want to scream at myself to shut up, to stay quiet, to listen to her voice.

Cyn reaches for a small, dark green bottle on the side table. It has a pipette, and she squeezes the nib, then drops some of the liquid drawn into the tube between my slightly parted lips. It hits my tongue, and that same strange warmth that enveloped me earlier, does so again.

Time passes, and the ghostly part of me floats about us both waiting for her to speak again. Arden and Lorcan come and go, and she remains stubbornly quiet, conversing only with her notepad, refusing their help, giving orders. Their concern is an oppressive energy that makes it hard for me to keep this form.

But eventually they leave, and I'm alone with Cyn once more. I watch her as she applies a poultice to my bare chest, then adds drops of something to a bowl of steaming water. Her touch is gentle, her hands lingering on my skin as she checks my pulse.

It isn't until the soft snores of Arden can be heard and the footsteps of Lorcan making his way downstairs a few hours later that Cyn speaks again.

"I never wanted to be tied to you, any of you. I resented my attraction to you all, and hated myself for it, but it doesn't change the fact that I wanted it," she whispers softly. "I wanted you all and I couldn't understand why, but now I do."

Cyn sighs, and for a long time she just stares off out of the window, her fingers wrapped around mine, her thumb drawing circles over my knuckles until, eventually, she returns her attention back to me.

"Blood pact or not, my fate is intertwined with yours, the same as it's intertwined with Arden and Lorcan's and there's nothing any of us can do to change it. I know who you are to me, what the three of you are to me, and I won't stand in the way of that."

Her voice trails off and she presses her soft lips against my cheek, her tenderness calming me. "Sleep now, Carrick."

And so I sleep.

"How are you feeling?" Arden asks me as he passes me a glass of water and I take it from him, chugging it back in one go.

"Thirsty," I reply, handing the glass back to him.

He grins. "Better?"

"What the fuck happened? I feel like I've been asleep for a week."

"You've been out for four days," he replies, sitting on the edge of the bed.

"Funny," I reply, rubbing my eyes and trying to shake the sleepy feeling from my bones.

"I'm serious. You've been in and out of consciousness for four days. We've been taking it in turns to look after you."

"We?"

"Lorcan, Cyn and me."

"Cyn?" I ask, my brows pulling together in a frown.

"She stayed by your side the first twenty-four hours. Refused to rest. Barely ate or drank."

I clear my throat, not sure how I'm supposed to react to that. Truthfully, I don't know how I feel other than better. I feel like I've had a really good sleep. My body doesn't ache. My chest is no longer tight and congested. My head and sinuses are clear. But more than that, I feel calm. There's no anxiousness or that constant feeling that doom is just around the corner.

I feel free.

I feel better than I have in a long, long time.

"If it wasn't for her, you'd be in a hospital on the mainland or worse..."

"It was that bad?"

"You don't remember?"

I shake my head. "Not really. I just remember feeling sick as a dog, and weak as fuck. I thought she'd poisoned me. If I had the strength to get out of bed, I would've hurt her," I admit, but I don't feel the same kind of anger behind that notion. I feel more shame than rage that I could ever consider hurting someone who has healed me now not once, but twice.

"Then it's just as well you weren't strong enough because Cyn healed you, Carrick, and she did it with her knowledge and skill."

A few days ago I'd be fucking furious at them all for allowing her to use her herbs to heal me. Today I'm not. I feel grateful to be here. I feel as though a heavy weight has been lifted off my shoulders, as though a chain has been removed from around me and I'm free to move again.

I feel alive in a way I haven't felt in a long, long time.

"Where is she now?" I ask, gripping Arden's forearm, needing to see her, to thank her.

"She's in the outhouse finishing off the first batch of diamonds for Soren."

"I need to see her, Arden."

"You need to rest. You're not at full capacity, Brother," he replies, placing his hand on my shoulder and pushing me gently backwards.

"I'm feeling better than I have in fucking years. I *need* to see her," I repeat, pushing upwards, and swinging my legs over the side of the bed.

Arden grins, his eyes falling to my crotch. "You might want to put some clothes on."

"What's the matter, Arden, afraid she might like what she sees?" I ask, standing.

"Just get dressed, arsehole," he says, and then pulls me into his arms and gives me a fierce hug.

"Anyone would think that you loved me," I say, holding him as tightly as he holds me.

"Don't ever do that to me again," he replies, his breath warm against the skin of my neck. "You might believe what everyone else says about us, but we both know we're more human than god."

I reach up and grasp his face, pressing my forehead against his. "Fuck, don't I know it."

"What's this, you two leaving me out again, are you?" Lorcan says as he steps into the room, a wide grin on his face. He strides over to us both, and wraps his arms around the pair of us. "If only they all knew."

"If only who knew what?" I question.

"That the Deana-dhe actually have hearts," he replies, with a wry grin.

"And we all know why that is," Arden says, serious now as I ease out of his arms.

Lorcan eyes me. "Cyn."

"Cyn," I agree.

As Arden searches for some clothes for me, Lorcan reaches

up and grasps the necklace that she gave him, ripping it from his neck.

"Thank fuck we're all on the same page, *finally*," he says, swiping the palm of his hand over the back of his neck, and rolling his head on his shoulders as though the necklace was a dead weight. I suppose it must've been.

Taking the proffered clothing from Arden, I get dressed. "What about Cyn?"

Lorcan and Arden exchange looks. "There's only one way to find out if she still feels the same way about us," Lorcan says.

"What do you mean *still* feels the same way?" I ask, but a sudden lightheadedness unsteadies me, and I reach out to my brothers to steady me.

"I wanted you all and I couldn't understand why, but now I do..."

I gasp, my skin covering in a rash of goosebumps as I recall a memory of Cyn speaking.

"Carrick, what is it?" Lorcan asks, but my only response is my fingers tightening around his arm.

"Blood pact or not, my fate is intertwined with yours, the same as it's intertwined with Arden and Lorcan's and there's nothing any of us can do to change it. I know who you are to me, what the three of you are to me, and I won't stand in the way of that."

Blinking back the memory, I shake my head, trying to make sense of it. I heard Cyn's voice. Fuck, her beautiful voice.

"Fuck!" I exclaim, shocked to my very core.

"Carrick, what is it?" Arden asks, holding me steady.

"I need to see her. Now."

"Carrick, talk to us," Lorcan urges.

"When I was sick, she spoke to me. I heard her voice," I say in a rush.

Arden squeezes my shoulder. "You were delirious, Carrick."

"Arden's right. It was probably some kind of hallucination or fever dream," Lorcan adds, glancing at Arden. I see the look he gives him, he's worried I'm not well enough to be out of bed just yet.

"You're right. *Fuck.* Ignore me," I say, plastering on a smile to reassure him whilst internally questioning myself. How can something that felt so real be a dream?

"Look, it stands to reason you'd dream about her voice when you've been so sick. We've all coveted it for many years now," Arden adds.

I swipe a hand over my face, then nod, forcing myself to ignore the niggle in the back of my head insisting that it wasn't a dream. "So what did you mean by finding out if she still feels the same way? How?"

"We take diamonds," Lorcan says.

"For what purpose? Don't get me wrong, I want to relive that night with Cyn again but I'd prefer to do it without the influence of drugs."

"Diamonds never manipulated our emotions, Carrick, they only enhanced what was already there. At the time we were too fucking stupid to realise it. If we all take the drug, then we'll know for absolute certainty that what we feel is real, and that she feels the same way too."

"But what about Cyn?" I ask. "What if she doesn't want to take the drug?"

"She'll do it," Arden says with an assuredness that concerns me.

"Why will she do it?" I question, not sure I want to hear his answer. A few days ago, forcing Cyn to do something against her will wouldn't have bothered me but I feel differently now.

"Because if she does, she won't have to stay here any longer. She'll be free to go."

"You're willing to let her go, after everything we've discussed?" Lorcan asks, his voice tight with pain.

"What's that old saying? If you love something, set it free. If it comes back to you, it's yours. If it doesn't, it was never yours in the first place," Arden explains.

"Love?" I question, meeting the certainty of his gaze.

He nods. "What else could it be?"

The silence that follows is deafening. The sheer fact that neither Lorcan or I protest, telling.

It's a trade-off none of us are happy about, but we're willing to do it for her.

Drug or no drug, that tells me all I need to know.

25

Cyn - Eighteen years old

Taking a deep breath, I push open the door to the chapel and step inside the building. It's cool inside, so much cooler than the oppressive spring heat that lingers even after the sun has long since slipped past the horizon. Sweat glistens on my skin and I swipe my hair up into a messy bun, appreciating the cool air passing over the back of my neck.

Heading towards the front of the chapel, I lower to my knees, press my sweaty palms against the cotton skirt of my summer dress and wait.

I don't know if they'll come, but I do know that I want to try and heal this disharmony between us. We'll never be friends, not with our history, but perhaps we can put an end to the hate, and the only times we've ever put our differences aside was when we were intimate with each other. Human touch, affection, physical closeness, *sex*, it all has the power to heal in a way that words sometimes can't. So last night I slid a note, and the drug I'd been working on, beneath Arden's door offering an olive branch. Offering them a chance to unburden themselves.

Offering them *me* on a silver platter.

I can't give them my voice, but for one night I can strip away our inhibitions. I can give them my pleasure and take theirs in return. And if my plan works, I can prevent us from ever harming each other in the future, knowing that without the drug, they'd never agree to it.

Sliding my fingers over the blade strapped to my thigh, I take in a deep, calming breath.

A blood pact isn't something I ever thought I'd consider using, given its power comes from a magic that I don't fully understand, but I'm willing to try anything to prevent them from hurting me again.

A blood pact isn't just an exchange of blood accompanied by a binding spell, it's so much more than that. For it to work, I have to give them a piece of my mind, my body and my soul, and I have to do it willingly. I've thought long and hard about this, and it feels like the right decision.

With my mind I will give them a drug that I made which will heighten emotion, sensation, feelings.

With my body I will give them my virginity, my blood, my pleasure.

25

Cyn - Eighteen years old

Taking a deep breath, I push open the door to the chapel and step inside the building. It's cool inside, so much cooler than the oppressive spring heat that lingers even after the sun has long since slipped past the horizon. Sweat glistens on my skin and I swipe my hair up into a messy bun, appreciating the cool air passing over the back of my neck.

Heading towards the front of the chapel, I lower to my knees, press my sweaty palms against the cotton skirt of my summer dress and wait.

I don't know if they'll come, but I do know that I want to try and heal this disharmony between us. We'll never be friends, not with our history, but perhaps we can put an end to the hate, and the only times we've ever put our differences aside was when we were intimate with each other. Human touch, affection, physical closeness, *sex*, it all has the power to heal in a way that words sometimes can't. So last night I slid a note, and the drug I'd been working on, beneath Arden's door offering an olive branch. Offering them a chance to unburden themselves.

Offering them *me* on a silver platter.

I can't give them my voice, but for one night I can strip away our inhibitions. I can give them my pleasure and take theirs in return. And if my plan works, I can prevent us from ever harming each other in the future, knowing that without the drug, they'd never agree to it.

Sliding my fingers over the blade strapped to my thigh, I take in a deep, calming breath.

A blood pact isn't something I ever thought I'd consider using, given its power comes from a magic that I don't fully understand, but I'm willing to try anything to prevent them from hurting me again.

A blood pact isn't just an exchange of blood accompanied by a binding spell, it's so much more than that. For it to work, I have to give them a piece of my mind, my body and my soul, and I have to do it willingly. I've thought long and hard about this, and it feels like the right decision.

With my mind I will give them a drug that I made which will heighten emotion, sensation, feelings.

With my body I will give them my virginity, my blood, my pleasure.

With my soul I will give them a promise to never harm them, and I will do it in a holy place.

My knees begin to ache from sitting in the same position before the altar, but I have faith that they will come. Minutes later the gentle creak of the oak doors opening validates my belief that they want this as much as I do.

Footsteps sound on the stone floor, and there's a sudden stillness in the air as if the chapel is taking a deep, calming breath, readying itself for what's to come.

"Lock the door," Arden commands, his voice breaking the silence, allowing me to breathe again.

Keeping my gaze fixed on the altar before me, I hear the lock click shut and footsteps crossing the stone floor. In my periphery, I see Arden make the sign of the cross before he drops to his knees beside me. The heat lifting from the bare skin of his arm has my body quivering in nerves and anticipation. On the other side of me, Lorcan mouths a silent prayer then drops to his knees too, his fingers brushing against the back of my hand in a way that can only be interpreted as comforting.

I wait for Carrick to join us, but as the minutes pass and I hear nothing but the soft breaths of Arden and Lorcan, my heart begins to sink inside my chest.

This won't work without him.

All three need to be here.

Lorcan must sense my disappointment because he squeezes my hand.

Then, right before Carrick's haunting voice lifts up into the air around us, I sense him.

My chest tightens, the hair on the back of my neck rises, and my skin covers in goosebumps as Arden entwines his fingers with mine. Linked by our hands, Lorcan, Arden and I hold onto one another as Carrick breaks our hearts with his voice.

As the last note leaves his lips, he approaches the three of us and stands in front of me. My breathing is ragged, my face wet with tears from the emotion his voice so easily pulls from my chest, and I'm trembling with words I can't express.

"Look at me, Cyn," he says, his voice even, commanding, as he presses his fingers gently against the top of my head. I slowly lift my gaze, locking eyes with him.

"You asked us to come here tonight, offering up something we've all coveted. But what makes you think we'd trust you after what happened?"

"She saved your life, Carrick," Arden reminds him, gripping my hand tighter.

"That shit was poisonous," he counters, not once taking his eyes off me.

"She warned you not to take it. She tried to stop you," Lorcan adds, exasperated, as though they've had this conversation over and over again.

"What makes you think this doesn't have the same ingredients, huh?" he asks, opening the palm of his hand, the drug sparkling like a real diamond in the flickering candlelight.

Releasing my hand from Lorcan's, I snatch it from his hand, place it on the stone step, then pull up my skirt and slide the knife free from the strap around my leg, smashing the handle against the drug before anyone can stop me.

"She brought a knife!" Carrick accuses, but before he can say anything further, I meet his gaze, flip the knife in my hand and offer it to him.

If he wants to seek revenge for what I did, I guess now's the time.

Carrick takes the knife from me, and for a split second I think he's going to slide the blade across my throat.

He doesn't.

Instead, he lowers to his haunches, picks up a shattered piece of the drug using the flat edge of the knife blade and says, "When Arden showed me this, I thought you'd given us a real diamond, that you were paying us to leave you alone. Then I read your note. You want us to take this drug, let it alter our minds and fuck each other until we find peace?"

I nod. *Yes.*

"And you think it will work? That any of us will find peace? That I will find peace from the nightmares that have plagued me ever since death had me in its grip?"

Truthfully, I don't know. I hope so, I do. But I don't give him false hope. Not that he'd believe me even if I'd answered yes. He waits, reading what he needs from my expression, then nods.

"Open your mouth," he demands. His voice is soft, laced with intent, whether it's good or bad, I've no idea.

I open my mouth, and he places the blade on my tongue.

"Lick it clean, *cailleach*," he says. "I need to make sure this is safe."

Folding my lips carefully around the blade, I meet his hungry gaze as he slowly pulls the blade free, depositing the drug on my tongue. I let it dissolve as he pulls back and waits.

If he's expecting my death, he's not going to get it. I've already tested the drug. I know the effect it will have on me, and I know that within five minutes every inch of my skin is going to be a thousand times more sensitive to touch than it is now.

I also know that I will see things that are unexplainable and feel emotions that are heightened. When I took this drug in my bedroom, I'd done so in front of my mirror. I'd made myself come five times over the course of an hour shrouded in a warm golden light. Somehow this drug allowed me to see the goodness my grandmother had spoken of. It allowed me to love myself.

Minutes tick by, bringing with it a languid warmth that both relaxes my body, and my mind. Without meaning to, I lean into Lorcan's side, needing the touch of the one person I believe has less hatred towards me than the others, searching for a sliver of kindness.

I sigh as his arms slides around my back, hauling me closer to his side.

"Cyn," he says as I reach for him. My hand presses against his chest and I feel the thrum of his heart as though it sits in the palm of my hand. I let out a breath, my skin prickling from the contact.

Arden shifts position, moving from beside me to behind me, until I feel the gentle caress of his breath against the back of my neck.

"Pass me the drug, Carrick," he says, the soft press of his lips against my bare shoulder, making me shudder. His featherlight touch feels like the plume of a swan's wing, stroking down my back.

"You're certain, Brother?" Carrick asks.

"Never more certain of anything in my life," Arden whispers.

Carrick nods, collecting the drug that looks even more like diamonds now that it's working its magic in my veins. Lifting the knife to Arden's lips, Carrick rests the blade on his tongue just like he did mine.

Less than a minute later, Arden groans. "Fuck, this is..."

His voice trails off as he slides his mouth up the column of my neck, telling me with his touch just how much the drug is affecting him. Reaching up, I grasp that back of his head, arching my neck to give him more access.

Next Lorcan takes the drug and the groan that parts his lips as I reach for the hard length through his joggers makes me shudder in pleasure.

"Cyn, fuck, that feels so fucking good. So good," he sighs, his body fluid, his muscles relaxing whilst his cock hardens beneath my touch. Needing to feel him in my hands, I slide my fingers beneath the waistband of his joggers, reaching for the silky, throbbing length of him.

"Yes," he hisses, arching his hips to press his dick into my hand, urging me to fist him. "Don't stop, Cyn."

Arden growls, his tongue snaking out of his mouth as his hand slides down my arm and across my stomach. The cotton material of my dress feels like a brick wall between us, and I want it off. I want to feel his flesh against my flesh, and I reach up with my free hand, pulling my straps down, telling him without words what I need. He doesn't need to be told twice.

Grasping the zipper on the back of my dress, he lowers it

slowly, chasing the zip with his tongue down the length of my spine, his mouth licking at the two indents at my hips. Breathy pants escape my lips as my clit swells and twitches, and my eyelids flutter shut, intense sensation taking over every rational thought.

"You taste like the summer breeze rolling across the ocean, Cyn. You smell like home," Arden mutters, his lips and tongue moving back up my spine, his hands sliding the dress from the top of my body, revealing my bare breasts.

"Fuck," Carrick mutters, his voice drawing my attention back to him as the cool air of the chapel slides across my puckered nipples only to be encased with warmth as Arden cups them.

My breath hitches in time with Lorcan's muted pants, his cock growing thicker and longer in my grasp as I pump him leisurely.

"I'm gonna come, Cyn. Fuck, I'm going to come so hard," he says, his words slurred with desire.

"This is the drug. That's all this is," Carrick says, fear and desire battling inside of him.

I shake my head. *No, it's so much more,* I mouth, urging him with my eyes and with my body to join us.

"This is a spell," he says almost to himself as he watches me writhe beneath Arden's touch, as Lorcan writhes beneath mine.

Please, I silently beg, parting my thighs, and drawing up the skirt of my dress so he can see my naked pussy, bare for him. Wet for them.

It's a sin to do what we're doing, here in this holy place.

I'm their temptation.

I'm their enemy.

I'm their original sin.

And in this moment, under the watchful eye of the stained glass image of the Virgin Mary, I'm theirs.

Carrick's gaze drops, hunger passing over his features as he stares at my glistening slit, and without taking his eyes off my parted thighs he lets out a long breath, his shoulders relaxing, the tension leaving his body as he makes a decision. Picking up a shattered piece of the drug he places it on his tongue, watching me as it dissolves.

I can't take my eyes off him, not when Lorcan convulses in my hand, calling my name as his warm cum spills from his cock. Not when Arden shifts his body so that he can take my breast into his mouth and lap at my aching nipples, and not when the stirrings of my first orgasm pulls deep inside my stomach.

With his eyes pinned on me, Carrick picks up the last piece of the drug, places it between his teeth, then leans over Arden, grasps the back of my head and kisses me. The gentle, sugar-coated taste of him, the firm length of Lorcan pulsating in my hands, the skilled mouth of Arden sucking on my nipple and the feeling of warmth wrapping around us all lifts me higher.

I feel like a leaf floating on a warm breeze.

I feel like a rainbow passing through the surface of a Mediterranean Sea.

I feel like the first snowflake of winter drifting to the ground.

I feel like a ball of molten energy as an orgasm is pulled

from deep within me, drawn to the surface of my skin from their touch, their kisses, their lips, teeth and tongues.

Carrick's groan and the sharp sudden scrape of Arden's teeth over my nipple detonates that orgasm and it rushes over my heated skin like a seed pod exploding across a forest floor.

My back arches and Carrick's lips are torn from mine as my orgasm takes over. Silent pleasure bursts from my parted lips as Arden captures me in his arms, holding me whilst I convulse and shake.

"Look at you," Arden whispers against my ear, adjusting me in his arms as I come down from one of the most intense orgasms I've ever experienced. Cradled in his arms he looks down at me, cupping my face in his palm. "You're covered in this golden glow, Cyn. You're so fucking beautiful I can barely stand to look," he admits, his black hair falling into his amber eyes that seem to shine from the inside out, his soul burning brightly from deep within him.

"I see it too," Lorcan adds, as I feel him gently wipe his warm cum from my fingers with his t-shirt.

I turn my head towards him, reaching up to press my fingers soaked in his cum against his lips.

Open up, I silently urge, sliding them between his lips as he licks them clean.

Smiling as he circles my fingers with his tongue, I look into his eyes and see his soul like lightning in a bottle, and it's *beautiful*.

"Place her on the altar," Carrick demands softly, clearing his throat as I turn my attention back to him.

I gasp, my eyes widening. His black eyes sparkle, his soul

glowing from within like the expansive silence of a peaceful night. All I see reflected in them is us.

Arden, Lorcan, *me.*

Scooping me up, Arden lifts to his feet and strides with me to the altar, spreading me across the cool marble like an offering. He reaches up and removes my hair tie, gently lowering my head back against the stone. Then his gaze slides down my body, his fingertips following the path of his eyes, stripping me of my dress until I am as naked as Eve in the Garden of Eden.

"Do you see what I see?" he asks Lorcan and Carrick.

They both nod, their fingers reaching out to hover over my body, tracing the light that ebbs from my skin in tiny particles that drift up into the pitched roof of the chapel above us.

"You're exquisite," Lorcan says, bending over to press a kiss against the flushed skin of my chest.

"Perfect," Carrick whispers, his chest rising and falling with emotion.

"You're ours," Arden says, stripping himself of his clothes, dropping them to the floor.

Lorcan and Carrick follow suit, until we're all stripped bare and there's nothing to hide the truth of our hearts behind.

Touch me, I silently beg, spreading my legs, arching my back and offering myself to them with silent words.

"Yes," Arden mutters, sliding his palm up from my ankle, over my shin, knee and thigh, cupping my pussy in the palm of his hand. "You're so wet."

"Fuck," Lorcan whispers, my nipples tightening as I rock against Arden's palm.

Reaching up, I grab Lorcan's hand, lowering it to my breast.

"You're so soft," he murmurs, gently squeezing my flesh, lowering his head to taste me.

I ache beneath their touch, but it isn't enough.

It's not *nearly* enough.

Tipping my gaze to Carrick, I reach for him, urging him to step closer. He moves towards me, his midnight eyes the embodiment of sin as they burn every inch of my skin. Heat fires in my blood as he presses his hand against my stomach whilst fisting his cock.

"I need to fuck you," he grinds out, his touch burning

"We take it together," Arden says, slipping his middle finger between my folds, gently parting me there. Bolts of heat rush upwards from my core as he gently circles my clit. "Spread your legs further, Cyn."

"Fuck, look at her," Lorcan says, the soft strands of his silvery hair passing over my skin.

A breath heaves out of my chest as their combined touch makes my eyes roll into the back of my head, and for a moment all I can do is feel.

I feel Arden and Carrick's fingers roam and explore.

I feel Lorcan's hot mouth taste and tease.

"Do you like that, Cyn?" Arden asks as he continues to play with my clit, and Carrick gently pushes my legs further apart, my thighs slipping over either side of the altar.

It's a question I cannot respond to with words, but I can with my body as I press my hand over his, showing him I need more pressure, more friction, just *more*.

Carrick sucks in a breath as Arden holds my pussy lips open, my desire trickling from my core onto the marble beneath me. It's a beautiful, natural reaction to the sensations we all feel, to the emotion emerging from deep within our hearts and I know that I will never regret this moment between us.

I will treasure it until the day I die.

It might be sinful to fuck in a place of worship, but this feeling inside...? That isn't.

There's nothing sinful about this, healing each other like this.

I want them to continue to touch me, to taste me. I want them to take my virginity right here in this chapel where our sins against each other can be forgiven together.

"Taste her," Arden commands.

They exchange looks and Carrick nods, releasing his dripping dick and traversing the altar. He stands at the far end, then climbs up, kneeling between my parted legs.

"I bet you taste as sweet as I imagined," he says, then lowers his mouth to my pussy.

The second his lips touch my sensitive skin, I jolt against his mouth. It's like nothing I've ever experienced before as he swirls his tongue and laps at the most intimate part of me. A rumble rises up his chest as he eats me out, all the gentleness of his kisses gone as he feasts on me. I grasp his head, pulling him closer, bucking against his face as Lorcan squeezes and grips my breasts, sucking, licking, sliding his tongue over the pebbled peaks.

And I'm gone, drowning beneath their attention, swirling in a whirlpool of heat and passion, desire and lust, sensation and feeling.

"Open your eyes, Cyn. Let me watch you as you come," Arden demands.

Slowly, I drag myself out of the arms of bliss as my eyelids flutter open and I'm looking up at Arden. He stares down at me, the slippery wet sounds of Carrick eating me out and Lorcan sucking on my breasts an erotic melody that only turns me on more.

"I want you to look at me, only me, when you come. Understand?"

I nod, panting as Carrick uses his tongue to rim my hole and Lorcan runs his teeth gently over my nipples, murmuring words of adoration against my skin.

You're beautiful.

You're perfect.

You're everything.

"I want you to listen to my voice and hear the sincerity in it," Arden continues, his amber eyes burning bright.

Yes, I mouth, tears pooling at the edge of my eyes at the way I feel. This is more than I expected. These feelings within me, overwhelming. Their touch ignites something inside of me that I don't understand, can't comprehend.

"Good girl," he says, lowering his mouth to mine and kissing me with more than just his lips and tongue, but with his very soul. "I see you, Cyn. I see what and who you are, and you *are* everything."

"Everything," Carrick repeats against my mound, pressing a kiss against my clit, sliding his tongue over my hot flesh.

"You're our enemy. You're our saviour. You're our sin. You're our *soulmate*."

I drag in a breath, my body shaking from the truth in his words as Lorcan and Carrick continue to assault my senses. I feel his words like I feel their touch. They sink into my skin, slide through my veins and tattoo my very bones.

My body convulses. My mouth parts. My toes curl. My fingers flex. My back arches.

I come.

I come as Arden presses his lips against my ear and says, "You're ours."

Then, as I shiver and shake, the chapel swimming with colour as tears bleed from my eyes, the three of them enter my body using a finger each, breaking my hymen and taking my virginity, together.

I don't feel any pain.

I don't feel anything other than belonging.

To them.

Slowly they remove their fingers, scarlet blood glistening on their skin, and I push upright staring at my essence painting their fingers red.

Now is the time to connect us together forever, to protect us from each other after the effects of the drug have worn off. Now is the time to make the blood pact.

I point to the knife discarded on the stone floor.

"You want the knife?" Lorcan asks, reaching for it.

I nod. *Yes.*

He hands it to me, no questions asked. Carrick doesn't try to take it from me and Arden simply watches me in interest.

At this moment, all of the uncertainty of our relationship is gone. All the fear and mistrust is dissolved. In its place is the honest truth.

This night, we are each other's.

Taking Lorcan's hand, I slide the tip of the blade across his palm, he winces but doesn't pull away, then I take Carrick's finger that's covered in my blood, and slide it across the cut, merging Lorcan's and my essence together.

He sucks in a shaky breath. "This is a blood pact."

Yes, I nod.

"You're binding us together?" Arden asks as I take his hand and cut his palm, urging Lorcan to slide his finger against the slit.

I nod again. *Yes*.

Lorcan follows my lead without question, and Arden accepts my blood from his best friend without fear. Finally I take Carrick's hand, cutting him too, and once Arden has swiped his finger across Carrick's cut I lift each of their hands, pressing their bloody palms against my chest making a silent promise in this sacred place, vowing never to harm any of them, knowing they can never harm me.

Time passes and with it the effect of the drug increases.

We kiss, we touch, we lick, we suck until I don't know where I end and they begin.

Our skin is slick with sweat, with cum, with blood.

Our essence combining.

They kiss me, I kiss them, they kiss each other.

We become one entity. We're soft palms and clenched fingers. We're bee-stung lips, sensual tongues, nipping teeth, gentle sighs and lustful moans. We move around each other in a languid dance like honey bees drunk on the sweet taste of nectar.

"I need you, Cyn," Arden says, sliding his hand up my chest, and gently gripping my throat.

Bending me over the altar, he presses my heated flesh against the cold marble and slides into me from behind. He's big, and the slight sting of his entrance snatches my breath momentarily.

"Breathe," he says. "Concentrate on how I feel inside of you."

Then with the greatest care, he fucks me.

He fucks me like I'm precious, something to be treasured.

Like I'm his everything.

"You feel so fucking perfect fisting my cock. You're fucking perfect," he laments.

Minutes later we come together, shaking and shivering, vibrating with an energy that is unexplainable, and when he pulls out of me, Carrick takes me in his arms and fucks me too.

God how he fucks me.

Every kiss over the past few years, every touch, every word thrown in anger and those released in hate are replaced with passion more powerful than words. Our bodies come together in a way that lays waste to all the past hurt, that heals it with touch.

We're two bodies drawing pleasure out of each other. We're two souls finding peace.

Finally Lorcan enters me, his eyes pinned on mine, his heart pounding against his chest so hard I can feel it vibrating in mine as though his heartbeat is my heartbeat.

"I don't want to forget this," he whispers against my lips. "I don't want to wake up tomorrow and think this was all a dream, a high that I'll never be able to reach again."

He moves inside of me, slowly and with deliberation, stoking another orgasm from somewhere deep inside. "I need to know you'll be ours forever, not for just one night."

I cup his face, press a delicate kiss against his lips, then cross my finger over my heart making a promise I can't possibly keep, but wishing with all my heart it remains true.

26

Arden - present day

Rapping my knuckles against the doorframe, I step inside Cyn's bedroom. She's sitting crossed legged on her bed wearing a woollen jumper, ankle-length skirt and thick socks. Dark circles rim her eyes as she lifts her gaze to meet mine, and guilt lacerates my chest at the exhaustion that paints her face. Placing her pencil within her notebook, she folds it closed and waits.

"He's awake, Cyn. You healed him," I say, a deep feeling of gratitude overwhelming me as I clear my throat.

She nods, smiling gently, and it's the purest thing I've seen in my life. Her kindness, her empathy, her goodness seeps out of her, and even from the other side of the room I feel the warmth of it.

"Will you come with me? He's with Lorcan in the den. We want to talk with you."

A flicker of something I can't interpret flashes in her eyes, and I expect her to deny me, but like always Cyn surprises me and slides off the bed and walks towards me. When I hold out my hand for her to take, she entwines her fingers with mine without hesitation.

Her touch sends electricity zipping over my skin and I shudder. It's as though, now that I've allowed myself to face the truth, my body is reminding me of the connection that was always there right from the very first moment I held her chin in my fingers that first day we met. It's the same feeling now as it was back then. It's undeniable, but my younger self was too angry, too ignorant, too self-centred to understand the gift he'd been given.

Now I get it.

It's not the blood pact.

It's belonging. It's fate.

She's *ours*.

I've never felt more certain of anything in my life.

When we enter the den, Cyn's hand is still grasped in mine, my thumb running over the back of her knuckles. Carrick sits in one armchair beside the fire, Lorcan the other. They both smile as she folds herself into the seat with the grace of a ballet dancer.

"Thank you, Cyn," Carrick says, the emotion within his voice like a fist around my throat.

We aren't men who get emotional. We're cold, aloof, guarded.

We're men who present ourselves to the world in a way that instils fear and commands respect.

We're myths, legends made up of stories based on fiction not fact. We've killed a thousand men each. We dance with the devil. We have sorcery running through our veins. We drink blood. We're immortal. We're demons dressed in human flesh. We're made from black magic.

But with Cyn, there's none of that. With Cyn we're human.

We're men with hearts that beat with love for her. With minds that are filled with thoughts of her. With souls that are forever entwined with hers.

And ultimately we're the story we told ourselves that would never come true, a wish we never believed we'd be granted.

"What you did for me, I can never repay you. You *saved* me," Carrick says.

Not you saved my life, but *you saved me*.

Cyn sighs, her breath a soft dance in the warm air. Turning to face him, her eyes drink him in. As they stare at one another, there's no animosity, there's no hatred, there's only acceptance, kindness, hope.

When she lifts her hand out to him, Carrick slides from the chair and onto his knees before her, taking her hand in his grasp. He bows his head and presses it against her knees in worship, perhaps even in prayer. They remain like that for some time, and I take his seat, watching how she brushes his hair, comforting him.

"What you did was extraordinary," Lorcan says after a while. "Your gift as a healer is exceptional."

She dips her head in thanks, a small smile easing up the corner of her lips.

"*You're* exceptional," Lorcan adds.

Carrick eases back, and looks up at Cyn. Right now he's the exact opposite of how the rest of the world sees him. To everyone outside of the four people in this room he's the man with the eyes of a demon and the cruel hand of a monster. He's the one who will take a life ruthlessly and without hesitation.

Right here and now, he's as vulnerable as I've ever seen him.

Reaching into his jean pocket, he pulls out a diamond and rests it on the palm of his hand, holding it out to Cyn.

"The last time we took this drug we were eighteen. We were young, foolish, filled with distrust and the binding chains of hate. You offered us a way to heal the pain between us. Back then we took the drug because we wanted your body more than we wanted to find peace. We hungered for you, Cyn. I won't deny that I still hunger for you. We *all* do."

Cyn nods, taking the diamond from his hand.

"That night we made a blood pact, binding us to you forever." Carrick heaves in a breath, bowing his head momentarily before lifting his gaze back up to meet hers. "When the effects of the drug wore off, I remembered everything that passed between us, but all I clung onto was the blood pact. I convinced myself it was that which bound us to you and not the connection that had always been there. I believed you cast a spell over us using dark magic, but in truth, it was us who'd turned that blood pact into something dark, something poisonous. Not you."

"We turned our backs on the truth in our hearts, Cyn. We denied our connection," I add, forcing myself to be honest. "I made Lorcan believe what he felt for you was wrong. I didn't argue with Carrick when he said you'd cursed us, I encouraged his belief to bury my truth. They trusted me to always give them the truth and I didn't because I was a fucking coward, and for that I will always be sorry."

Cyn acknowledges my apology with a slight dip of her head and a tiny smile that shows a tremendous amount of forgiveness when I deserve none. She's a fucking wonder. She really is.

Swallowing hard, I try to say the words that will form the sentence which will give her the opportunity to be free of us, but I can't.

"Arden," Lorcan prompts, urging me to say what we all agreed to earlier.

My gaze meets his and I grit my jaw, the selfish part of me doesn't want to offer Cyn an escape. I want to fucking keep her, despite what I'd said earlier.

"Arden, say it, or I will!" Lorcan insists, determined to put things right.

Of the three of us he was always the one who understood Cyn, who protected her and shielded her as much as he could. I know he feels guilty about not standing up to me or Carrick more, but that shouldn't be his burden, that should only be mine. I didn't listen. I refused to see.

It didn't make him weak, it made me an arsehole.

What is it? she asks with a pinched brow and curious look.

"Your debt, making the diamonds," I say, forcing myself to say the words. "I had every intention of making you test the drug when the time came, not because I believed you'd somehow tainted it, but because I wanted you to want me just like you did that first time we took the drug."

"Fuck, Arden," Carrick mutters, glancing over at me.

"That morning in the kitchen the day after we brought you home, I swore I wouldn't hurt you. I lied. I would've hurt you to get what I wanted."

"You're an arsehole," Lorcan mutters.

I can't deny it.

This is not what either of them were expecting me to say, but I owe Cyn the truth, and nothing but the truth. It's the least I can do. So I spill my own secrets, uncover my lies, so that she can make her own decision. In my truth I give her power. It's the only exchange I can give her that's worth a damn.

"The difference is now I don't want to hurt you, and despite wanting you more than I've ever wanted anything in my life, I won't coerce you into doing something for my own gain. I won't treat you like I treat everyone else outside of this room by offering you a solution for something in return. I won't be fucking selfish."

"Arden, where are you going with this?" Carrick asks, a note of panic in his voice.

"He's letting her go," Lorcan whispers, the pain in his voice undeniable.

Cyn's breath catches as she glances between Lorcan, Carrick and me.

Sighing, I scrape a hand over my face. "Earlier I'd told

Lorcan and Carrick that I would offer you the opportunity to test the drug with us so that we might confirm how we feel, and in exchange I would clear your debt and you'd be free to go, but I don't need to do that. I already know how I feel. You're ours, Cyn. You always were. I don't need to take diamonds to know that. So, I guess what I'm saying is that you're free to go. No one's going to keep you here."

Cyn exhales a shaky breath, her chest heaving at my confession as confusion shades her eyes. Casting her attention to the diamond sitting in the palm of her hand, she swallows hard. Then after a moment she stands.

I expect her to leave, to pack her most personal belongings and wait for one of us to accompany her back to the mainland.

She doesn't.

Instead she hands back the Diamond to Carrick, pushes back her chair, unzips her skirt and allows it to fall to the floor. Then she steps out of the crumpled material and removes her woollen jumper, leaving her in her cotton underwear and knee high socks.

"Cyn, what are you doing?" Carrick asks, fucking breathless given the way his chest heaves.

She looks down at him still kneeling at her feet, and reaches up to unhook her bra. He gasps, and my fucking dick hardens at the delicate slope of her breasts and the pink buds of her nipples. Then fixing her gaze on me, she removes her knickers, sliding her socks down with them until she's naked, bare before us.

And then something miraculous happens.

She speaks.

And if we weren't utterly under her spell, captivated by her body, her heart, her beauty, her soul, we sure as fuck are now.

"Touch me," she says, her voice as soft as silk, as smooth as honey.

"Cyn?" Carrick gasps, reaching up to cup her hand.

"Your voice," Lorcan says, disbelief followed by amazement as he drinks her in.

But my words, they won't come. I'm too dazed, too shocked to do anything other than grip the armrests and hold on tight because her voice is that of an angel, and this fierce sense of protectiveness rushes through me at the sound of it.

How can I let her go now? How the fuck can we let her go now?

"I knew I heard your voice. I knew it," Carrick says, the first of us to recover.

"Touch me," she repeats, lifting Carrick's hand to her hip.

"Fuck, Cyn. Fuck," he mumbles, lifting up onto his knees and pressing his cheek against her stomach, wrapping his arm around her waist.

She rests her hand against his head, stroking his hair and says, "I'm glad you're okay, Carrick."

He looks up at her in awe, and as their eyes lock he leans forward and presses a kiss on the mound of her pussy. She smiles down at him, clutching his face gently as he dips lower and presses another kiss where her pussy lips meet.

She moans, and the sound goes straight to my dick.

I'm rock fucking hard.

Opposite me, Lorcan slides from his seat, dropping to his

knees at the exact same fucking time that I do. The sound of her pleasure, her voice, a fucking siren's call.

"I don't want to leave," she says, as Carrick presses kisses over her lower stomach, her fingers grasping his hair as she moans. "And I don't need to take diamonds to prove to you that I want the same thing as you do."

Opening up her palm, she allows the diamond to slip from her hand and roll across the floor.

"Cyn–" I begin, but she cuts me off.

"I don't need to take it. The truth is, I've known for some time that you're mine. I knew it that night in the chapel, but the way you acted towards me afterwards made me question my feelings. The blood pact also complicated matters," she says wryly.

"As did your relationship with The Masks and Malik Brov," I say, addressing the elephant in the room.

She sighs. "Yes."

"Does it complicate matters now?" Carrick asks.

"I miss my friends," she says, giving us a sad smile that fucking hurts like a knife to the gut. "I loved them, but I cannot speak of them right now, it hurts too much."

"But does it change how you feel towards us?" I press.

"I'm here, aren't I?" she replies softly, the tears I've been expecting to fall ever since we brought her home, gathering at the edge of her lashes.

"Jesus, Cyn," Carrick mutters, the guilt in his voice untethering my own.

We did that to her, we caused her this suffering and whilst I will never be sorry that those men are dead, I do regret the pain it's caused her. Yet, I won't lie to her about how I feel, all I can offer is the truth.

"They will always remain our enemies even in death, Cyn," I say, "But I will respect your love for them even if I can't understand it."

"Thank you," she whispers.

"Did you learn to speak again in their presence?" Lorcan asks after a moment, a dash of jealousy casting his face in shadow as he glances over at me. I get it. I feel it too.

"Yes," she replies, her body language closing down any further questions. Despite wanting to hear how that came about, I'm willing to wait until she's ready to tell us.

Eventually, I break the silence. "What now?" I ask, giving Cyn the choice to decide how we move forward. As much as I want to fuck her, to bury my dick deep inside of her and claim her once and for all, I will let her take the lead. It's the least I can do.

She locks eyes with me, draws in a deep, shuddering breath and says, "Crawl to me."

The sultry hint to her voice makes me want to do what I've never done before for any woman. Submit.

But that's what I do.

I crawl to her.

Fuck, I'll kiss her feet if she asks me to.

When I reach her, she tangles her fingers in my hair, pulling on the strands. "I want you to repent your sins with your lips and your hands. I want you to make me come," she says, and fuck if I don't almost come there and then.

"Show me how much you want me," she continues, turning

her attention to Lorcan, who rips off his t-shirt, baring his flushed skin to her, his platinum grey eyes swimming with desire.

Unzipping his fly, he pulls out his cock, precum beading from his slit. "Is this good enough?"

"It's a start," she replies, and I have to bite down on my bottom lip at her attitude.

Fuck, who is this woman?

Cyn licks her lips, then sits back down on the armchair, spreading her legs, revealing her glistening slit to us. Her confidence is an aphrodisiac. Her voice a fucking fish hook in my heart, reeling me in.

Carrick grips her knees, staring at her pussy as she runs her fingers through her folds.

"We hated each other for so long," she says, playing with herself, slowly undulating her hips against her hand. "I'm done with all the hating."

"No more," Carrick agrees, Lorcan muttering his agreement and me nodding with a kiss to her thigh.

"Do you want to taste me, Carrick?" she asks, the lyrical sound of her voice and her dirty words making all three of us groan.

"I've thought about nothing else for years now," he admits.

She nods. "Taste me then. Show me how sorry you are for hurting me."

"Every fucking day, Cyn. I will repent my sins against you by worshipping you every fucking day for the rest of my life."

Sliding his lips and tongue up the inside of her thigh, Carrick takes his time, teasing her as much as she teases us.

When his mouth reaches her pussy, he licks her from crack to clit then sucks her folds into his mouth.

She cries out, her nipples peaking.

Lorcan curses, freeing himself of his clothes, discarding them in a frantic rush as Carrick eats her out, lapping at her pussy, thirsty for her.

"Let me taste her, brother," Lorcan begs, squeezing Carrick's shoulder, his cock bobbing as they change positions.

"Finish what I started," Carrick says, reaching for her breast, lifting the weight of it in his hands.

Cyn cries out as Lorcan hauls her hips towards the edge of the seat and places her thighs either side of his head before burying his face in her pussy.

The slippery wet sound is a shot of desire straight to my dick and it punches against my jeans, straining against the zip. I stand, a burst of frantic energy forcing me to rip off my clothes before I drop back down beside Lorcan and grip his hair in my hands, yanking him off of her.

"I'm thirsty too," I growl, wanting in on the action. I need to taste her too.

Lorcan grins, his mouth and chin glistening with her arousal.

"Kiss him," Cyn breathily demands.

I glance at her, then at Carrick who is watching us all, dick in hand, pumping his fist up and down, up and down. I can't deny her. I don't want to.

"You know you want to taste Cyn on my lips. Fucking kiss me," Lorcan grinds out, gripping the back of my head as he yanks me towards him.

We kiss. Two powerhouses coming together, tongues duelling, hearts pounding, dicks rubbing against each other but as much as I'm enjoying him, I want Cyn more.

Ending the kiss with a sharp bite to his bottom lip, I turn to Cyn, grabbing her hips and pull her from the chair. I lay her down on the rug in front of the fire, burying my head between her legs, slaking my motherfucking thirst.

In my peripheral vision I see Lorcan and Carrick settle down on either side of her. Carrick grasps her chin and kisses her, and Lorcan squeezes her breasts in his tattooed hands, taking the globe of her tit into his mouth.

The sounds she releases from her lips makes me almost violent in my assault on her pussy. I can't be gentle, this isn't the languid fucking under the influence of diamonds. This is pure lust, pure animalistic need. This is the truth of our hearts grasping at the connection that binds us together, tightening it, wrapping us all in its embrace.

"I'm going to come," Cyn breathes, her chest heaving, her hips bucking against my face.

The strain in her voice is addicting, I want to hear her beg for release. Fuck, I want to hear my name on her lips. Pulling back, I smile up at the shock on her face.

"Don't stop. Don't stop."

"You want to come?"

"Yes," she hisses, arching her back as Carrick lowers his mouth to her breast and swirls his tongue around her nipple, whilst Lorcan continues to assault her other breast.

"Tell me you want this. Tell me you want us. Now. Forever."

"I want this," she cries. "Now, forever."

"Beg me, say my name, Cyn. Let me hear it on your lips. I've waited so fucking long to hear my name on your lips."

"Arden, please. Make me come."

"Good girl," I reply, then lower my mouth back to her clit and slide two fingers inside of her pussy, curving them upwards towards her stomach, reaching for her g-spot.

She groans, calling out my name.

"Arden, please. Carrick, Lorcan, please don't stop. Don't stop."

She climbs higher, her pussy clenching around my fingers, her clit twitching beneath my lips, her desire trickling down her slit. When I stroke my fingers inside her, beckoning her orgasm to life, she comes. With an arched back, strained neck, and fisted fingers, she comes screaming our names until she's breathless.

Climbing over her, Lorcan and Carrick move to the side, allowing me a moment to press my body against hers and kiss her senseless, and despite wanting to enter her. I don't. Instead I say, "I want to fuck you, Cyn. I want to bury my cock inside of you and never come up for air."

"Not yet," she says breathlessly.

"Not yet?"

"I need time to be certain."

"Certain that you want us, but I thought–"

"No, I need to be certain that I can trust you to take care of my heart. We need time to start over. Will you give me that?"

I pull back, lifting her up into a seated position. "We'll give you whatever you want," I say, knowing I would burn the world down if she asked me to.

"Whatever you need," Lorcan adds, brushing his lips against her temple.

"We'll give you it all," Carrick finishes, taking her hand and kissing her palm.

"Thank you," she replies softly, opening her arms and welcoming the three of us into her warmth.

And in that moment, as the four of us hold onto one another, I make a silent promise to her that no secret unearthed and no lie spoken will ever get between us again.

27

Cyn - Eighteen years old

"Come closer, child," the old woman says, her wispy grey hair falling over her face in a shroud as she looks up at me from beneath a curved spine. Her face is illuminated in candlelight, shadows creeping across her features as she shifts her head from side to side. "You need not fear me."

I shake my head, not because I'm afraid to step closer, but because I need her to know that I don't fear her. There's nothing about this circus or the people within it that scares me.

"Ah, those boys outside then," she asks, cocking her head to the side as I take a seat opposite her.

I shake my head more vigorously this time.

No. Well, not exactly.

Her wrinkled lips spread in a knowing smile, revealing tobacco-stained teeth and pale gums. She casts her gaze to the closed curtains behind me, which are blocking her view from Arden, Lorcan and Carrick, but clearly not her senses.

The three of them remain outside of the tent smoking the joint filled with cannabis and another secret ingredient that I added to give it that extra kick. I'm hoping the high will distract them long enough for me to have this conversation without interruption.

"I see, so they challenge you. You once feared them, but no longer. You're not friends, but not enemies either."

I nod minutely.

"And yet..." her voice trails off as she waves her hands in the air before her face, like she's trying to rid herself of an annoying wasp.

And yet, *what*? I want to ask.

Of course, I don't. Instead, I watch her with interest, this wizened old lady, bent and brittle with age, as she takes a moment to rid herself of whatever it is that's bugging her.

"You are connected to them in a way that cannot be undone. Isn't that why you're here?"

I gasp, and she grins.

"Don't be so surprised. I have lived a long time, met many people, and witnessed a lot of magic. You are not so difficult to read, child," she replies, and I know at that moment that she's a true *cailleach,* a witch, a wizened old hag.

Of course I don't say that out loud.

"You know I can help with that too. You need only ask," she

says, interrupting my thoughts with a sly smile lighting her watery blue eyes.

I shake my head. *No.*

Leaning forward in her seat, she narrows her eyes at me. "Are you certain? You have a powerful voice. A voice that could stop a man in his tracks, and bring three others to their knees," she says knowingly.

A shiver tracks down my spine. Her words are more of an omen than an observation.

"Oh please, there is no need to fear me. This is who I am. There are things I sense about a person, and I'm sensing that there is more to you than silence. Do you wish for me to read your palm?"

Shaking my head, I reach into my handbag and pull out my pen and pad. She clicks her tongue, muttering about understanding me well enough without the need for it to be spelt out, but I ignore her and quickly scribble my response.

No, thank you, I write.

The old woman reads my words, then lifts her gaze to meet mine. Her left brow rises a millimetre. "Then *why* are you here?"

I cast a look over my shoulder, making sure that Arden, Lorcan and Carrick are still outside the tent and haven't snuck in whilst I've been distracted.

We made a blood pact. I want you to bless it. Will you?

"*You* made a blood pact?" she asks, narrowing her eyes at me.

Don't sound so surprised, I make a lot of things, I retort, my words a scrawl of annoyance across the crisp white paper.

"That's not what I meant," she responds, narrowing her eyes as she peers up at me from beneath her bushy, white eyebrows. "So you're a witch too?"

I chew on the inside of my cheek, debating whether to tell her the truth. Then I realise it was a rhetorical question because she already knows. I write my response anyway, showing her my answer.

I prefer the term healer.

She stares at my words on the pad. "This isn't the sixteen hundreds, you don't need to fear a hanging," she says with a smirk.

Can you help me or not? I ask.

"That all depends."

On what? I scribble. *I can pay you.*

"This isn't about money, though it *will* cost you five hundred euros..."

I roll my eyes. Sure, it's not about the money.

What then? I write.

She raises her brows. "Your palm. Give it to me," she says, snatching the pad and pen from my hands and dropping them to the floor.

I look at my pad trapped beneath her foot and sigh. Why does it feel like she's trampled on my words and silenced me with that one thoughtless action... Oh wait, that's because she has. Her swollen foot stuffed into a pair of leather sandals crushes my notepad as she peers at my palms gripped firmly in her crooked fingers.

"You're troubled. Your voice was stolen through trauma not illness..." she observes, tilting her face up briefly.

No shit, I internalise, rolling my eyes.

"You don't suffer fools, and despite your perceived weakness, are in fact as strong and as stubborn as a century-old oak tree."

Now that I can agree with, though, being likened to a thick, gnarly oak tree isn't quite the look I was going for. Still, I'll take it. Better to be strong and steadfast like an old oak tree, than vulnerable like a sapling.

"That wasn't meant as a compliment," she points out, glancing up at me. "Just because an old oak has roots deep enough to withstand many storms, doesn't mean that one day it won't get felled by a man with an axe." She looks at me then, her eyes filled with portent as she flicks her attention from my face to the curtain. "Or should I say, *three* men with axes."

Fucking great.

If she notices my unspoken cursing, she doesn't acknowledge it and goes right back to staring at my palms. When she lifts my fingers to her nose and breathes in deeply, her eyes fluttering shut, I have the urge to rip my hands out of her hold and run.

"You are very gifted indeed. This blood pact is powerful. I can smell their souls on your hands," she says, admiration in her voice as I snatch back my hands. "You are tied together, you and them. Is that what you wanted?"

I'm not sure how to answer that, and in truth, I wasn't even sure if it would work. Chewing on my bottom lip, I point to my pad crushed beneath her foot.

"I can understand you perfectly well without it," she says.

I jerk my chin.

"Fine, if you insist on using this notepad to converse, who am I to stop you?"

I did it to protect myself, I write after she hands them back to me.

"But you're not afraid of them anymore, so why tie yourself to these three men forever if that's the case?"

We were high...

I look away from her intense stare, hating the way heat creeps up my chest from the lie. We were high when we made the blood pact, but it was more than that. She knows it. I know it.

"Have you ever heard of the phrase *soul tie*?" she asks, surprising me.

Like a soulmate? I ask, wondering where this is going.

She shakes her head. "No, there is a distinct and important difference. A soulmate," she continues, "Is a deep and instantaneous bond that is powerful and everlasting. It is love in its purest form."

I snort, yeah I can categorically say we do *not* share that bond, no matter what Arden had said.

"A soul tie is something a little more complicated."

Go on, I urge, jutting my chin so she knows I'm getting impatient.

Rude? Perhaps, but I can hear Arden's voice getting louder outside the tent and if she doesn't hurry up and help me, they'll barge in here and ruin everything.

"A soul tie takes time to form, and can even happen with someone you aren't fond of. Well, at least in the beginning. Truthfully a soul tie can be far more powerful than that of the bond between soulmates. With soulmates there is mutual give and take. It's a little more complicated with a soul tie. Sometimes they come hand in hand, other times not. Perhaps one day..."

I fold my arms across my chest defensively. *Never.*

She cackles again and I'm pretty sure I hear Carrick tell the circus hand standing outside of the tent to *get out of his fucking way.*

"You have unwittingly... or perhaps not," she adds, giving me a pointed look, "Tied your soul to these men with this blood pact. If they're a part of you, and you're a part of them then they can't hurt you because they'd be hurting themselves, am I right?"

I press my lips into a hard line and nod.

"Wrong," she says, clicking her tongue. "We all know those closest to us are the ones who have the power to hurt us the most. You've tied yourself to these men for a different reason, haven't you, Cyn?"

I shake my head, panic seizing my heart. "You thought that eventually their disregard for your well-being and happiness would turn into respect and love? That binding your souls would make them want to protect you, not hurt you?"

Tears well in my eyes, and I blink them away furiously. How can she possibly know? How can she possibly see the real truth behind my actions?

"You cannot force a bond any more than the sun can force the moon not to shine. You have played a dangerous game, little witch..."

I didn't mean to... I just thought that if I gave myself to them... That if I bound us together they'd ... What have I done?

"I am going to impart some wisdom, child, in the hopes that one day you'll remember it. There is no act that we do not mean, and no spell that cannot be undone. If you wish to release them from this blood pact, then only you can do that."

Tell me how, I beg.

The old woman stares at me, pity in her eyes. "This blood pact, how did you do it?"

Why does that matter?

"It matters."

My skin turns a fiery shade of red as the slow heat creeping up my chest and neck reveals the memory across my face.

"You gave them your virginity, didn't you?"

I nod. Shame filling my stomach, making me want to throw up. I always wanted to give myself to the man I loved. I didn't want to lose my virginity to the boys I both loathed and am dangerously attracted to. But I was desperate.

"Which one took it?" she asks, her expression serious.

I press my eyes shut briefly, blinking back the tears. *They all did...*

"It's not possible," she says, her voice soft enough to make me want to cry even more.

I drop my gaze to my hands, telling her exactly how they did it.

"They all entered you with their fingers?"

Yes, I nod.

"They broke your hymen simultaneously?" she asks.

Yes.

"Then you applied your blood to a cut on their body that you inflicted, am I correct?"

Yes. I carved the tip of a blade into their palms, and the blood pact was made.

"And now it is done, the result isn't what you expected."

I drop my gaze, sighing. *Nothing's changed, they're the same as they always were.*

"I see."

I made a mistake. It doesn't feel right.

"Regardless, it is done. *I* cannot undo it."

"So you're telling me we came here for nothing?" Carrick says as he flings back the curtain and steps inside the tent. "Or are you just a fraud, old woman?"

Behind Carrick, Arden and Lorcan step into the tent.

"I am no more a fraud than your friend here is," she replies, looking directly at Arden. "I see you have the gift too. Interesting."

"Tell us what we want to know. How do we break the blood pact?" Arden retorts, ignoring her curious remark that leaves me with even more questions.

She folds her hands in her lap and presses her eyes shut, before slowly opening them again. "Only death has the power to break a blood pact."

"Oh, fuck this," Lorcan mutters.

"It's time to go, Cyn," Carrick snaps, stepping towards me.

I move to stand, but the old woman reaches for me, grasping my hand.

"Consider your blood pact blessed," she says, before dropping my hand and easing back into her seat.

"We don't want your blessing," Arden retorts, stepping in front of me and blocking my view. It feels like an act of protection, but I know that the only people Arden protects are his two best friends, not me. Never me.

"That may be, but you have it anyway."

I push past Arden, glaring at the witch.

"There is no sense in being angry at me. You got what you wanted," she says, folding her arms across her chest as she looks up at me.

I shake my head. *But this isn't what I want. I made a mistake.*

"No, child, you didn't."

And with those parting words I'm yanked forcefully from the tent.

28

Arden - present day, two months later

"So where's the woman capable of such devious magic?" Soren says as he leans back in his chair, eying me.

The dim lighting of his backstreet club, and the smoke from his joint, only heighten the shadows across his face, making him seem even more sinister, or at least that's the effect he's going for given his full body tattoos. His face is tattooed to look like a skull, and from what I can see of the rest of his body not covered by clothing, his body a skeleton. But he doesn't scare me. A man who needs to change his image to instil fear, isn't a man worth fearing.

"She's not here, and there's no magic involved in making

diamonds," I reply, picking up my glass filled with a shot of brandy and knocking it back. He must be fucking delusional if he thinks I'd introduce him to Cyn.

"But there is skill required, is there not?" Soren asks, focusing on me, his green eyes slithering over me like a snake in long grass.

Sliding my glass across the table, I motion for the waitress to pour me another. She glances at Soren who nods, giving her permission. Like all the women in the Skull Brotherhood, they're treated no better than animals, to abuse, fuck and order around. This particular woman is naked except for a thick gold chain wrapped around her middle, the other end attached to Soren's wrist. She's beautiful, with pale skin and chocolate brown eyes, her ash blonde hair braided in long plaits down her back.

"Some, but no more than any other scientist who has studied chemistry. She's a dime a dozen," I lie, giving the woman a cursory nod in thanks.

"And yet she has the skills to make a drug that is more potent than viagra, as mind-altering as LSD and without any kind of lasting side effects," he counters, fingering the diamonds laid out on the velvet cloth in front of him. "Tell me again that she isn't valuable."

"We don't have to tell you a damn thing," Lorcan says, sitting forward in his seat to the right of me. His animosity is palpable, but it doesn't seem to bother Soren who just grins, his filed down teeth a row of sharp little points begging to be pulled out of his head.

"This is true, you don't. But I do have to wonder why the

Deana-dhe are now encroaching on *my* territory. Drug manu-facturing isn't usually where your interests lie."

"This is just a side-venture for short term gain. We're not interested in making it a permanent thing," I explain, trying to appease the fucker.

I don't care if we've ruffled his feathers, but I do care about getting back to Cyn. It's only been twenty-four hours and already I'm desperate to return home. Sitting here with this dickhead is the last thing I want to be doing, not when I could be with the one woman who holds my heart hostage. This time Carrick was the lucky bastard who got to stay behind and watch over her.

"If that's true, then I want to make you an offer," Soren says, leaning forward, his hands clasped on the table before him.

"And what's that?" Lorcan asks, eyeing him.

"Five million for the woman," he says, watching our reac-tion with interest.

Five million? In another lifetime I might've accepted his offer.

But Cyn is priceless, and there's no way in hell Soren is getting his hands on her.

"She's not for sale," Lorcan snaps, and I have to reach under the table and squeeze his thigh so he doesn't do something stupid and launch himself at Soren.

Don't get me wrong, I want nothing more than to slide the blade I've got tucked in my boot across his throat and watch him bleed out, but now is not the time nor is it the place. We might be the best fighters in the world, but we're in his lair, surrounded by his men, and there's only two of us and over fifty of them.

Soren rolls his tongue over his pointed teeth, narrowing his eyes at us. "So you are going to expand your business, then?"

"No, but we're not selling her either," I explain.

"She's valuable to you," he remarks.

I grit my jaw, he doesn't just mean she's valuable because of what she can produce, and we both know it. However, admitting that she's valuable to us personally is akin to admitting weakness. The Deana-dhe don't have any weaknesses.

At least we didn't until very recently.

But he doesn't need to know that.

"She won't be making any more diamonds for you or anyone else. She will, however, be spreading her legs for as long as we decide. She's not for sale," I grind out, hating that I've lowered what she means to us to just sex, but this is what Soren understands, and it's the only way I can protect her in the short-term until I figure out how we can deal with this issue. We need to unearth some of Soren's secrets, in order to secure her safety. Either that or kill the bastard.

Soren laughs. "I always wondered how you three entertained yourselves. Rumour on the street is that you're eunuchs."

Lorcan leans forward in his seat, his silver-grey eyes boring into Soren's sly green ones. "I think you'll find that's what happened to the last man who pissed us off."

Soren snorts. "Looks like we have something in common then. Removing body parts is my specialty," he replies, the threat blatant. "I have quite a collection. Maybe you'd like a tour of my vault where I keep them?"

"Another time perhaps?" I reply evenly.

Around us the air thickens with tension, and Soren's woman takes a side step away from him, her gaze wary. Sensing her fear, he reaches out a beefy arm, wrapping it around her waist and yanking her none too gently back to his side. She whimpers, his skeletal fingers digging into her hips.

"Very well," he says, reaching down and sliding his fingers through the woman's pussy, then tasting her like he's just helped himself to some honey from a jar. "I understand you're busy men. Pass my regards on to Carrick, will you?"

"Of course," I reply, grabbing the bag of money he pushes across the table, and slinging it over my shoulder.

We head towards the door, one of his men holding it open for us. Unlike Soren, only a quarter of his face is tattooed with a skull, which means he's a lower ranking soldier. According to our sources only Soren has a full face and body tattoo given he's their leader, the rest of the Skull Brotherhood have portions of their face and body tattooed depending on their position in the hierarchy.

"Oh, and one last thing," Soren says, forcing us to stop and turn.

"Yes?" Lorcan grunts, strung tighter than I've ever seen him.

"When you tire of your bitch, pay me a visit. I'll gladly take her off your hands."

Lorcan's teeth grind together so loudly it sounds like the ground tearing apart. Any minute now, he's going to erupt and there won't be a damn thing I can do to stop him.

"Don't worry, we will," I reply, twisting on my feet and glaring at Lorcan to move.

We pass through the club, Soren's men and their women watching us as we leave. Some have even stopped fucking so they can get a good look, whilst others continue to slam into their women, eyes pinned on us both.

"Fucking deviants," Lorcan mutters as we cut a path through the club.

"Let's just get the hell out of... *Fuck!*" I exclaim as a sudden, violent wave of nausea washes over me. The room spins and my knee buckles, but Lorcan grabs hold of my arm, preventing me from collapsing and half drags my stumbling arse out of the door.

"Give me the nod and I'll go back in there and fuck them all up," Lorcan says as he shoves me against the car door and I suck in lungfuls of crisp, autumn air. "I told you not to drink his fucking brandy. He must've spiked it."

"Not that." I shake my head, the familiar feeling of an impending vision.

"Arden, shit!"

"Vision," I manage to utter, before the first tendrils of darkness grasp at the edges of my sight.

"Now?" Lorcan exclaims, pulling open the car door and shoving me into the backseat. I don't even have the ability to sit up, so I just lie there as he climbs in the car and starts the engine.

"We need... to get out... of here..." I mumble, passing out just as Lorcan puts the car in drive and hits the gas.

◇

I come to several hours later on the boat crossing from the mainland to our island, my head in Lorcan's lap whilst Donovan, the skipper, sails us home. It's late, cold, and I feel as though a fucking sledgehammer has been taken to my head.

"You were out a long time, Brother. I was beginning to worry," Lorcan says, easing me upright.

"What did I draw?" I ask, looking around me in the small cabin of Donovan's boat.

"You don't remember?"

I shake my head. "No."

"You passed out in the car, then came to about an hour later. You were frantic, needing a pad and pencil, so I pulled into a gas station and managed to grab what you needed. You spent the rest of the journey to the port drawing this," Lorcan explains, sliding a piece of paper across the small table towards me.

"I don't understand?" I say, dropping my gaze to the drawing.

Lorcan runs a hand over his face. "Me either."

We both stare at the drawing and a sense of dread fills my veins as I try to understand its meaning. I've never drawn anything of the past, only the future. But in this sketch, Cyn is surrounded by The Masks, smiling broadly up at Jakub who's grinning back down at her. Next to him is Leon and Konrad, arms thrown over each other's shoulders. They look nothing like the men we know, and if I hadn't met them in person myself I would question who these men are. I can't help but wonder what it means.

"That's Cyn and The Masks," Lorcan points out unhelpfully.

"No shit."

"She's *happy*," he says, and my stomach churns at the thought that those men ever made Cyn smile.

"So are they," I point out.

The Masks didn't deserve fucking happiness, and they sure as fuck didn't deserve to see Cyn smile. It kills me to know she was happy with those fucking arseholes.

I fall silent as I try to comprehend what this means. It's been years since my last vision and now I have one that depicts a scene from Cyn's past where, evidentially, she was happy.

It doesn't make any sense.

"You're not wrong there. But it has to mean something, right?" Lorcan asks.

"Maybe."

We fall silent as Donovan raps his knuckles on the window indicating that we're nearing the jetty. Through the window I can see the familiar outline of the monastery against a starry backdrop, the windows lit up from the inside.

Lorcan squeezes my shoulder. "Come on, let's go home. We can figure out what this means once we've got some food in our bellies and Cyn's kisses warming our lips."

"Sure," I say, giving him a tight smile as he pushes open the door to the deck and goes to speak with Donovan.

Picking up the bag of money, I take one last look at the drawing, my gaze travelling over every detail. Then my eyes snag on something I hadn't noticed before. I blink, squeezing my eyes shut briefly just to make sure that I am actually seeing what I'm seeing. But when I open my eyes it's still there.

"Fuck!" I exclaim, loud enough for Lorcan's head to snap around and for Donovan to ask me If I'm alright.

"What is it?" Lorcan asks.

Pushing open the door to the deck, he meets me halfway, and I grip his arm, pulling him to one side and out of earshot of Donovan. "This isn't a vision from the past!"

Lorcan frowns, the wind whipping his hair around his face, the salt spray from the ocean wetting our skin. "What are you talking about? The Masks are dead, Arden. We saw that with our own eyes," he says, shoving his hair out of his eyes.

I grip the drawing tightly and stab my finger at the spot I need him to see. "Look at her right hand. Look at what's on her ring finger, Lorcan."

He drops his gaze, taking the drawing from me. "It can't be."

"Three butterfly tattoos," I say.

"But she hasn't got any butterfly tattoos on her finger yet."

"Exactly."

"What are you saying?" Lorcan asks, rounding on me.

"I'm saying this hasn't happened yet."

"But that means..." Lorcan shakes his head in disbelief.

"That The Masks are not dead."

Throwing a wedge of cash at Donovan, we jump from the boat the second it sidles up to the jetty, and sprint up to the house. Lorcan hasn't said a word but I know what he's thinking because I'm thinking the same thing too.

Cyn lied to us.

She didn't grieve because she couldn't bear to acknowledge

their passing. Cyn didn't grieve for The Masks because they never fucking died.

We trusted her.

We opened up our motherfucking hearts to her.

Rage swims in my chest like a swarm of angry wasps as I push open the door to our home and shout, "Cyn!"

Fury paints my vision as I stalk towards the kitchen, the most likely place she'd be at this hour. "Cyn!" I yell.

She lied to me.

Lorcan follows me into the kitchen, his expression a reflection of mine, but she isn't here.

"Cyn! Carrick!" he yells, heading towards the den.

They're not there either.

"Where the fuck are they?" I grind out, taking the stairs two at a time, but all of the bedrooms are empty.

She lied to us.

"Arden," Lorcan says as I step back out into the hallway, ready to commit murder.

He's looking at something on the wall, something I hadn't noticed on my way past.

It's blood.

"Something's not right," he whispers.

Dropping the bag of money at my feet, I pull up my trouser leg, and grab my knife strapped to my ankle. "Stay close," I say, creeping back down the hallway.

When my feet hit the top step of the stairs, I hear groaning and lean over the balustrade. Below Carrick is clutching his head, blood running in rivulets down his face, his other hand pressed against his stomach, more blood seeping through his fingers.

I run, reaching him just as he collapses to the floor.

"Carrick, what the fuck happened?" I demand as Lorcan falls to his knees beside us.

"They took her," he says, his words slurred despite the rage and the pain behind them.

"Who, The Masks?" Lorcan asks, gripping Carrick's shoulders and giving him a shake.

Carrick's eyes roll back a little, his head dropping forward as he swims in and out of consciousness.

"Carrick! Was it The Masks?!" I shout, forcing his head up, fear making me quick-tempered.

"They fucking took her from me," he replies, frantic now as he tries to push up to his feet.

I grasp his shoulders. "Carrick, was it The Masks?"

The hand holding his face drops and bile rises up my throat at the knife wound slicing through his temple, across the bridge of his nose and his cheek, flesh and bone revealed beneath it.

He shakes his head, spitting out blood.

"It was the Skull Brotherhood," he says, before slumping in my arms and passing the fuck out.

29

C yn - present day

I promised my childhood friends, The Masks, and the woman they love six months.

Six months to strengthen their bond. Six months to build their home. Six months to prepare themselves for what was to come.

I gave myself six months to do the same.

Six months to make diamonds.

Six months to heal the rift between myself and the Deana-dhe.

Six months to lay the foundations of our relationship.

Six months to get them to fall so deeply in love with me that no matter what secrets I held, what lies I'd told, they'd forgive me.

And I did that.

I hope.

"You're not what I was expecting," Soren says, his penetrating green eyes boring into my skin as the train we're travelling on rumbles through a dark tunnel towards a foreign land way beyond the shores of Great Britain.

"You're exactly what I was expecting," I reply, recognising his image from the drawing Arden sketched all those years ago when he was under the influence of a vision.

"Plain, barely worth looking at," he muses, blowing out a steady stream of smoke from his joint, his thick fingers made thin by the skeletal tattoos imprinted onto them. "Not a scrap of meat on your body. No arse or tits to speak of."

"Is that why you tattooed your skin, because you were barely worth looking at without it?"

"Feisty. I'll enjoy breaking you," he says, before jerking forward and taking a swing at me, his fist meeting my jaw before I can even dodge it.

My head rings, dark spots dancing across my vision. Blackness threatens to make me pass out, but I shake my head, refusing to fall under its grasp. Spitting out the blood pooling in my mouth from my split lip, I glare at him.

"Does hitting women make you feel more of a man?" I taunt, glancing at the naked blonde woman, covered in a patchwork of bruises, who refuses to make eye contact with me.

"Haven't you noticed, I'm not a man."

"You're made of flesh and blood. You're a man."

"Just like the Deana-dhe. They bleed too. According to my second in command, Carrick bled a great deal trying to protect you from my men. If he survives the beating they gave him, I'll eat her heart," he says, pointing to the woman shivering in the corner of the cabin.

"You bastard," I seethe.

"It's true, I am. I'm also not to be underestimated. Arden thought he could keep you to himself, that I would be too scared to make a move because they're the infamous Deana-dhe. He's a fool."

"They'll kill you."

Soren laughs. "Only if they can find us first."

"Oh, they'll find you."

Soren makes a noise in his throat. "Even if they do, they're just three *men* against a clan of fifty psychotic monsters. They're no match for us."

"Who said it was just going to be the three of them?" I ask.

"The Deana-dhe work on their own."

"Not this time. This time they'll have friends."

"You seem very certain of yourself, witch. Care to share your knowledge with me?"

I bark out a laugh, forcing myself to be brave.

"No."

"Tell me."

"Eat shit," I reply right before he slams a fist against my temple and I'm dragged into the blissful arms of darkness.

EPILOGUE

Arden - present day

In my hand I hold my knife, my father's skin wrapped around the handle. His butterfly tattoo, a constant reminder of who we are and the power we hold.

We're the Deana-dhe.

Brothers in arms, purveyors of truths and lies, dealers of debts.

Legends.

We're also *human*

We're men who hate, who hurt, who bleed.

We're men who love.

And it's that humanity that has us seeking the help of three men who we thought were dead.

The Masks.

Jakub, Konrad and Leon Brov, the sons of the man who murdered my father.

Cyn's story, and that of her time spent with them is detailed in her leather-bound notebook. Written amongst her recipes is the story of her time with The Masks, their friendship and the secrets of Ardelby Castle. Left for us to find, Cyn gave us her truth and allowed us to uncover her secret.

We've spent our entire adult lives recognising the power in truths uncovered. We've used information to manipulate and coerce, to get what we want. We've sold information to criminals without any thought or care of the consequences. We've allowed stories to be weaved about us, letting them grow and mutate, safe in the knowledge we were unreachable, untouchable, unhurtable.

Until now.

In the pages of Cyn's notebook we learned how The Masks found love and thus their humanity. She lied to us to protect them. Her goodness, and her instinct to heal helped three troubled men become more than the victims of abuse, but to become human.

Just like us.

Picking up the telephone, with Carrick and Lorcan watching on, I dial their number obtained by a debt called in. It takes time to ring through, but eventually someone answers. There's no voice on the other end, but I know it's them.

"I know you're alive," I say, my voice coated in warning, years of animosity seeping through my voice.

Cyn's diary might suggest that they're changed men, but I know that their kind of darkness isn't something you can shed yourself of completely. They're still dangerous. They're still Brovs.

The line remains silent, but something clicks and I know I've been put on loudspeaker. My fingers curl into fists and I'm tempted to hang up, to deal with this on our own. Then I look at Carrick, at the badly sewn scar zig-zagging his face and I swallow my pride. As much as we're capable fighters, there are too many of them and I can't risk Cyn's life because of my pride. Grinding my jaw, I lock eyes with Carrick and Lorcan and say, "The Skull Brotherhood have Cyn, and we need your help getting her back."

T*he End... for now.*

C*urses & Cures* will be released in early 2023 and will complete Cyn's and the Deana-dhe's love story. Expect violence, sex, a touch of magic, and cameos from some of your favourite characters.

ACKNOWLEDGMENTS

So there we are, the first part of the Deana-dhe and Cyn's love story is complete. I hope you enjoyed it!

Book one of the duet was all about establishing the Deana-dhe's history with Cyn, and their human side given they have such a mysterious reputation. In book two the men all criminals fear will be emerging full throttle because no one fucks with their soulmate, right?

I knew the moment that Arden, Lorcan and Carrick appeared on the page in the Academy of Stardom series that they needed their own story, and as soon as Cyn appeared in The Dancer and The Masks, I knew she belonged to them. I love their chemistry.

BUT, writing this book was hard work, not because of the characters or their story but because life stuff has been tricky this year. If you're in my reader group on Facebook (Queen Bea's Hive) you'll know that I've had to take care of my parents a lot this year through their own ill health and it meant pushing back the release of Debts & Diamonds which I hated having to do.

So I want to take this opportunity to thank my readers for being so kind and supportive, and not complaining about the later release date. I get to do what I love because of you all, and I get to look after the people who need me the most because you understand that I'm also a mother, daughter and friend, and not a machine. You are the best readers, and I adore you.

Special thanks to Heather Long, Liz Ryan and Krystal Bosmans for their help with all the scientific, biochemistry and plant expertise! I may not have gone into great detail, but the information you supplied me with helped me to understand the process of her making her tinctures and tonics (hahaha Courtney, couldn't resist) enough to make those scenes realistic.

Thanks to my beta team: Gina, Lisa, Clare, and Jen for being my cheerleaders. Love you ladies!

Thanks to Janet, my proofreader and plot questioner, lol, you get me.

Thanks of course to my alpha, PA and good friend, Courtney, for getting me through the days when I truly didn't have it in me to write, and the guilt I felt about that. Love you girl.

And finally, a huge hug to my mum and dad. Like Cyn, I always, *always* take care of the people I love. You're never a burden. I love you.

Thanks for reading.

Bea xoxo

ABOUT BEA PAIGE

Bea Paige lives a very secretive life in London...

She likes red wine and Haribo sweets (preferably together) and occasionally swings around poles when the mood takes her.

Bea loves to write about love and all the different facets of such a powerful emotion. When she's not writing about love and passion, you'll find her reading about it and ugly crying.

Bea is always writing, and new ideas seem to appear at the most unlikely time, like in the shower or when driving her car.

She has lots more books planned, so be sure to subscribe to her newsletter: beapaige.co.uk/newsletter-sign-up

ALSO BY BEA PAIGE

The Deana-dhe Duet (dark reverse harem)

1 Debts & Diamonds

2 Curses & Cures

Grim & Beast's Duet (M/F second-chance, bodyguard romance)

#1 Tales You Win

#2 Heads You Lose

Their Obsession Duet (dark reverse harem)

#1 The Dancer and The Masks

#2 The Masks and The Dancer

Academy of Stardom

(friends-to-enemies-lovers reverse harem)

#1 Freestyle

#2 Lyrical

3 Breakers

4 Finale

Academy of Misfits

(bully/academy reverse harem)

#1 Delinquent

#2 Reject

#3 Family

#4 Academy of Misfits box set

Finding Their Muse

(dark contemporary reverse harem)

#1 Steps

#2 Strokes

#3 Strings

#4 Symphony

#5 Finding Their Muse box set

The Brothers Freed Series

(contemporary reverse harem)

#1 Avalanche of Desire

#2 Storm of Seduction

#3 Dawn of Love

#4 Brothers Freed box set

Contemporary Standalone

Beyond the Horizon

For all up to date book releases please visit

www.beapaige.co.uk